Carroll, Gladys Hasty
    The light here kindled.   [1st ed.] Boston,
Little [C1967]
    282p.

I. Title.

The Light Here Kindled

By Gladys Hasty Carroll

Novels

AS THE EARTH TURNS
A FEW FOOLISH ONES
NEIGHBOR TO THE SKY
WEST OF THE HILL
WHILE THE ANGELS SING
CHRISTMAS WITHOUT JOHNNY
ONE WHITE STAR
SING OUT THE GLORY
COME WITH ME HOME
THE ROAD GROWS STRANGE
THE LIGHT HERE KINDLED

Collected Short Stories

HEAD OF THE LINE

Nonfiction

DUNNYBROOK
ONLY FIFTY YEARS AGO
TO REMEMBER FOREVER

The
Light Here
Kindled

GLADYS HASTY CARROLL

Little, Brown and Company · Boston · Toronto

Published simultaneously in Canada
by Little, Brown & Company (Canada) Limited

PRINTED IN THE UNITED STATES OF AMERICA

To
Anne and Warren

The light here kindled hath shone unto many,
yea in some sort to our whole nation . . .

William Bradford, *Of Plymouth Plantation*

The
Light Here
Kindled

1

THERE was this very old woman living last year in a way you could hardly have believed if you had known of it; not many did, and those few only superficially and in part. Her home, oddly enough, was in the house where she was born, and when the census taker found her and asked the date of her birth she showed him where it was entered in delicate tracery on the flyleaf of a big Bible bound in rotting brown leather — *Jane Ellen Foye, November 27, 1870.* Since Jane had been her mother's name, she said, she had always been called Ellen or Ellie as long as there had been those who called her by her given name.

It was also recorded in this Bible that on February 12, 1887, she had married Ethan Dockham, born July 28, 1864. This entry, like the one just before and those which followed, was in her own firm, square script, for Jane Foye of the delicate hand had died in the early summer of 1886, having been a widow for fifteen years following the death of Simeon Foye from tuberculosis contracted in a Southern prison camp. Of Jane and Simeon's three children only Ellen had lived long enough to be named. Of Ellen and Ethan Dockham's six, two had died in infancy, a son in a logging accident at the age of nineteen, a daughter in childbirth at the age of twenty. The other two had survived their father, who was killed on a railroad crossing in a blinding snowstorm in 1910, but Charles Dockham, who never married, was buried in French soil in 1918, and Minnie Dockham Travelli died of pneumonia in California in 1934. It was put down there in the Bible, and the census taker found himself reading on, though it was all a long time ago now, and no concern of his.

"Your daughter Ethel had no children who lived?"

"No. No, that was her first time. I always thought maybe if I had been with Ethel — but she and John lived up Massachusetts way. He was a stonemason, John was. After that he came home here for a while and married Minnie and they traveled out west. Always planned on coming back to settle but never did. John died before Minnie. Says here . . . well, of course he was older, but wasn't either one of 'em old. Fur from it . . ."

"They had two children."

"Yes. Junior and Betty. John's sister, that went out with him and Minnie, brought them up. Cora — that was John's sister — never had any young ones herself.

She used to write once in a while and send pictures of Minnie's. Betty wrote and told me when Cora died, four, five years ago. Betty had just been married then. No word has come since. I don't doubt she and Junior've got their hands full with their own families."

The census taker gave himself an inward shake and returned to his assignment.

"How many acres in this farm?"

"Twenty-five, more or less, deed says. Used to be about fifteen of field and ten of pasture. All so grown up now, except for maybe an acre right around the house, you can't hardly tell one from t'other."

"Any stock?"

"Two cows. A dozen hens. A pig."

"How do you — keep the cows giving milk?"

"Chester Morrison, has a dairy farm a mile below here, takes 'em to bull. When they come in, takes my calves in trade for grain."

"Dogs?"

"No. None I own. One runs out of the woods every once in a while and stays a spell and leaves. Same with cats."

"No television, I gather. I see you don't have power."

"No. No."

"Battery radio?"

"No."

"Car?"

"No. Charlie had one. A model T. I kep' it until John and Minnie left. Then I sold it."

"Well — I guess that's all."

As the census taker rose he glanced around at the old kitchen with its scrubbed pine floor, big black wood-stove, braided rug, bare dropleaf table, iron sink, zinc pail of water with a gray enamel dipper in it, homemade couch with a cretonne cover, ticking clock with a fat, redbreasted bird painted on the glass below the face, uncurtained windows; and looked again at Ellen Dockham, who had risen instantly when he did, as a business executive does to close one interview before telling his secretary to send in the next in line.

"No telephone, either?"

"What would I want with a telephone, at a hundred dollars a pole all the way in here? It's 'most a mile to the main road."

The census taker knew that; a narrow, rutted, ungraded mile. He rubbed his chin and grinned.

"Hard to believe, Mrs. Dockham, that you were born in 1870."

She shrugged as if to say, "Believe it or not, as you wish."

He added, "You certainly don't look ninety years old."

She was a woman, so this pleased her. She smiled slightly, passing him to open the door so that he could be on his way.

"Oh, well," she said, "after anybody's been getting old long enough, they start to get younger, I guess."

The most recent census was taken in 1960. Last year Ellen Dockham was still there, and for her nothing had changed.

In the nation's capital a High Source was being interviewed by newshawks and doves and television
cameras. He sat at a bare shining desk, smiling and
bowing, and though some of the questions were rather
sharp, a few even so hostile that he paused to place his
smile in a glass of water and became exceedingly
grave, his voice never lost its gentle patience, its reflection of a seemingly limitless understanding of and
sympathy with everyone everywhere, or its recurring
deep notes as he clearly implied that those who dis-
agreed with his judgment or doubted the purity of his
motives must more earnestly seek enlightenment.

The nation was at war, military or other, within
and without, through and through and over all hori-
zons, but for the purpose only of the establishment
and preservation of peace and brotherhood, recogniz-
ing no enemy except the evil in human nature which
alone kept any man from loving his neighbor. This
evil must be exorcised, and the pain of the process was
regrettable but unavoidable; when it was over those
who had suffered it would be forever thankful for it.
It was for the good of all, and after it there would be
no more pain. There was war against foreign Commu-
nists, and against native extremists; against dictator-
ship abroad, and against opposition at home; against
ignorance, and against intellectualism. There was war
against poverty, and against wealth; against business,
and against the right to work; against pacifism, and
against patriotism; against God, and against atheism;
against crime, and against the police. There was war
against age and youth, inflation and frugality, emo-

tion and reason, injustice and justice, violence and nonviolence, guns and plain talk, organizations and isolates, billboards and trees . . .

"Mr. Source, sir, is it your belief that we can win all these wars in our time?"

"As you will readily understand, Phil, much of the information available to me is strictly classified, but let me say this: let me say that it must be clear to all that we have already made much progress, that we have set our shoulder to the wheel and placed our hand upon the tiller, that we are the richest and most powerful nation on earth, and that with God as our guide we are more than halfway up the mountain. If we do not falter — and let me assure you that we shall not falter, however fierce the struggle, for we know we have the full support of the overwhelming majority of our people — if we do not falter, which I promise you we shall not, we are bound to discover the Holy Grail which is man's brotherhood toward man. We shall hold to this course *because we know that it is right.*"

"I regret that our time is up and we cannot ask more questions of Mr. Source, whose presence here today is very much appreciated. The name of our next week's scheduled guest will be announced following station identification."

"The preceding program has been brought to you in living color through the courtesy of Freedom capsules, which may help to free you from some of the symptoms of the common cold. They are available at drugstores everywhere on prescription from your doctor. Contribute to Radio Free Europe. The Iron Curtain is not soundproof, and only through the broadcasts of Radio Free Europe can the millions beyond it hear the truth."

From the hub the spokes of the wheel to which the High Sources had set their shoulders ran out across the rich and powerful nation toward a rim which did not exist; the ship on whose tiller they had placed their hands trembled on the crest of each giant wave and creaked ominously as it settled into the troughs; the face of the mountain was a smooth, sheer cliff and its peak, which no man had ever seen, was obscured by clouds.

Everywhere there were people in the numbers in which, in a less motorized and scientific age, there had been flies. Masses of people who needed people and so, the song said, were the luckiest people in the world. People thronging among the spokes, stumbling, falling, and either getting up or lying there to be trampled on. People hanging like swarming bees to the rigging, or slipping on the wet deck and rolling off into the water and swimming aimlessly or going under. People with edelweiss in their hatbands and blisters in their boots climbing in formation or stopping to rest or to get warm or to find shelter from a sudden blizzard which obliterated the trail, if there was one, or turning back in confusion and despair on the faint chance that there might be a better way up this mountain or even perhaps some way around it.

Each human being was in living color, but their sur-
roundings were in shades of gray. Nowhere was there
the relief of a solid block of black or the revelation of
a streak of radiant white.

2

A FEW miles from the campus of a teachers college which until a few years ago had been called a normal school, its students — not all but perhaps half of them — had just arrived at a rocky point on the riverbank for an annual cookout supper which was all that was left of a traditional event known as the Hare and Hound Chase. In the early years of the Normal School the first pleasant day in November had been declared a half-holiday, and students selected as hares had set out immediately after lunch for a secret destination which they were instructed not to reach until after two hours of hiking. In those days, as the hares went they dropped bits of paper here and there along roads or in fields and tied white strings to occasional bushes and tree branches in the woods. At three o'clock the hounds — the remaining students — were released from in front of the administration building

and raced with light laughter and small, excited
screams (for nearly all were girls) in search of flutters
of white. The race was to see who of the hounds
would be the first to see each signal and cover the cir-
cuitous route which led them to the unknown place
where the hares had congregated and were building
fires over which coffee would be boiled in great,
sooted enamel pots, frankforts roasted and rolls
smoked, while apples and potatoes were baking in the
coals. The pots the hares had taken with them. The
coffee, frankforts, and rolls they had bought at the
country store at the crossroads nearest the picnic site.
The apples and potatoes they had bought of a farmer.
The water for the coffee was dipped from the river or
a brook or a spring.

For some years now the population had been spread
out so far on all sides of the college town that there
were no open fields and woods within hiking distance,
and the Hare and Hound Chase had become a dull
ride in buses to the public picnic grounds on the
rocky point where there were permanent fireplaces
with iron grilles and a safe water supply from foun-
tains. The food came in trucks from the college kitchens, and was not improved by the trip. Those of the
students who had not preferred or who could not
afford to go into town for cheeseburgers and Coke
that night shivered as they came off the buses into
the damp November dusk which smelled of the pol-
luted river water and of the chemicals used in the
battle against the pollution.

The number of men students now nearly equaled

the number of girl students at the college, but more men than girls preferred and could pay for cheeseburgers and Coke. The majority here were girls, though all had haircuts similar to the men's, and nearly all wore trousers.

The few couples getting off the buses, seeing that supper was not yet being served at the long tables in the grove, disappeared among the trees. Some of them, experienced upperclassmen, were dragging blankets with fringe which caught on bushes, tugged briefly and let go.

Audrey Mason was a freshman, a small girl in a seagreen hood which surrounded her thin face and either was the exact color of her enormous eyes or had given its color to them. Her jacket was gray as the November dusk, but she wore a skirt, which made her conspicuous in this company. It was a dark wool plaid, pleated and short, showing her bare knees above high black boots. Audrey was either all eyes and knees, or all skirt, depending on where attention focused. But no one seemed to be paying her attention, and she was not aware of attracting any.

She circled like a moth around the nearest spot of light, but the chef was there, turning thin slices of meat on the grill for the flames to lick, and midway in her second slow circle he shot a glance in her direction which seemed to say that it was bad enough to have to come out here to cook without having his rude kitchen invaded by kids hoping in vain for a whiff of the breast of chicken or maybe filet mignon he would have liked to be broiling on a first-class hotel range.

" 'Tain't ready," he growled. "When 'tis, be on platters on the tables."

And cold by the time it reached there. Dry as a chip, tough as leather, cold as stone.

She went off at a tangent toward another spot of light, but this and those beyond, manned by student assistants of the chef, were already close-ringed by so many shivering girls that, as Audrey came near, she could not even see the flames, much less feel their warmth.

Suddenly she turned away and strode to the river's edge. Fog was beginning to rise there, but above the fog, in the west from which the dark current ran, the pale pink reflection of a November sunset, like a lost, torn banner, flew from the top of a leafless tree.

She stood staring, two great green eyes and two pale, knobby knees. As the color began to fade, she stared the harder, as if by staring she could hold it there. She saw it as a curtain which might at any minute separate, be rolled back, gather in rosy folds to frame — what? A bridge to another world? A balcony on which such a creature as she had never seen would appear and speak words of such wisdom as she had never heard? A recreation of the incredible past? A preview of the mysterious future?

It only grew fainter. Fainter and smaller. But as it disappeared, she noticed a small glow, apparently resting on the water a few hundred feet upstream. Was this one of the unidentified objects coming to be known familiarly as UFO's? Her knees felt stiff, as if they might be freezing. She sat down where she was, hugging her ankles, pressing her hooded chin to her knees, and stared at the glow.

A minute later a figure rose as if from the water, was briefly silhouetted against the light, and sank or moved on into the dark.

She knew then that the glow must extend to the riverbank, for this was no man from Mars. The figure was that of Walter Ross, who had no qualifications for walking on water, or even standing on it for an instant.

She would not have recognized the full-length silhouette of any other student at the college, but Walt's was unmistakable not only because of his unusual height, the breadth of his shoulders, and the way his big head set so low between them that he appeared to have no neck, but because it had been familiar to her for years now. In high school at home he had been a year ahead of her and already infamous by the time she got there. It was Walt Ross, son of the town's only lawyer, who had been caught smoking in the school belfry and suspended for a week, but not until after the football season when his shoulders were needed in the line. It was Walt Ross whose fingerprints had been on the steering wheel of a car which the police had found two blocks from where it had been parked by its owner and who consequently had to report to a probation officer on the twenty-third of every month for a year. It was Walt Ross who was thought to have stolen the Latin examination questions from the principal's desk in the night because no one else was known to be tall enough to pull himself over the sill of the window which through an oversight had been left open; though there was no proof and he would not admit it. Walt Ross who probably spiked the punch at the junior prom, broke the plate glass window, pushed the gravestones off their foundations, tossed the loaded pistol under the bleachers. All the high school girls had been afraid of him until they found that he never appeared to be aware of their existence. Then most of them hated him.

Audrey did not hate him. She had been afraid of him for a while. Until she had stopped being afraid of anyone or anything in particular, only of everything in general.

People at home had always said they did not understand how the Rosses could have a son like Walt. So different from his older brother Matthew, who was just like his father, quiet and scholarly, at the top of his high school class, Phi Beta Kappa at college, and now an editor of the *Cornell Law Review;* and from his sister Sharon, who was just like her mother, pretty and gay and popular with everyone. Nobody had been surprised when Walt did not get his diploma at graduation and was sent away to some boarding school; they only wondered what school would take a boy with a record like his.

Audrey had been surprised to find him in the entering class at the Teachers College, but had not written home about it, thinking it might worry her parents. All the parents at home were afraid for their children — girls or boys — to be where Walt Ross was. Then she had forgotten about him.

She forgot about him again now, and stared at the glow.

Sometime afterward — she had no idea how long — she heard slow footsteps approaching her through the dark. She shrank deeper into her hood, hugged her knees tighter, and the footsteps passed a few feet away. But not far beyond they turned and came back. Very slow, like those of a man searching the ground for something he could not see and did not want to step on. They came nearer and nearer, and stopped just behind her.

She did not move. She scarcely breathed.

"This you, Audrey?" asked Walt Ross's low rumble.

"Yes."

There was a moment in which neither of them moved or spoke. It seemed long, and, when it ended, as if it might have been forever.

He sat down behind her in the dark.

He said, "I thought I saw you here."

"How could you see me in the dark?"

"Before it got quite dark. The light from the sky was on your face. Just your face."

"I was looking at the sky. It was pink."

"So was your face. Like a — flower or something. A pink flower. With two green leaves."

This was Walt Ross? He was so near that she could feel his shoulder behind her head, his body behind her shoulders — the high back of a wing chair; a warm chair; a chair with one arm, as he supported himself by a hand on the stone she sat on.

"You mean my eyes. You couldn't have seen my eyes from away down there."

"I did."

"You couldn't have."

"Well, I won't swear. Maybe I — just remembered. I knew it was you."

Warmth was spreading all through her. In the silence her body spoke to her and her mind answered.

Feel the goodness in this man . . . But they've always said Walt Ross was bad . . . Feel his gentleness. You heard it in his voice, too. Could such gentleness be in a bad man? . . . I would never have believed . . . Do you now? Do you believe what they have always said, or what you feel and what you hear? . . . I don't know. I haven't known what I believed, for a long time . . . Do you want to know what you believe about this man? . . . Yes. Oh, I do, I do. I am so lonely . . . Then wait. Wait and listen. He is lonely, too . . .

"You said, 'From away down there.' So you did see me."

"Not until after dark. Then I was watching that glowing spot. I thought it was hanging over the water. I thought maybe it was a UFO. Until you stood up just this side of it."

"Did you know it was me?"

"Yes."

No, I thought it was Walt Ross.

"Do you know what the glow is from?"

"No."

"You couldn't, very well, from here, I guess. It's a fire I built."

"A fire — you built?"

"I didn't want to eat with the kids. I didn't need that bus ride. I didn't want to eat downtown either. The joints will be jammed tonight. So I walked over here and brought some frankforts and rolls and made a fire down there beside the river to cook them over. I cut some sticks to spear them with."

"Why did you come here? If you wanted to be alone."

"Well . . . It's a place you can build a fire without getting into trouble . . . And the fact is, I didn't want to be alone if I could find you. Not that I expected to be that lucky. But I knew you were coming."

"How?"

"You signed up, didn't you, on the bulletin board?"

"Why did you want to find me?"

"I thought then — because I wanted to talk to somebody."

"Did you try to find me on the campus?"

"No. I didn't want to talk to anybody on the campus. Until today I haven't wanted especially to talk to anybody anywhere. But today I began to think of talking to you, outside somewhere, in a place kind of like this. And there was going to be this cookout, so I looked at the list and there was your name. I knew I'd never go looking for you in the mob. But somehow I walked over here and found a place to build my fire. I can tell you I could hardly believe it when I looked up here and saw your face in that pink light. Just your face. Like as if it was floating."

I could hardly believe it . . . I would never have believed . . .

"Why do you suppose you suddenly thought today of wanting to talk to somebody?

"I know why. Because I'm going away in the morning. And if I went away in the morning without talking to somebody tonight, I'd go without ever having really talked to anybody in my life."

Going away in the morning . . .

"Where are you going?"

"I've enlisted in the Marines. I've got a reservation on the first plane out. I'm reporting at Parris Island tomorrow night."

"Why? Why have you done that?"

"Because I had to. I've got to get out of here. I've stood being nothing I wanted to be and doing nothing worth doing as long as I can. I don't know whether we ought to be fighting in the Far East or not. It's all too complicated for me. But a lot of guys are and that's the kind I belong with. The kind of guys that take care of themselves, wherever they are, or die trying. I've had enough of being helped and hearing that helping other people is the only good thing there is to do in this world. More than enough. I figure that helping myself is my business and if that doesn't help other people nothing I could do would . . . You see what I mean, Audrey?"

"Yes. I see. I do see."

". . . My fire must be about right to cook over now. Want to come down?"

She nodded. He got up and came around in front of her, and reaching for her hands, pulled her up.

She tipped back her head to look full into his face. Dark as it was, she could see a smile around his mouth.

"Hey!" he said exultantly. "This sure is my lucky night."

He had kept one of her hands and began to draw her with him.

But she said, "Wait . . . I like the way you say my name. Only — I can't explain — I don't want to say yours. The one I have always heard you called by. What can I call you?"

They stood still. He was thinking.

Then he said, "Somebody I never saw again after I was about five years old always used to call me Ranger. Because we listened together to *The Lone Ranger* every night. I liked that."

She laughed softly. Soft as it was, the sound startled both of them, making their eyes widen.

She said, "I like it, too. Let's go, Ranger."

They began hurrying, almost running, toward the glow.

That day Chester Morrison had driven his jeep through the woods, bringing Ellen Dockham's mail. Once a week he opened her box at the outlet of her road, and delivered the contents to her with her grain. Usually there was the *County Gazette,* published Fridays, to which her father had been a subscriber, and then her mother, and which her husband had continued; she kept on with it because its print and makeup had so long been familiar that it was a part of home like the handhewn beams which jutted from the corners of every room, like the damp, earthy smell of the cellar; the news in it now was all of strangers engaged in activities she did not understand, or disapproved of, or thought unimportant. The *Gazette*, which she always looked at but seldom read, and a bundle of advertising circulars which she saved for quickening the fire usually made up her mail. But today there had been a letter which she read twice by daylight, and now was reading again by holding it close to the chimney of the oil lamp on the kitchen table.

It was from Suse Wentworth, who had gone to district school with her — a little girl when Ellen was a big one — and then on to the Academy in the village, as Ellen had not, and who had married a village boy who later became a doctor and practiced in Philadelphia. After he died, Suse had gone out west to live with her married daughter. Once when the young folks were on their way to Quebec they brought her to visit Ellen while they were gone and she had stayed two weeks.

"My dear Ellie," wrote Suse now, "can it be that this will find you still there where I spent the happiest fortnight I have had since Paul died? I know you told me you are no letter writer, but ever since I left your house I have longed to hear from you. I wish I knew if you get my Christmas cards. I wrote the Morrisons a

year ago or more, begging for news of you, but no answer. Oh, Ellie, I am so alone in a crowded house, so
poor in the midst of plenty. The days are so long, and
oh, Ellie, the *nights!* I can no longer rise from bed or
chair without help, and I hate so to ask, even if some
one is near, but I am always waiting, wishing I knew
how long I have waited, but do not want to admit I
cannot see the hands of my watch, and clocks don't
strike any more. Everyone here is so busy. Nine beds
are always ready for sleeping, but I don't know who
sleeps when, since the grandchildren grew up; except
that no one except Max, my son-in-law, who goes to
business, is ever around before noon. I think the lights
are on all night. Maida, my daughter, is president of I
don't know how many women's organizations and always going to meetings, dinners, lectures and such.
Her three girls have rooms and get their meals here —
Kimberly, the second one, while her husband is in
Vietnam; she is working on a newspaper to buy a
house for them to live in when he comes back, if he
comes back. Suzanne, the oldest, has a friend they call
Nat who lives here with her, I guess. They are always
coming and going together and don't get along well
with anyone else. Especially they don't get along with
Kim, because they spend most of their time and en-
ergy opposing the war Kim's husband is fighting in;
they parade and protest and carry signs and make
speeches. The way those two girls dress makes me
ashamed of them, Ellie. They look like tramps. And
then there's Maisie, Maida's youngest. She goes to a
junior college here, but all she is interested in is danc-

ing and singing and playing a guitar. That sounds gay but it isn't. The songs sound like dirges, she gets so little sleep her eyes look like burnt holes in a blanket (a green blanket, from the stuff she smears on her lids), she spends hours working on her hair so it will come out as straight as a horse's mane, she never smiles, and she talks in a kind of croak. I shouldn't be telling you all this, Ellie, but I have to tell someone. Sometimes I am sure I am losing my mind. Day in and day out, year in and year out, I have nobody to speak to about anything I care about, nobody who wants to hear anything I might say, no reason at all to go on living — but I don't know how to stop. Are you still there, Ellie? Do you still sleep upstairs, and do the stairs still creak? Does your spring still bubble up among the smooth stones like champagne? Do you still have a wood fire? Can you smell it and hear it crackle? Do you still bake beans on Saturdays? Did you have vegetables right out of the field last summer? Ellie. I'm hungry. I'm lonely. I'm afraid . . ."

Ellen said aloud, "Poor Suse. I've got to write something to her. It'll be hen-scratching, but I'll put down something before Chet comes again."

She mounted the creaking stairs, carrying her lamp, thinking of what she would say.

Yes, Suse. I'm still on the same old stamping ground. I don't know as you can make out to read this. I wish they would get you into a car and bring you for another visit. We did have a real frolic before, didn't we? I guess young folks today are a sight different than we was, judging by what you say and what I see in the papers. Remember how we could all cook a meal and seam up sheeting and make patchwork by the time we was eight years old? I earnt the money to pay for my first slate picking potato bugs. Grampa give me a penny for every whiskey bottle I filled with them. I can still remember you speaking a piece in a school concert. One line in it was "Far down the dusky dingle the cows are coming home." Or maybe it was "dusty dingle." Your mother had made you a brown plaid dress trimmed with yards and yards of black braid and put your red hair in a black lace snood. You had the handsomest hair I ever saw. You try to get so you can come again. I raised a good crop of Green Mountains this year, and enough beets and carrots and cabbage to carry me through. Chet butchered for me, so I've got a tub of nice salt pork for my beans. I always put your Christmas card up on the mantelpiece by the clock. I ought to send you one but I don't get anywheres to buy anything. I wish I was more of a hand to write . . .

That night the water froze in the cattle trough, so hard that she had to take an axe to it in the morning. The cold was unseasonable for November.

3

IN THE spring the annual Literary Convocation
was held by the women's club of a Midwestern
city. The clubhouse had been built of granite at the
turn of the century as a Universalist church and had
many of the architectural characteristics of a Greek
temple, though behind its columns the size, design,
and colors of its windows were as elaborate as those of
a cathedral. As time went on, its congregation had become so sharply divided between those who wor-
shiped Jesus Christ and those who were convinced
that Jesus was a man as other men that no one pastor
could serve them all, and they had gradually drifted
away to more or less orthodox institutions until the
few who were left could maintain neither conviction
nor services. Thus the building had been closed, and
eventually purchased and renovated by the Women's
City Club. Actually, it had required very little reno-

vation; only modernization of the kitchen and vestry, and removal of steeple and pews. They had retained the fine pipe organ, and from it strains of classical music flowed softly down the two spiral staircases to reach the jeweled ears below the flowered Easter hats of the ladies gathered in the clubroom for coffee and a social hour preceding the literary program.

Mrs. Maxwell Frome, president of the City Club, moved with the ease of long experience from one role to another, all things to all the women about her, leaving with the chief book reviewer of the *Evening Bulletin* the speaker she had just driven in from the airport and pausing to kiss the tiny, tremulous charter member at the coffee urn — noticing as she did so that the supply of teaspoons was diminishing and must be replenished — on her way to look in on the shyer and more domestically inclined of the membership and compliment them particularly on the hot, crusty little cheese biscuits before catching up with the society editor of the *Morning Herald* to make sure she would mention on her page that the flowers, which were everywhere in tall silver vases and shallow copper bowls, had been flown up from Florida, the gift of another charter member who now made her home there.

The president had in her time taken one by one, with meticulous attention to detail, each step which led to her present eminence from the day when, a Philadelphia Junior Leaguer and Max Frome's bride, she was accepted into the City Club as a probationary member without voting privileges. As in childhood and girlhood, with her parents who had grown up in a small Maine town, she had slowly and conscientiously learned the ways of living, dressing, speaking, thinking which would make her a congenial companion for those born to the Main Line, in Max's home city she had begun by slowly and conscientiously acquiring the breezy manners, the outwardly more democratic attitudes, the greater interest in all that was new, the more flamboyant taste in dress and interior decoration, the happy pride in tangible, personal possessions natural to the daughters of the frontier who were the wives of her father-in-law's — and now Max's — business and professional associates. First assigned to the kitchen, she had made a small name for herself with her Dutch coffee cake, and never forgot how she gained in courage and dedication from the kind comments of older club members. More confident and with wider acquaintance, she had been promoted to carrying silver trays of very small sandwiches and frosted cupcakes into the clubroom, refilling teapots and coffee urns, where the august pourers smiled at her and said, "Thank you, Maida. What a lovely dress, dear! I hate you for being so young, but I like your hair style. Who do you go to?"

In due course, rising in her orbit as Max rose in his, she had been awarded full membership, appointed to hospitality committees, study committees, charitable committees, placed in charge of publicity, made program chairman, elected third vice-president . . . second . . . first . . . Until now that she had overall responsibility for the Women's City Club — as for the

Women's League of her church, the board of directors of the Sarah Anderson Settlement House, and F.F.L. (Female Friends of the Library, the oldest women's organization in the city) — there was no part of the operation in which she had not served a devoted apprenticeship until she became an expert. Though she was fully aware that there were those who resented the firm assurance of her touch and who replied to, "Isn't it marvelous the way Maida Frome delegates authority?" with "Don't you believe it! She keeps an eagle eye on everything right down to the points of the desk pens, which window is open how many inches, and when the water comes to a boil," she was no more troubled by it than a high-powered car is by leaving the others behind when the light changes. Rumor had it that any day now she might be named to head the Community Chest, the first woman who ever had been. In charge of an organization she was a complete, unsurpassed, freely acknowledged success.

The one area of organizational work in which she had so far failed seemed for the most part to have escaped the notice of her fellow club members; to the few who spoke of this gap it had apparently not occurred to lay the blame at her door. But Maida Frome put it squarely where she would have placed the blame for a scratchy pen, a draft on a sensitive neck, a scarcity of polished teaspoons, or a burnt biscuit; and this matter was far more serious than any of them.

Too few young women were applying for admission to the City Club, the Women's League, or F.F.L., or offering to give time at the Settlement House. Far too

few. Almost none, in fact. The great majority of those
now active in the women's organizations were in their
forties and fifties, and most of the rest were in their
sixties. Traditionally, members of the Women's City
Club on reaching the age of seventy were retired to
honorary titles. Something had to be done to attract
the young or there would soon be a serious shortage,
first of able workers and then of financial support.

Something had to be done. But what?

She moved casually and without apparent insist-
ence from group to group, suggesting that the members might like to find their seats in the auditorium,
and as the clubroom was clearing joined the speaker
— a chubby little novelist with sky-blue hair, laughing blue eyes, and a mink shrug, now properly surrounded by the other officers of the club who would
accompany speaker and president to the platform.

The program was scheduled to be opened at 11:45,
and the hands of Maida's watch read 11:42.

"I see the members and their guests are beginning
to go upstairs," she said brightly. "All looking forward eagerly, I'm sure, Miss Halstead, to what you
have in store for them this morning. Shall we follow
along, if you are ready? Lorene, will you lead us, since
your chair is at the far left and we are going up by the
right stairway? Then the rest of us in the order of our
chairs. Perhaps you will come between Ruth and me,
Miss Halstead. That's fine. I hope everyone took time
to notice the flowers. It was so sweet of dear Alma to
send them to us, and Dorothy and Leah made such

charming arrangements. Aren't we fortunate in the weather? It is perfect for shrugs."

Lorene may not be past fifty, but Ruth is considerably older than I am. Eleanor and Louise are getting on toward fifty, and Marjorie must be nearly seventy, for she has been club secretary for thirty-one years. There won't be one person on that platform who is even in her early forties, to say nothing of in her thirties, as most of us were when we began holding office.

The organ music quickened as the officers and the speaker proceeded down the wall aisle and across the platform, and rose to a crescendo as soon as they were seated, silencing the hum of voices below. With the dying of the last note a vice-president came forward to greet the audience. It was precisely 11:45. Another vice-president read a few notices. Another introduced the program chairman, who began introducing the president.

The president remained unhappily aware of the age of each. *Something* had to be done, and soon. But what?

Graciously acknowledging the applause which greeted her as she rose, she recalled the happy occasion of Nina Lee Halstead's first appearance on this platform, shortly after the publication of her novel *Stand Not upon the Order,* which had been a close contender for the Pulitzer prize; recalled also that Mrs. John Steeves ("our hostess at the coffee urn this morning") had introduced her that day as club president. She listed several titles of more recent Halstead books, with lively references to some of their characters, and spoke of the effort which had been made from time to time to bring Miss Halstead back for another engagement.

"But Ruth Grienblom is the first program chairman to succeed in doing so, in part no doubt through Ruth's well-known gifts of persuasion, but also in part due to the fact that Miss Halstead, who has been committed not only to an artistic career but to the bringing up of a family as well, has only recently been free again for occasional speaking engagements . . . It is a joy and an inspiration to have her with us, for, as her novels prove, she knows the challenges, the frustrations, the cost, and the rewards in the way of life of women who, like ourselves, strive to be good wives, mothers, and citizens; to do our civic duty without neglecting our domestic duties and likewise without stifling our own need to grow, to learn, to develop, to appreciate, and to create as individual human beings. Our speaker today is one whom we have all long thought of as a personal friend — Nina Lee Halstead, American novelist!"

After the program, which was warmly received, the officers of the club had Miss Halstead and the press as luncheon guests in the board room. Photographs were taken. Then Maida Norris Frome drove Nina Lee Halstead to the airport.

On the way she said suddenly, "The chief problem we have now is attracting young women to our organization. At state and national conventions, I gather that this problem is very general, at least in cities.

Perhaps less so in small towns. Is that your impression?"

Miss Halstead said it certainly was her impression that few of those in her audiences were young. She added rather ruefully that she had assumed it reflected the age of her public rather than that of club memberships, and that younger women preferred other programs.

"No. We have pretty much the same audience for whatever we offer, and so naturally we try to offer what interests them. There is no incentive to do otherwise. We are given no reason to think that young women consider important *anything* that we have always considered important, and still do. So little meeting of minds seems possible between those of different generations now . . . You have daughters, don't you?"

The laughter went out of Nina Halstead's blue eyes. They became grave, though not despairing.

She said, "Yes, I have daughters. Two. And I *am* a daughter. My mother has never had any interest to speak of in anyone or anything she did not recognize as a part of her home and family. It must have been very difficult indeed for her to understand my urge to participate in and try to contribute to the lives of many people, most of whom were total strangers. I am not sure that she ever has understood it, particularly since doing so has often taken me far from those with whom she would have liked me to spend every waking hour. I suppose that it is even more difficult for us to accept in our daughters a trend toward cutting themselves off entirely from those with whom they grew up — from the people, from the places, from the values and standards to which they were born — and especially the trend toward ignoring themselves, neglecting their own potential, trying to avoid any real and lasting involvement, always just looking and never buying, always doubting and never convinced. But this seems to be the next step for civilized women, the majority at least, for those who are not so individual as to avoid any pattern. It is not a step we expected. Nobody warned us. But our mothers did not expect us to go out to make contact with the world and try to change it, either. And nobody warned them that we were going to until we had done it. Yet something in their way of life led to ours, and something in ours has led to the present, which we can only hope is not so chaotic, not so self-defeating, not so pointless and unhuman and alarming as it seems to us."

"But in the meantime what happens to all we have undertaken?"

"We continue to carry it as long as it seems worthwhile to us, as long as we are able. Then it may die. As we shall, having done what we could of what we believed ought to be done. That, I believe, is what we were sent here to do. To the extent that we have done it I feel we have met our responsibilities in this life. In their turn our children will do what they can and must."

There was no parking place near the entrance to the airport offices.

As a porter reached into the Frome car for Nina

Halstead's bag, she covered Maida's gloved hand with hers.

"God made the plan, you know," she said. "Each succeeding generation has its own place in it, and each individual. There is a reason and a purpose in whatever we are and do and whatever happens to us. A good reason and a good purpose. Trust Him, my dear."

Following the porter, she turned and waved. The laughter had come back to her eyes.

A renowned columnist had lately written in a great metropolitan newspaper, announcing his retirement, that the unresolved problems of humanity were as grave as any that had ever burdened man. He was retiring, he said, because "There has crept in a sense of futility because of the transgressions of politicians" and it was "as good a time as any to stop." He complained of his government, which was endorsing "an evangelistic concept of world stewardship," and of a society "both kith and kin" to the total welfare state. He grieved for the American Constitution as being eroded by "the swollen powers of the President" and the "judge-made legislation" of the Supreme Court. He said that the leaders of one of the major political parties alarmed him by their deviousness and naked, driving ambition, and that those of the other were "cowardly and confused." He asked of his own professional colleagues, "Where is the old general-assignment man with the cold objectivity in questioning officials? I'll not look for my kind of stuff any more." He was an old man who had been working in the field of journalism for almost six decades, after dropping out of Princeton in his freshman year for lack of funds. He had covered his first beat on horseback, earned the Legion of Honor with his despatches from the Versailles Peace Conference, twice won Pulitzer prizes for interviews with Presidents of the United States. He had traveled a long way in search of the truth and typed out his findings, hunt-and-peck, day in and day out, year in and year out, as clearly and honestly as he could. He was tired.

Kimberly Tucker, Maida Frome's second daughter, waiting at her desk in the city room of the *Evening Bulletin* for her next assignment, read the story in *Time* magazine and sighed. She knew Rick, her husband, would see it. *Time* was the one magazine which always found him, every issue of it, sooner or later, though often crumpled and muddy, and once so mildewed that some of the pages were stuck together and illegible when pulled apart. He always read it and kept on reading it until the next issue came, doggedly trying to find out what was happening to the principles he was fighting for, in the country for which he daily outwitted death in the hope of returning to it a whole man and a free one.

Dear Rick! Marvelous, adorable, incredible Rick!

Kim had found him on the bank of a tidewater river, standing tall in a small boat to tighten a noose around an old railroad tie which served as a post to hold up the wharf where she sat alone sipping coffee from a paper cup while inside a hut built into the

bank a green crustacean she had pointed at as he
crawled about a tank was turning red in a copper pot.

She had stared disbelievingly at Rick, exactly as she
had at everything since she first reached the salt
marshes in the little rented car which had been delivered to her when she stepped off the plane. At the salt
marshes . . . at the impossibly old houses cheek-by-
jowl with prefabricated developments, and at other
impossibly huge old houses standing on high points of
land like castles with equally old tiny houses scattered
over the lower levels round about, each with its own
fields and each tiny one as well kept as the great one
. . . at the plainness of the churches in the little vil-
lages and the slenderness of their steeples . . . at the
giant elms lining the streets and at the dark, prickly
green of the forests . . . at the sky which was blue
and the water which was bluer . . . Until she had
left the car by the roadside, on a bed of brown
needles, and made her way down a steep ramp to a
wharf, and sat there alone, entirely alone with the
smell of pine and fish and seaweed and steaming
coffee. Until Rick came down from the blue sky or up
from the blue water and stood there, bare to the waist
and barelegged, barefooted, brown as the pine needles, wet with salt spray, brown and shining as if he
had been carved from dark wood and polished, so
brown his blond hair looked almost white and his eyes
had no color at all staring back at her.

Then suddenly he had reached for one of the crates
piled on the wharf and bent and begun filling it with
lobsters.

Kim Frome was on vacation. It was the first time she had ever been anywhere, done anything, entirely alone. No one at home knew why she wished to do this. Her mother had suggested that they spend the summer abroad, the two of them, as a graduation gift; this had been her sister Suzanne's graduation gift. Her father spent every summer at the lake, fishing. Suzanne had said, "I don't wonder you don't want to go with Mom. It would be deadly. I *know*. Like chained to a talking guidebook. And the everlasting shopping for clothes, and presents to bring home for everybody and his brother! Look, can't you tactfully suggest they stake *me* to the trip with you? Nat's dying to go, and she can afford it. Her Dad gives her whatever she wants. He's got a lovely guilt complex. She stayed over there two years once." But Kim had not wanted to go abroad with her mother, and even less with Suzanne and Nat, or anywhere with anyone. She had always been with someone. She just wanted, she told them, the experience of being by herself somewhere she had never been before. So here she was.

And here was Rick. She was still alone, yet not alone.

She went no farther.

They rode the waves and pulled in the traps and climbed the cliffs and lay among the dunes and ran in the rain and sat in the sun and watched the moon rise from the water and set among the pines for days and nights that ran into weeks and on into months.

"When I do this," Rick said once, smoothing oil

across her forehead and the bridge and point of her nose with one long finger, rubbing it gently over her cheeks and shoulders with two big palms, "I can't help wondering how long it would have taken us to get to know each other if you hadn't been a redhead with the kind of skin that blisters at a touch of sun or wind."

They knew each other well by then.

She knew that he was a lobsterman because his father and one of his grandfathers had been lobstermen. The other grandfather had been a lighthouse keeper. Some of his great-grandfathers had been whalers, and there had been at least one sea captain who had rounded the Horn many times in a sailing ship. But there was something Rick liked better than being out on the ocean in his boat and that was making things of wood and repairing wooden things. He had furnished a room called the parlor in his mother's house with pieces he had found in the cellar and dark attic and barn loft and made beautiful. Since he found no desk he had made a desk from applewood after a hurricane laid waste the orchard, and it was as beautiful as the old pieces. All this he had done while he was still in high school. Since then he had repaired fine old furniture for many summer people, and made reproductions for some. He did this in his mother's woodshed in off seasons, hoping someday to build himself a shop. He said he had already carved his sign and gilded it. It was a mermaid holding a banner on which were the words RICK TUCKER, JOINER. When he had a shop to put his sign on, he said, he would never set another lobster trap. She knew all this about him, and much more.

He knew that she had always lived in the Midwest, her father had an insurance business, her mother was a clubwoman, she had two sisters; and that her grandmother, who lived with them, had been born not far from here. He knew these things, but they did not matter to him. They were of no importance beside all else he knew of Kim — the way her long flaming hair blew out in the wake of his boat, her habit of closing her teeth over her lower lip in sudden delight or wonder or admiration, the crinkling at the corners of her eyes when she laughed, the notes in her voice which, always unexpected, made his own voice hoarse if he tried to speak, her arms when she raised them, her body when she ran, her feet clinging to rocks, the lightness of her touch, that she had been graduated from college in June.

She knew what was important to him because he told her. He assumed she knew without being told, but still he told her.

As the summer went on his questions about what she had done in college, what she had learned there, what it meant to her, how she hoped to use it became more frequent, more persistent, more penetrating. This worried her a little, for her replies did not satisfy him. It would have worried her more if she had not known that everything else she said and did and was fully satisfied him.

"There must have been more than that, baby," he

said sometimes. "A whole lot more. I never got to talk before with anybody who had graduated from college. Heck, that's where the brains are. I mean the ones with brains who know how to give out with what they know. They must have said better than you say they said. Honey, you just didn't listen."

"Maybe I was too busy taking notes. Anyway, I only like listening to you."

"Okay, so you listen to me now. If they didn't tell you what you wanted to know, you could have looked it up in books. They must have every book there is."

"They've got a lot of books, darling. But I didn't know what I wanted to know. So how could I know which of all those books to look in?"

"I know what I want to know."

"What do you want to know, Rick? I think you know everything worth knowing."

"Well, you're wrong, baby. I want to know how to take care of you."

"Rick! You *do!* Nobody else does, nobody ever did; but you do. If you didn't, nobody could teach you, even if anybody else knew."

"Wrong again, Red. Sure I know how, right here, right now."

"You're sweet."

"Because right here, right now, there's nothing but you and me and the sky and the water."

"That's the way I like it. That's all I want."

"It's the way I like it, too. But it's not all there is. So it's not all we're going to get. We're going to be in a heck of a lot of hot water, Kimmy — worse off than caught lobsters — if we're not smart enough to keep out of it."

"We're smart enough."

"Says you. You went to college for four solid years and, as far as I can see, never learned one thing about how this great country got made out of all this land and all this sky and all this water, and what people knew and did that kept it growing greater. So how do you know how to help keep it on the right track, headed in the right direction, so when your kids are your age they'll have a country to be proud of, to count on, to want to live right in?"

He was speaking low and quietly. There was no anger in his voice, but something was there which she had never heard before. She lifted her head from his shoulder and drew back to look at his face in the moonlight. He was staring past her, his gaze unseeing on the waves breaking against the cliff.

She said humbly, "I don't, Rick." She could remember being taught that nobody knew which was the right track, the right direction; that truth was relative; that the good mind was an open mind; that strong conviction was at best amusing and at worst the mark of the bigot, and nothing mattered very much except that everyone be freely given as much as possible of whatever he thought he wanted.

She wondered if he had heard her. She put her hand on his and said again, "I don't, Rick."

Then he pulled her against him and she lay there waiting.

"Okay," he said. "So you don't know. So I've got to

find out and then I can tell you. Because in the long run it's the only way I can take care of you. And because your kids are going to be my kids, too."

They kissed and it was better than ever. An ominous, spiraling cloud had passed. A wave of relief and thankfulness washed gently over her.

"Whatever you think, Rick," she whispered. "Whatever you say. Whatever you want."

"That's my girl."

They kissed again, and it was better than before. Once more there was nothing but him and her and the water and the sky.

The end of August came and they had been married a week when he told her what the next step was going to be. It was a hot night and they lay, on the mattress he had brought from his mother's house, in the loft of a woods cabin which was used as a hunting camp in the fall but now was their honeymoon house. There was no light and she could not see his face, only hear his voice and feel his heart beat.

He said he was classified 1A in the draft, but he was not going to wait; he was going to enlist in the Army. He was going to do this to prove his loyalty to his country at a time when he was hearing of others of his age whose principles, totally incomprehensible to him, made them prefer prison sentences to serving in the armed forces. He remember how he had felt as a little boy — and how he still felt — when he heard the national anthem or "God Bless America," when he saw the flag over a public building, when he watched a parade of veterans. He was going to do it because it

was what he was able to do — all he was able to do —
right now in the defense of freedom and the way of
life he wanted for himself and his family. He was going to do it because of all he would learn; and, with
that as a basis, when he came back he would get the
education he needed in order to understand what he
must do next, and how to go about it.

"Oh, Rick! I thought you were going to have a shop
and make things, repair things. I thought you were going to put up your mermaid —"

"That was a long time ago. Maybe I will someday. I
don't know. I have to find out. You're my mermaid
now."

He said they would have another week of nights
here in the woods, of days in the boat, and then he
would take her back to her family to stay until his
tour of duty was over.

She sat up.

"I don't want to go back there. I don't want to go
anywhere. I want to stay here. With you. Forever."

"So do I. But we can't. Too much else has to be
done. I have to go and this is no place for you to stay
without me. You wouldn't like it. I wouldn't like it. I
want to think of you with people you belong to."

"I belong to you."

"Sure. But you belong to them, too. We've still got
our folks, but you're a stranger to mine and I'm even
more a stranger to yours. I want to take you home and
begin to get acquainted with them."

"This is home."

"No. It's a good place while we're in it, but it's not home. When I get back we'll have one."

"Wherever you are is my home."

"But that's just it. While we can't be together, I want you to be with your own folks where you grew up, and I want you to feel it's home."

Kim had tried, beginning the moment she returned to her parents' house after seeing him off on an eastbound plane. She had tried very hard. She could have managed better if Suzanne and Nat had not been there. As it was, now a year since Rick's last leave before going to Vietnam, she concentrated with an almost desperate intensity on their correspondence and on earning and saving money for a home they could share when he came back. Her grandmother was the only one she could talk with about this, and show her bankbook to, who understood what she was trying to do and how important it was that she do it. When she had mentioned her savings at first, her father had been amused, saying that a furnished apartment was more practical in every way for a young couple. Her mother had grieved, and still grieved, that Kim was cutting herself off from social life, from fun, from travel, from all that had meant growth to her when she was Kim's age, from everything except what she did for the newspaper and at the desk in her room; she would never know why Kim had married Rick nor grant that such a marriage had a future. Maisie obviously thought that of all the beautiful, melancholy things she had ever heard about, Kim's situation was

the most beautiful and heart-breaking. She had written several very bad songs about it, and liked to sit
crosslegged on the floor with her guitar between her
knees, staring at Kim and waiting for an inspiration
for another. Suzanne and Nat, having stated flatly that
what Rick had chosen to do and whatever Kim did to
aid and abet him was immoral, the ultimate in im-
morality, were ready to pounce on her with proof of
this point whenever the three were in the same room.
If she answered, they looked at each other with awful
significance as if to say, "Wouldn't you know? Didn't
I tell you? Isn't it horrible?" and swooped on her
again. If she did not answer — as more and more she
did not — they looked at each other as if to say, "You
see it's hopeless," and ignored her, avoiding her eyes
as others might the touch of a leper. Sue and Nat, of
course, professed infinite compassion for and understanding and admiration of the leprous, as for all the
diseased of body and mind, for all the poor, for all the
ignorant, for all the criminals; in short, for all those
they thought needed and would accept their support,
their ministration, and their indoctrination. They
loved everyone, in theory, except those who felt capable and desirous of living their own lives without in-
terference and of maintaining or bringing about a social order which would make this possible. Those
were The Enemy who must somehow be overcome
and slaughtered, or at least incarcerated and made im-
potent; and for this action Sue and Nat, the great
lovers of humanity, had all the zeal of Joan of Arc's
inquisitors and executioners.

Kim wrote Rick nothing of all this. She had no idea what he would make of Sue and Nat of the college Class of '60. During the few September days he had been at the Fromes' they had been on a picket line in Washington, D.C., protesting the war and the draft and cheering the young men who were burning their draft cards, and the family had said only that Sue was on a trip east. Maisie had been at home, but Rick had not tried to figure her out. Nobody did; it was useless. Kim wrote very little about her family, only enough to reassure him that she was with them; and nothing of what she read in newspapers, saw and heard on television of the activities and efforts of many who had had or were getting the educational advantages he thought he wanted for himself. It seemed cruel to add this to the burdens and uncertainties he already carried. She wished he need not know much of what was going on in his country and affecting his future until he came back to it. Surely a shock then would be more easily borne than disillusionment now.

But *Time* reached him and he sometimes asked for her impression of conditions he read about there. Almost certainly he would ask, "What do you think of what this Arthur Krock wrote when he retired?"

She was tired of trying to think of new ways to say she did not know what to think, that they would think it all through together when he came home, that he must believe as she did that however it was, whatever happened, they could handle it, or adjust, or find a way when they were together again . . . "You will know, Rick. I don't, but you will. I know you will. Don't worry about it now. Just keep your mind on what you're doing and take care of yourself. Please, please take care of yourself. For me. Nothing else will matter to me when I have you, Rick. Nothing."

And that was true. But she knew more mattered to him than being with her, was to him an inseparable part of being with her.

She saved up little things to tell him, to make him smile.

Tonight she would write him about the man in the secondhand furniture shop where she had stopped during her lunch hour because, walking past, she had seen Hessian andirons in his window, but they were reproductions; not recent reproductions but not original. Anyway, they might not need andirons at first, for they might not have a fireplace at first, but she hoped they would quite soon, for there had been a fireplace in the hunting lodge.

"He was there alone, Ricky, and half asleep in an overstuffed chair. A funny, kind of fat little man with small scars all over his dark face. I expect he had dreadful pimples when he was a boy. His coat was too tight and pulled apart between the buttons so they looked as if they would surely pop any minute, and under it he had on a faded plaid cotton flannel shirt he'd probably worn all winter without washing it. The door stood open and I didn't think I'd made a sound going in, but as I stood there looking down at the andirons he opened his eye and said, 'No, madam, they're not the best ones. I had a pair of the real thing once. That must've been ten years ago. But you can't tell. I might just get another pair termorrer. 'F you live in town and want to leave me your number, I'll let you know if I do. 'Bout the only chance of getting anything special is to leave me your number. Wait till you see it in the winder and you'll likely wait forever. Things come in here and go out again within an hour if they're good for anything. Didn't used to be like that but 'tis now. Anything's got any age on it, a dozen's waiting to grab it. Same with any nice, beautiful piece of furniture. I don't care what 'tis — table, chair, bedstead, chest of drawers, bookcase, sofa, I don't care — if it was a nice, beautiful piece twenty years ago, or even ten, its better than anything they're throwing together now and I can sell it for half as much. Anything you want, you name it, and leave me your telephone number. Would you believe, I've got dozens of telephone numbers I can call and say, "I've got a nice, beautiful chest of drawers" — or "a beautiful table, nice one" — and they'll tell me, "You bring it right over"? They don't even come to see it, most of 'em. I don't think that's right. I tell 'em they'd better come and look at it, but they say, "No, no. Get it over here as soon as you can. If you think I want it, I want it." They know if I say it's a nice piece, real beautiful stuff, it is. Let me tell you something. Last night I delivered a walnut desk to a man. Nice, beautiful walnut, not a scratch on it, and nice and clean inside. I make all my deliveries nights after I close up here. His wife had come in asking about a desk for him because something is the matter with his legs so he can only get around in a wheelchair. Well, when

I got there with it, he wanted me to help his son take the desk he'd been using up into the attic . . . So I did, and after we settled the new desk he said, "Now seems as if we need something to kind of hold down the opposite side of the room. Maybe a table . . . You got a table you think would fit in over there?" I said no, I didn't. I didn't have a thing in a walnut table. I told him I'd put him down for one if it come in, and keep his telephone number. And then I happened to think, and I told him, "You've got a nice, beautiful table, with a marble top, right up in your attic. Better than anything I've had lately for that spot. Want us to bring it down and see how it looks?" He said sure, so the boy and I brought it down, and I asked his wife for a rag and if she had any Pledge, because it was covered with dust. So I cleaned it up good and he thought it was great, but then she said, "That stand don't look right now." So I said, "No, madam, course it don't. That's a nice, beautiful little pine stand but it don't look right with this walnut and marble, that's for sure. Up in your attic, though, where this table was, I see a nice dark lamp stand with a marble top, a real beautiful one. If you want me to, I'll get it." So I brought that down, and put the pine one in the hall, and polished up the one from the attic, and set on it a bowl of flowers they had there — nice, fresh flowers — and you ought to have seen his face! He was so tickled, you know what he done? He took ten dollars out of his billfold and tucked it into my pants pocket! I told him he didn't need to but he said he hadn't been able to get up attic for so long he'd forgot all about them marble-topped tables his mother used to have, and but for me he might never have laid eyes on 'em again. I feel good about that every time I think of it' . . . Oh, Rick, you'd like him, wouldn't you? I know you would. I like him *so* much. I'm going to keep going in there on my lunch hours to keep acquainted until you come to go with me. Some days I'll buy something, so I won't feel I'm just a nuisance to him, though I really don't think he would feel that way. I'm sure he really likes people. Of course I left him my number. Not my name yet . . ."

She could not decide whether she hoped the secondhand dealer would have the designated reason to call her. What if Sue or Nat should answer the ring and he said, "Madam, I've got your Hessian andirons"? What a red flag to a pacifist!

That Thursday night Walt Ross's parents and his sister Sharon saw him off on a plane for Philadelphia, where he had told them he was to spend the weekend with a friend before returning to Parris Island. He had been at home on leave since Sunday, sleeping late, eating well, driving the Cadillac, being polite to neighbors and family friends, having his picture taken. Now they waited with him at the gate, Sharon clinging to his arm and smiling up at him as if she thought he would like for onlookers to suppose she was his girl friend, his mother handing him a box of fudge she had made herself ("before you woke up this morning,

dear. I really think you have caught up on your sleep.
You look rested"), and his father sneaking a look at
his watch as often as he could.

The gate opened. Over the loudspeaker came the
announcement, "Boarding now for Flight fourteen to
New York, Philadelphia, and Washington. Passengers
boarding now for Flight fourteen —"

Walt said, "I guess this is it. Had a great time,
folks." He picked up his bag, shook hands with his
father, put the bag down to hug and kiss his mother
and Sharon, clutching the box of fudge awkwardly to
keep it from gouging into their backs, fumbled for his
ticket, picked up the bag, and somehow was through
the gate at last, lost in the crowd spilling across the
runway, up the steps, and blinking as he peered into
the interior of the plane.

She was not there. Of course she was not there, nor
would be. He had not really thought she would, had
he? Not *be* there. It was one thing to write . . . It
was all very well . . . But deep down a guy knew
. . . He was no fool . . . not fool enough to let
himself count —

"You have a reservation, sir?"

Sir!

He showed the girl in the uniform whatever it was
he had in his hand.

She said, "Aisle seat, sir. Number twenty-one. Glad
to have you aboard."

He found the number, stowed his bag and the box,
flung himself into the seat, felt the jab of the seat belt
buckle, swore, pulled it out and sank back, knocking

his cap low over his eyes. One thing a Marine could always do, given the chance; he could sleep.

He knew that behind him there were a woman with a small boy, two blondes with tall hairdos, and four men making remarks about the blondes. He knew that in front of him there was a naval officer with his wife. Now a dozen or more men were filling up the seats, shouting back and forth to one another about the convention they were leaving, and asking how soon drinks would be served. They had already had enough. It was going to be a noisy ride. A couple of old women came in, scared-like; then a very elegant woman with a nursemaid carrying her baby . . . A man wearing a soft hat, with a briefcase . . . A fat little woman in a long, dowdy black coat and a black hat with a veil who hesitated beside him and said, "I'm sorry to wake you up, but my seat is twenty-two, by the window."

"Audrey!"

"You were expecting, maybe, somebody else?"

He lurched into the aisle, and thrust her hatbox under his seat. He stood over her, looking down at her. She took off the hat with the veil and handed it to him. She took off two coats and handed them to him; the inner one was an olive raincoat with a belt. He put them all on the hatbox, and stood there looking down at her. It was Audrey.

"You *must* have been expecting somebody else," she said. "You won't even sit with me."

"I guess I have to sit with you. The seats are assigned."

"Like at convocation. If you aren't in your seat when they take attendance, you get marked absent and there goes a perfectly good cut."

"Yeah. And the monitors may be up there in the balcony now, getting out their pencils and little black books. But to heck with the monitors. I can see you better from here . . . Audrey, you're different. You've — changed."

"For the worse?"

"No." He almost shouted the word.

"Sit down, silly."

"Wait. It's partly your eyes." He was almost whispering now.

She closed them.

"They're greener. Or else they're bluer."

She opened them.

"Ranger, if you don't sit down, I'm going to get off."

He sat down, and she instantly slid a hand under his arm and smiled at him.

She said, "That's a good boy."

He had never been so happy in his life. He was through with school, and through with boot training. He could climb a pole and work at the top of it with his head as clear as a day when you can see the snow on top of a mountain a hundred miles away. He could tramp for miles in the heat on one swallow of water and whistle before he took the next one. He could wade into a river up to his neck in the dark and swim against the current until told to get out, and find his way back to where he had come from. Height couldn't scare him, heat couldn't stop him, water couldn't drown him. He was a gorilla, he was a whale, he was an eagle, he was a Marine. And Audrey Mason, a girl who had known him all his life, knew all the worst about him — worse than there was — trusted him; trusted him and liked him; trusted and liked him enough to save up her cuts and her money and start out alone, by bus to Boston, by taxi to the airport, and board a plane for the first time in her life to fly with him to Philadelphia. That was something, man. That was something for a girl like Audrey to do. And here was her hand under his arm, her face smiling up at him in a way she had never smiled at him before, a way nobody had ever smiled at him before. Man . . .

"What was the idea of the veil?" he asked. "And all the coats — is it that cold in Dewey?"

"Silly! I didn't wear them out of Dewey. I had the hat in the box and the black coat over my arm. I put them on in the taxi. You should have seen the driver watching me in his mirror." She laughed, and his stout Marine heart skipped a beat. "Weren't they cute? I got them at a rummage sale. I knew well enough your folks would see you off, so I had to have a disguise or my folks would have known by tonight where I was — or at least that I was far from the campus."

"I never thought of that."

"Lucky for me I did . . . I wonder what I can do with that hat and coat. If we just leave them here, would anybody notify anybody?"

"I doubt it."

"Just the same, we'd better not risk it. We'll find a trash can in Philadelphia and drop them in."

"Do you mind having to be so sneaky?"

"No. I think it's fun. I don't really have to be. It's nobody's business where I am. But you know how people start making other people's business their business and start thinking and saying a lot of things that may be true — and may not, too."

"I know that all right."

"Yes, you do. If anybody knows, you do."

"I'd almost forgot, though."

"I guess you would, being a Marine. Tell me all about that. Everything you've written me, and everything you haven't. I want to know all about it, the bad and the good, the awful and the absolutely great. Come on. Make me feel as if I'd been there, too."

She gave an excited wriggle and then a sigh of content as if certain of being satisfied, clasped both hands around his arm and burrowed her cheek into his sleeve. He bent his head until his chin rested in her soft hair, and began to talk.

They did not notice when the plane took off, though they had responded to the request that they fasten their seat belts and later to the flashed permission to unfasten them.

Walter Ross, U.S. Marine, was back on Parris Island Monday morning and Audrey Mason was in attendance at her classes. Of those who noticed their return, no one knew where they had been. If many had, few would have believed that though they had stayed three nights in the same hotel, they had rooms on different floors, they had not slept together nor had to fight it, yet they had known from the first minute of meeting again that they were in love. Except while they slept they had been constantly together, and throughout each long day they had been teaching each other and learning from each other what it is to fuse two separate hearts, to combine two solitary spirits into one flame.

Men were in their seventh orbit around the earth, one of them walking in space to remove equipment from a rocket they had overtaken, and on a college campus a high government official was dedicating the cornerstone of a library to honor the father of space exploration. Under that cornerstone had been solemnly placed a capsule for the ages, containing, along with the official's speech, a miniskirt, a Bugs Bunny comic book, and the current issue of *Playboy* magazine. Just off the campus, prevented by police from passing through its gates, Suzanne Frome and her friend Nat and two or three dozen other young people from scattered parts of the country who looked much as they did — the same haunted eyes, thin faces, shaggy hair, shapeless sweaters, tight slacks torn off somewhere between knee and ankle, runover loafers — made an endless, ragged circle, carrying on cardboard signs in crude letters the words they chanted in hoarse voices. STOP THE WAR. STOP THE KILLING. STOP THE WAR. STOP THE KILLING. STOP . . . STOP . . . STOP . . . This group followed this particular high official wherever he went to speak. His itinerary was their itinerary. Like groups followed other high officials, attended the christening of submarines, the takeoff of warplanes from home bases, the construction of missile sites. STOP . . . STOP . . . STOP . . . Protest was rampant. There was no action, no philosophy, no attitude, no opinion, no faith, no system, no practice without its opposition, its train of protesters so dedicated that they thought of little else than how better and more conspicuously to make their protest.

Stop the war. Stop communism. Stop crime. Stop the police. Stop segregation. Stop integration. Stop profits. Stop poverty. Stop ignorance. Stop intellectualism. Stop disease. Stop the population explosion. Stop the slums. Stop the disfiguration of the whole face of the country. Stop private control. Stop federal control. Stop disciplinary methods. Stop juvenile delinquency. Stop death. Stop the high cost of living. Stop the overcrowding and understaffing of hospitals. Stop unemployment. Stop producing. Stop recession. Stop escalation. Stop the highway accidents. Stop the drought. Stop prayer. Stop flag-waving. Stop violence, drug addiction, promiscuity, excessive desire for material things, and senseless destruction. Make a law. Make it illegal. Break the law.

Surrounded by opposing factions of eloquent, hostile, often fanatical placard-carrying protesters, the majority of the citizenry stood swaying in a physically comfortable but mentally and emotionally threatening environment. They were warm, well fed, supplied with astonishing artificial aids and artificial organs, within a corral of shining promises that whatever need might arise would be met. By edict fear had been banished from the realm. But the two most basic and devastating fears of humankind obeyed no social edict, and from their winds, which gnawed at the very vitals, the citizenry had no protection. To dare to live a man must have faith in himself and in his ability to meet challenge and to build on his success or failure. To dare to die he must accept the inevitability of death, know God, and trust Him. With faith denied and daring talked out of him, trained out of him, dieted out of him, bred out of him, a man becomes a pitiable creature, beyond reach of God and totally dependent on other men's mercy, which, having been a man himself, he uneasily recalls has limits. So he huddles there in the sunny corral, alone though pressed against others to feel the winds less, suspicious even of white, fleecy clouds, wishing he could pray. If he could, he would plead, "No change. Please, no change at all."

But outside are the placards. STOP PRAYER. STOP . . . STOP . . . STOP . . .

Though no movement, no trend, no current is ever stopped short unless by divine miracle. Since mankind must work out his own salvation, the present is rooted in the past and the future in the present. What happens today is the outgrowth of what happened yesterday, and what happens to a man tomorrow depends upon what he and his fellowmen do today. If he has known freedom and wishes to know it again, though now enslaved, he will do so only if he begins to push forward toward that end with his whole mind, his whole heart, and every muscle in his body, and never stops pushing, however strong the forces against him, however long the road. Change is constant. Whatever is not growing better is growing worse. We move always away from something and toward something else, whether we choose to or not; nor may we choose the rate of speed, though our effort — or lack of effort — may affect it. Such choice as we have is one of direction. A civilization goes toward opportunity, morality, self-respect, wisdom, love, and truth, or goes away from them. It goes toward God, or away from Him. This is natural law for humanity, and no man can break or repeal or amend it.

For hygiene and convenience every item of food to be consumed was packaged or wrapped. Empty boxes and papers overran the kitchens, spilled out of pockets, blew from cars, dropped from careless hands. Every city and every smallest town had to provide a place for their burning, crews to pick them up, trucks to carry them away. Trash cans, often overflowing, occasionally empty, but always battered and ugly, stood by every house door and apartment door, waiting to be dumped or filled. A campaign was launched to beautify the nation. Now trash cans in the form of bright new containers labeled EVERY LITTER BIT HURTS appeared on every corner, lined the walks in parks, the roadsides, the beaches. Advertising signs on major highways were replaced by other signs reading $100 FINE FOR THROWING TRASH ON HIGHWAY; SPEEDING IS PUNISHABLE BY LOSS OF LICENSE; STAY ALERT; FOOD AND FUEL AHEAD. This was a change, but where was the beauty?

To promote education for all, to prevent dropouts from school, the government provided free meals, high school diplomas were guaranteed to all who attended classes for four years, teachers' salaries depended upon how many education courses they had taken, and a plan for government-financed college education for all young people was under serious consideration. But what was a teacher beyond the number of courses he had taken? Who decided what he was to teach? What was a student beyond a name on a chart? If he was studying, what was in the books he studied? If he was learning, what was he learning? What was the future of the student who was staying but not learning? Would the system destroy him? Who was to do the work he might have done successfully and proudly? Where were the highly intelligent to be instructed and trained in what they needed to know? Where was wisdom to be found? No institution which is for everyone serves anyone well.

There was a concerted effort to bring unemployment to the vanishing point, but no day in the year without its hundreds of thousands on strike for better working conditions, mainly higher wages, which when they got them would increase the prices of everything they wanted to buy. The struck industrial plants were dark, or lit only in one corner for skeleton office staffs who ran a gauntlet of surly and often obscene abuse as they grimly came and went, and sometimes were targets for bricks, stones, and clubs.

There were public nurses, free clinics, free drugs, free hospital care. All were so much in demand that nurses were in short supply and those nurses on duty, like the doctors and surgeons, had become over-worked and scarcely able to maintain a professional, much less a friendly and kindly, attitude toward pa-tients; stocks of drugs ran out; hospitals grew alarm-ing overcrowded, despite new wings being added, new buildings going up day after day. Where was the health they had been expected to insure? The citizen who had not lately been in a hospital bed, was not awaiting word that one was now available to him, did not have a half-circle of small bottles around his plate at each meal and pillbox in his pocket, was not ex-hausted every day before time for his coffee break, did not require sedation to sleep, but felt well, looked well, and acted well was so rare as to be an object of suspicion. Acquaintances thought him a show-off, and friends worried about what he was hiding.

Sexual promiscuity had become more than a way of life for many; it was defended, promoted, praised as an article of pseudo-faith, the basis of a pseudo-reli-gion. The refusal to give one's body was selfish, even miserly; it was there to be given. The really sweet and generous girl would sleep with almost anyone, as often as invited, or without being invited. Why not? What was so special about it? Besides, varied sex relations were essential to knowledge. How much could be learned from one in comparison with what could be learned from many? Dark, light, old, young, tall, short, lawyer, teacher, cabdriver, landscape gardener . . . Now consider other nationalities — French, Ital-ian, Norwegian, Turkish — and other races — Oriental, Negro, Jewish, Indian! All there to be learned from. One had only to get where they were. Sooner or later (but not much later) one must travel as others were doing. "I was out west near a reservation all last summer but I'm determined to get to Europe next year, money or no money. I'll bicycle, and *somebody* will feed me wherever I go, I know that." "Oh, but darling, you must get to Hongkong as soon as you can. I was there all last year and really the whole world is in Hongkong." "I know what you mean, but I have a feeling — I really can't explain it — that I'm supposed to go to Nigeria first. After Europe, I mean. Maybe I'll find a way to get to Nigeria from Europe. Oh, I don't know. I may never come home — wouldn't that be marvelous? . . ." But where was love? Where was commitment? Where was responsibility? Without these the body is no better gift than an empty and cracked cup; and a lifetime is not long enough for learning all one man and one woman can teach each other . . . Kim and Rick Tucker knew this now, and Audrey Mason and Walt Ross were beginning to realize it. But what would convince the sex cultists who read no more of any human book than a paragraph somewhere in the middle, before picking up and glancing into the next?

Ellen Dockham sat on a milking stool just inside the open shed door, a grain bag across her spread knees, cutting seed potatoes with a jackknife which had belonged to her grandfather. Each section to be planted must have at least two eyes in it, and three were better; then one would surely put out a strong sprout. She did not have to look at the basket from which she was taking whole potatoes, at that into which she tossed the sections, nor at the potato and knife she held. For this work, as for much of what she did inside the house and out, she saw with her earth-stained hands. She could see the floors and the ground here with her feet, and the sky with her nose.

"I could do as well, almost," she thought, "if I was blinded. Still in all, I'm glad I ain't."

It was good not to have to depend altogether on nose and ears to know which way the wind was blowing when she could not feel it, as now, or to have to piece together what they told her with memory pictures of the small, new leaves of the shade trees, tender yet tough, sweeping the sky and dancing wildly as they swept, of the budded lilac bush beside the sink drain plucking up her enormous skirts and joining in with the astonishing ease and grace and featherweight step of most huge women who venture to trip the light fantastic, of the scudding spring clouds which might or might not pelt the new grass with raindrops as they flew overhead. Though there had been winds and days much like this in every one of Ellen's many years, no wind, no day was ever exactly like even one other; each flew in with the first streaks of light newborn and wearing a quiver of surprises. It was good to see as well as to feel, and hear, and smell every waking hour as it came, to absorb the truth of today without adulterating it, to be able to leave yesterday undisturbed where one could go back to it at will and find it just as it was, completed, serene, and perfect.

This knife now . . . It had been in her grandfather's pocket the day he died. The day he fell face-down on a towering hayload being rushed to the barn ahead of a thunderstorm. This was some years after the death of Ellen's father. Her grandfather had been carrying on the farm with her mother's help. Her mother, who had been raking after, and a neighbor, who had been pitching on, had pulled him off the load as soon as it was under cover, carried him into the house and laid him on the kitchen couch. Ellen could remember it. She had been about five years old at the time, and had been watching the lightning from the window before they brought him in. He was eighty-three. But she could not see his face because her mother was at the head of the couch, bending over. She could see only his faded blue overalls, their cuffs bunchy with hayseed, and the steel bottoms of his boots.

The neighbor was by the door, turning his big straw hat and twisting its rim.

"Ellie, go into Grandpa's bedroom and bring me a sheet from his cupboard."

Suddenly Ellen had been afraid of the lightning and the thunder. She never had been before. She and her grandfather had often watched and listened to it together, from the kitchen door or just inside the shed or barn. But she thought it had never been so bright then, or so loud. Still she went into his bedroom, climbed on a chair to turn the wooden button, and found the sheet. She was afraid she would never get back to the kitchen, but she did, and her mother turned and took the sheet from her. When she turned toward Ellen again, she had covered the whole couch with the white sheet. It was a big sheet, for her grandfather's bed was a big bed though he was not a big man, and now it touched the floor along the side and across both ends of the couch where he always rested after supper and which he had told her he had made when he was first married and had just finished building the house. He had worked on it summer evenings in the yard, he had told her; and "your grammy — that you never saw, God love her — held the lantern for me."

Her mother had something in her hand.

"What's that?" asked Ellen.

Her mother glanced at her in a strange way and opened her hand.

It was her grandfather's knife.

"Why did you take Grandpa's knife?" Ellen asked. "He needs it for — he needs it for everything, all the time."

Her mother was looking down at it and kept on looking down at it.

At last she shook her head and said, "No. He don't need it, Ellie. You and I, we need it now."

"Why?"

"Because — we've got to learn to use it. The way he did. All the ways he did."

That was yesterday. Today Ellen was as deft with

the knife as ever her grandfather had been, and as accustomed to its slight weight in her pocket, the reassurance and companionship of its small nudge on her
thigh. This was her knife, this her milking stool, these
her Green Mountain potatoes which had grown a
dozen to a hill last year and cooked up nice and mealy
in the pot every night of the winter now past. Winter
had passed and spring had come and here was a dry
wind blowing out of the northwest from behind the
barn, bringing with it the smell of manure she had
that morning forked into depressions she had made
with her hoe where Chet had plowed, harrowed, and
furrowed for her. The robins were back and running
over the worked ground, looking for worms. There
was music in the top of the sugar maple, and when
she stepped out of the shed door, shaking the grain bag
and brushing off her apron, a cloud, a host, of evening
grosbeaks flew off toward the pond with a flutter of
wings.

A cloud, a host, of golden . . . What was it? A
cloud, a host . . .

No matter. Tomorrow she would plant.

4

THEY said it was a nation of laws, not of men. But it was a democratic nation and in a democracy men — and women — make the laws, and the society of which they are a part passes judgment on whether it is essential or even desirable that the law be kept. Who can deny that an immoral law is better broken, that it is nobler openly to break an immoral law and pay the penalty than meekly to keep it and go unpunished? But what are the standards by which a law can be shown to be immoral? Did those who voted for it consider it immoral? Why not? And is it moral to allow one who has broken an immoral law to undergo punishment? Is it noble of me to break any law which I have convinced myself is immoral? Should I be punished for doing what my conscience tells me I should do? And if I have no conscience, should I be punished for that, since no man can give himself a conscience?

What is your conscience, anyway? Where did you get it? Are you sure it is a reliable guide? If you are doubtful and concerned, where do you go for answers?

"I can't see that what you are suggesting," said one lawyer to another, "is according to the terms of this will you wrote yourself."

"It is not far from what he told me while we were walking our dogs in the park," replied the other, though no one could testify to this but the dogs, "which is why I phrased it quite loosely. I think we can get it by Probate."

"My old man would sure be mad if he knew I'd driven into Chicago right down State Street in the rush hour tonight," said a boy sitting in a Thunderbird on the shore of Lake Michigan. "I told him I was going to your house for dinner and around the corner to your little old school dance in Oak Park."

The girl beside him asked drowsily, not really caring, "What if he should go looking for you at the dance?"

"He won't. He's playing poker tonight."

"But if he did . . ."

"He'd be in a sweat, and good enough for him. If he hadn't pushed to find out where I was going, I needn't have lied."

"He'd say, well, it's his car."

"*Who* says it's his car? It's the family car. Heck, I only have it twice a week. If he'd get me one of my own, I wouldn't have to take this one. Shouldn't wonder if he's coming round to that idea. The old lady's working on it."

One Washington legislator said to another, "I know you're against this much money going to my state, Mac, but I've got to have it. This bill has got to pass. I'm running scared and for good reason. Everybody at home is talking about how much went across the river from us last term. They're for balancing the budget and all that, but the way money's flying now, the dish being passed around and around and around, they're in no mood to keep on saying 'No, thank you' until it's empty. They think it's up to me to stop it long enough to dip in and get that dam. Either I do or I'm a dead duck this election. And from all I read I judge there is a lot of heavy artillery aimed at you, too, fella. So what do you want to promise them for next session that I'll help you get if you'll vote for my bill?"

The other legislator hunched his broad shoulders in a gusty sigh and said gently, "Okay, Bob. If we must, we'll go all over it again. I was sent down here for the same reason you were sent up — to do everything possible to cut down on federal spending, leave tax monies with the states so they can afford to keep out of the control of the federal government, and leave private concerns enough to produce with, and expand with, and initiate with. I'm still working for the voters who sent me down here. If there aren't enough of that kind left to send me down again, I'll stay there and see if I can cultivate a new crop. Private enterprise could build your dam and ought to be allowed to. We started out together here, working together on a lot of stuff, but that was quite a while ago and don't pretend it wasn't. Times have changed, I know, and you've changed. I haven't. I'm not making a deal, and I'm not voting for your bill . . . But if it's any comfort to you, I see it as pretty certain to pass."

"It had better," the first legislator said gloomily, "or Ken Saunders will be up here next session instead of me. And you can figure about what help *he*'ll be to you!"

Back home, in a mountain town some distance from the capital of the second legislator's state, an old man and his youngest son sat at crowded and untidy roll-top desks putting together a weekly newspaper. Both were in shirtsleeves. The old man wore suspenders, which he still called galluses, and had a thumb thrust under one. The mail had just come in and he was riffling through it. Suddenly he paused and tore open a long envelope. It was the weekly "Letter from Your Congressman." As he read he chuckled several times, and when he finished tossed the folded sheet across to his son's desk.

"Read that, Andy," he said.

His son glanced around at him and grinned.

"Good, huh? All of a sudden, you've got the look of a war-horse smelling gunpowder."

"That's what he sounds like in that letter. It's all about what he says he takes pride in, and you can tell he does, too. What he's voted *for* in the last two years and what he's voted against. Everybody ought to know without his telling 'em, but put it in caps, boy — every danged word of it. People that wouldn't vote to send him back want their heads in a noose, and will deserve it if they get it. Trouble is, we'll all be strung up with them. Still, we'll know why it happened and who's to blame. That may help us some. Read it, boy, read it."

When Andrew Pollister, Jr., looked up from the last paragraph, his father had put on a suit coat misshapen to accommodate the flabby, aging body of a sedentary son of working farmers and stone masons, covered his bald head with a straw hat, kicked off his slippers, and now stood with a foot on his teetery swivel chair, grunting as he tied his shoelace.

"Where you going, Dad?"

Andrew Pollister, Sr., let his shod foot down with a thump and straightened his arthritic back with difficulty.

"What do you think of it?"

"Of what? The letter? It's great, of course. Question is, will it make more people mad than it pleases?"

"We'll find that out soon enough. Print it."

"Sure will. I asked you where you're going."

"Home, boy. The stuff is all in. You can put it to bed. You're a sight better at that than I am. Only I want that letter to start on the front page. In caps."

"It will."

Andrew, Sr., reached the door open onto the sidewalk. Andrew, Jr., could see the crippled feet cringing from the pressure of leather, even though the shoes were too big and slits had been cut along the insides, next to the big toes.

There the old man stopped and turned. Between

the hat brim and the sweatstained open shirt collar he still had that look of a war-horse smelling gunpowder, a horse trained to battle and glorying in it, urged on by lively memories of earlier victories, the sweet and spicy taste of them still in his mouth and hungry for more.

"I'm going to celebrate that letter and those votes, boy," he said gleefully. "If you're right and this is the last thing to celebrate, I'd better make sure of this celebration. If you're wrong and there's going to be more reason by and by, this'll get me in practice. I'm going to have your mother call up the Hickses and the Flynns and the Shapiros and the Roberges and the Petrovskis and the Sylvesters and anybody else she wants to that we know is on our side and ask 'em if they want to meet us over at the Rockaway for supper. While she's doing that I'm going to climb into a bath-tub and if I ever get out I'll put on a clean shirt and a necktie and my Sunday suit, and she'll dress up and we'll ride out. After we eat, we'll tell 'em to come back to our house and she'll play the piano and we'll all sing. Soon as you get through here, come home and sing with us. Do you good."

"I'll try to make it," Andy said. "Now have yourself a ball."

He grinned again, waved, and spun round to hunch over his desk and reread the letter from the Congressman whose campaigns the *Clarion* had enthusiastically supported for more than twenty years. Even Andy could remember when every other newspaper, not only in Mac's district but all over the state, had

supported him editorially. Now the *Clarion* was the
only one. Most of the weeklies strove for political
neutrality, but all the dailies were strong for Murray
Danforth, Mac's opponent, a tousleheaded young fellow from New York who had been in this state only a
couple of years but had brought with him some smart
new ideas about urban renewal and civil supervision
of courts and police and getting federal money to buy
up timberlands to be made into parks. And papers
strong for Danforth didn't stop with their editorials
and printing his speeches; they glorified him in every
news story he appeared in; every time he shook somebody's hand he was described as "mobbed by well-
wishers"; and he was photographed starting his car,
eating at a hamburger stand, entering a Boston theater
with his wife, who had been a Hollywood starlet before he swept her off her feet, boarding a plane, sharing a bag of popcorn with a Negro child, putting his
arm around an old lady in a home for the elderly,
trading jokes with a man named Cohen in a gas station, draining a Coke bottle, waiting in a trench coat
for a factory gate to open, staring soulfully at a view
from the top of an observatory, and so on, ad nauseam.
While mention of the current Congressman was confined to the lower inside corner, midway of the paper,
under small, misleading headlines, and implied that
he was talking but nobody was listening. Even there
it was surprising how often, when he was quoted, the
type was scrambled.

What was it about hair, Andy wondered. All of a
sudden it had come about that if anybody had enough

hair, he was great, and, whatever slot he wanted, he was *in,* unless somebody with more hair wanted it.

In the picture the *Clarion* always ran with the "Letter from Your Congressman" Mac had a reasonable head of hair, but it was the same photograph as when Andy first went to work on the paper, three years ago.

"His forehead better not be any wider when he comes home to start campaigning. That much I know," Andy muttered.

He stood up and stretched. As his arms fell to his sides, his attention was caught by a sheet of drawing paper tacked to the wall above the editor's desk. Though no doubt white once, it had been there so long in the rising smoke from the editor's pipe that it was as brown as wrapping paper. For all Andy knew it had been there before he was born. Certainly it had been there when he was in grade school and first began hanging around this office.

There was no decoration, only words, on the paper, but the words were hand lettered with great care and sense of design. In caps, of course. The editor of the *Clarion* had always believed in the effectiveness of caps.

AN AMERICAN CREED

I DO NOT CHOOSE TO BE A COMMON MAN. IT IS
MY RIGHT TO BE UNCOMMON IF I HAVE THE ABILITY
AND THE COURAGE. I SEEK OPPORTUNITY; I WILL
PROVIDE FOR MY OWN SECURITY. I DO NOT WISH TO
BE A KEPT CITIZEN, HUMBLED, DULLED, WITHOUT
SPIRIT. I REFUSE TO BARTER INCENTIVE FOR THE

DOLE. I WILL NOT TRADE FREEDOM FOR BENEFI-
CENCE, NOR MY DIGNITY FOR A HANDOUT.

I WILL NEVER COWER BEFORE ANY MASTER NOR
BEND TO ANY THREAT. IT IS MY HERITAGE TO STAND
ERECT AND UNAFRAID, TO THINK AND ACT FOR MY-
SELF. THIS I HAVE DONE.

> "LET EVERY MAN PROVE HIS OWN WORK;
> THEN SHALL HE HAVE REJOICING IN HIM-
> SELF ALONE AND NOT IN ANOTHER, FOR
> EVERY MAN SHALL BEAR HIS OWN BUR-
> DEN"
> . . . PAUL'S EPISTLE TO THE GALATIANS

This I have done . . . These were probably not
the editor's own words — Andy had never asked —
but if not they were the words of a brother in time
and spirit; for this Andrew Pollister, Sr., *had* done,
and was able so far still to do because of the foundation it had been possible for him to lay up in an earlier day, in what seemed now another world. Because
he had always thought and acted for himself, even in
childhood on the hill farm, throughout his nearly seventy years, he could not conceive of doing otherwise;
and perhaps, if he did not live too long, he always
could. Nor could he conceive of any sensible person
doing otherwise, whatever the conditions. This left
him with a residue of confidence in his fellowman,
and therefore of hope, which welled up richly when
he saw what he believed to be true and right well expressed, simply and clearly; because surely only those
who had not encountered this truth, so expressed,

could doubt it. Now that it was here and would appear *in caps* in his paper, he could put on his hat and shoes and go off like a boy let out of school to eat and sing with his cronies, longtime friends of his own age, or somewhere near it, whose principles he knew to be the same as his own and with whom he could easily communicate. Lucky guy, despite his aches and pains.

For behind him, as he went, unseen forces were moving in as if to cut off his return, and fog seemed to roll up from the floor, down from the ceiling, in from the sides of his office, with the intent of slowly wiping out the proud words behind his desk.

Andy's arms, hanging at his sides, felt heavy. He walked slowly to the open door and his feet felt heavy. He stood looking down the quiet, sunbaked street.

Somehow it had become not quite honorable to be or wish to be other than a common man, to use abilities others did not have, to show courage openly. One was taught to be as much as possible like everyone else, to conceal his special abilities, to agree that it was every man's right to die in his bed, to close his eyes lest he be called as witness. He could want and demand opportunity, but not actively seek or make it; opportunity was either given to you or withheld. One who said that he would make his own security was marked as a man with no concern for others; it was of no consequence whether or not he achieved security, without aid, except that if he did he had quite certainly done so at the expense of his fellow citizens. Anyone humbled and dulled by being helped had been wronged; to be helped was his right and if he did not know this those who helped him were at fault. Trade freedom for beneficence? Nonsense. There were new freedoms now — the freedom from want and the freedom from fear. And there was no beneficence in giving. It was the duty of one who had to give, and the right of one who had not to receive. Dignity, like opportunity, was not to be earned but was due every man, and the debt paid or unpaid by others. *No one* should cower, or feel threatened. It was *everyone's* natural right to stand erect and unafraid. Unless, of course, he "rejoiced in himself alone," which was antisocial and immoral and not to be tolerated, since the only proper rejoicing was in the welfare of others; and what was old Paul thinking of when he said that every man should bear his own burden? In a good and great society, no man would bear his own burden, only the burdens of everyone else.

But Andy Pollister had to bear his own burden, which was that he could not rejoice in himself or in anything he saw about him or in anything he foresaw of the future. He was twenty-two years old and alone with his inheritance. There was no one for him to eat with or sing with, tonight or any night.

He was stopped before he had started.

It had not been his expectation, or that of anyone else, that he would one day have a desk in the *Clarion* editor's office. The editor, though glad to have him, was still puzzled by it. Andrew, Sr., and Lillian Pollister had always wanted the best for their six children, of whom Andy was the youngest and the only one still living in the state. Gran, the oldest, named for his mother's father, had won appointment to Annapolis, and, now nearing forty, was a rear admiral, commanding his own ship in the troubled Far East. The four girls were graduates of various colleges — Simmons, Sargent, Mount Holyoke, and the State University — and all but one married. Their husbands were a doctor, a college professor, and a bank president. Lura, unmarried, was a university librarian in California. They all came home for Christmas if they were in the country. It was a family tradition. But they were too many now for the size of the Pollister house and all but Lura slept at the motel. Lura; and Andy, of course. Andy had the bedroom which had been his since he took it over when Gran left for Annapolis; and Lura had the girls' bedroom which had been hers and Molly's before they went away to school, when Marilyn and Dot had come up to it from the front room downstairs and Andrew, Sr., and Lillian regained use of their parlor.

As far back as he could remember, Andy had wanted to be a newspaperman, but he had dreamed of being on the staff of a big city daily. To this end he had been first a delivery boy for the *Clarion,* then a legman for it weekends and vacations; and he had been the first underclassman ever to be named the editor-in-chief of the monthly high school paper. That had been a good year, his junior year in high school. He had not only edited the paper, but had been anchor man for the track team, the juvenile lead in a community play, drummer for the town band, marshal for the seniors at graduation; had joined the church, and had his first date. Oh, that Kathy Christianson, with her two thick tawny braids which she could — and did — sit on, her dimples giving the lie to her somber blue eyes, and her sloping shoulders which the soft pink and white stole of her junior prom formal only pretended to conceal! . . . Senior year had been good, too. He had his driver's license, was again editor-in-chief of the *Hilltop,* sure of giving the valedictory address, not only admitted to one of the great universities of the country but a Merit Scholar; and he and Kathy were working conscientiously at not going steady with the result that when either of them dated anyone else, they returned to each other as if it were the night before the Fourth and a spark from a single, fizzling Roman candle had set off a whole package of sky rockets. That summer they had given up the losing battle and made the most of every free hour — canoed on the river, ridden the waves and had cookouts at the beach, danced in the street on band concert nights, and lingered on her porch steps, dreading to say good night.

Kathy had seen no sense in his going to college. No sense at all. She was going to work in the local bank. Within a year she would be a teller. And the bank was just across the street from the *Clarion.* Within a year —

But Andy had his dream.

"You wait," he told her. "We're only seventeen. Someday I'll be doing a column for a New York paper and we'll have an apartment on Washington Square. Or I'll be writing features for a Washington paper and we'll have a house in Alexandria. I'll get assignments abroad. We'll go to Europe. We'll go to Japan. We'll go to South America. You just wait, Kathy. You'll see."

They had kissed, and she had cried. He had held her close and dried her eyes and that made her cry again. So they kissed again, and she cried harder. There seemed no way out of it but to square his shoulders and go, because he had to get ready to take her away from the local bank and the local paper, far away from this little mountain town, out into the world where so much waited to be done . . .

But Kathy had not waited. Within the year she had married a boy in training at the air base, and now she was with him in Germany. It was Andy who was here. Alone.

Because nothing had been as he expected.

The campus of his university was mostly asphalt, separated from the sprawling city which surrounded it by an iron fence with ornate gates. He had a single room with cement floor, blank plaster walls and one window, in a building like a factory. The students he encountered in the halls, lavatory, or elevators approached him only to ask if he had anything in his room to drink or, sometimes, if he wanted to come in for a drink or to go out for a drink. He did not drink. He went to classes and listened to lectures, went to the cafeteria and thought about them, went to the library and did assigned readings, returned to his room and thought about them. At first he was mystified, incredulous. It could not be, he thought, that the great scholars who lectured, the presumably greater scholars who wrote the books, were saying what it seemed to him that they were saying. Topics for papers were assigned and he wrote the papers with great care, handed them in, sometimes had them returned to him and sometimes not. If they were returned to him, the grades scrawled on them in red pencil were usually C, sometimes D, once or twice B. The grade did not matter so much. It was the occasional comment in red pencil which at first surprised him, then worried him, and finally angered him.

You must be joking!

Why do you say this? You can't believe it. Or do you?

Absurd, on the face of it. See Norton.

He had seen Norton, the sociology assistant, and Rushworth, the English assistant, and Schwedes, the world history assistant, and the other candidates for graduate degrees who read and graded papers for the professors who lectured before his classes and were always the first to leave the classroom, gathering up their notes during their last few sentences, then turning on their heels and walking away. He had seen the assistants who only sometimes motioned to him to sit down while they lay back, feet on desk, and told him with raised eyebrows and fake friendliness or with sharp glances and biting sneers what they thought was wrong with his thinking. None of them was of any mind to listen to what he thought was wrong with theirs. Thus parting with them was usually abrupt, with no change of point of view on either side.

He was angry when he went home at the end of the first semester, and ready to believe that Kathy was right, that no one was going to educate him but himself and his life experience, and that as soon as he could get a job on a city newspaper they should be married even if they had to live for a while in two rooms of a fourth-floor walk-up. But that was when he had found a letter from Kathy waiting for him, telling him she had flown west on a visit to the parents of the Air Force mechanic she was going to marry in May. He had spent most of his between-semesters break walking in the snowy woods, noting the tracks of small animals and an occasional deer, hearing the wind in the tops of the pines, and trying to make up his mind whether to go back to the university or look for a job where he could begin at the bottom, no matter how far down the bottom was. His parents had watched him anxiously whenever he was in their sight, but asked no questions.

Finally he had gone back, in the hope that among new lecturers and new assistants he would find one from whom he could learn something that seemed to him both new and true, or at least that from one of them he would hear of a book which would show him how to interpret what was going on in the country and the world in the light of what his own experience so far had been. But it did not happen. Everything was more confusing, more disturbing than before, if only because his former instructors now obviously expected him to be difficult and had alerted others to a common problem. To find a Merit Scholar a problem intrigued them all, apparently. But they found no solution as winter ran into spring, and neither did he.

The end came in early May when an hour examination in English was returned to him with a failing grade, written all over in red pencil, and with a note in the same color taped to the inside of the bluebook's back cover.

"Every other bluebook from this class took me only a few minutes to grade." (*Sic. Twenty-seven parrots?*) I have spent over two hours and a half on yours, mainly to explain to you why it is a useless, egotistical disgrace. You have no right to so much attention from a grader unless you manifest signs of a sincere will to learn or else display occasional flashes of intellectual brilliance. I find no trace of either in this bluebook and am willing to have this judgment checked by anyone teaching at this university. Nor am I ashamed of the apparent mercilessness of these remarks. I am convinced you lack neither the intelligence nor the application to earn an honor grade in this course — only the moral character, specifically the mixture of openness and humility that forms the personal virtue known as 'humanity.' I would be, I have been, willing to try to help you improve your performance, but I regret to say that it seems clear to me I have done you no good. This is the last (possible) attempt. There is nothing more I can do for you but pray."

Andy Pollister had not gone to bed that night. He had gone to his room, locked his door, sat at the desk or paced the floor or stood at the window listening to the songs and shouts of some of his fellow students who were having a party on the floor above and tossing their bottles into the street five stories below. The sound of the crashes came back up as a dying tinkle almost inaudible among the soprano shrieks of the guests.

He was trying to figure out what was so meritorious about an essay examination on presumably debatable material which could be read and graded in a few minutes. To what noble use was put the time of the grader thus saved? Why was it useless to disagree with another's philosophy of life? Why was it an egotistical disgrace for a young man to defend his own convictions when they were under fire, to remain unconvinced that he was wrong even though he was a minority of one in a group of thirty — or of thirty million, for that matter? Was only submission proof of a sincere will to learn? When had "humanity" become a virtue, and "open-ness" (unhyphenated) and humility become its chief or only characteristics? Above all and most importantly, even crucially, who in this university or anywhere else had the right to say that Andy Pollister lacked moral character?

Graduate-degree-candidate Zecker was right on one point. Like Norton, Rushworth, Schwedes and the rest, he had done Andy Pollister no good, and this was indeed his last attempt, since it was the last chance he was going to get. And he might as well skip the so-called prayer since it was unlikely that Andy's God would recognize it as such and listen to it.

Andy began pulling stuff from the drawers of his desk and dresser and throwing it into bags. He left the room, and the dormitory, and the asphalt campus at the crack of dawn, unshaven because if he had encountered in the lavatory a student who was on his way to bed, he probably would have punched him in the nose. And it was not freshman but faculty noses that he longed to punch. But he told himself it would be like driving his fist into jellyfish, and hurried down the deserted street toward the bus station, his bags bumping against his knees.

He did not go home, of course. He could not go home in May, for this was the month Kathy was to be married. There would be stories of her bridal showers in the *Clarion*, talk of her attendants, her dress, her veil. Then there would be rice and confetti on the church steps and on the lawn in front of the Legion Hall, and a picture of Kathy and her groom in the paper, Kathy in the white gown, the white veil . . . He could not go home in June because Kathy would be back from her wedding trip, even at the teller's window in the bank perhaps, anyway coming and going on the street, the somberness vanished from her eyes — and he had thought *he* would be the one to take it away! — her dimples playing, her braids bouncing. He could not imagine Kathy without her braids.

He did not go home until September, after she had gone to Germany, and only for the Labor Day weekend.

By then he had run the full gauntlet of returning nights to a cheap room from days of making the rounds of newspaper buildings, seeing his money dwindle until he could scarcely swallow for thinking what the swallow cost, making the rounds of employment agencies and sitting for hours on a bench until told that another applicant had been hired, giving up the room and spending his nights in hotel lobbies, the subway, the bus stations, the parks, as long as he could in each without being told to leave, always hungry but thankful that it was summer, substituting for bus-boys, dishwashers, and porters on vacation for money to buy a place to sleep in, and doggedly continuing his rounds of the newspapers. By August he had his job. He was a reporter for the *Sun*, sitting nights in a police station and following in a cab when the police answered a call. It was grim, depressing, and exhausting work, but he was on a metropolitan evening paper, and he went home Labor Day to explain to his parents why he had done what he had done, for he doubted that they fully understood it from what he had said in letters.

He had not been sure that they understood it when he told them, though they gravely nodded their heads. He doubted that they understood it yet. With little formal education of their own, they had a deep if blind respect for educational institutions. It seemed to him they assumed — and perhaps still assumed — that he had lost his way because of Kathy, though they never mentioned her name. Knowing what love between them had meant for nearly fifty years they had some idea of the disruption which would have followed the loss of it when they were young or for that matter at any time. So they grieved for him, mutely, and waited for his pain to pass, if it would.

He had returned to the *Sun*, and to the police station in the fourth district. Following patrol cars in cabs and policemen on foot he heard the screams of women and children kicked into corners by men crazed by drink; saw girls pulled from the river and begging to be set free to go back into it; trailed dope pushers; heard the sobbing of old men whose little shops had had their windows smashed, their contents ransacked, their cash registers cleaned out and safes broken open, and who had themselves been trussed up and beaten by bands of hoodlums who raced away on motorcycles. He became a creature of the night in a world rocked by crime, trying to write about it for those who never went here, and prevented from picturing it as it really was by rules imposed by others who had never been there but who earnestly believed that everyone but the criminal was guilty of the crime. They concentrated on concealing from one another the identity of the criminal, while studying his childhood environment and influences, his recent environment and associations, his educational level, his skills if any, his emotional state; and on drawing plans and voting money for institutions to oversee his reeducation, his retraining, his rehabilitation, in short his rebirth. When all this was done and well done, the former criminal would be worthy of membership in society. Perhaps so. But would society by then be worthy of him? And first the criminal must be caught up with, or the numbers of people kicked into corners, driven into rivers, trussed up and beaten, raped, murdered, to say nothing of the amount of property destroyed, would become intolerable, if it was not already. Only the police were trying to catch up with him and protect society from him while it worked on its plans for him. At present he was neither open nor humble and seemed void of all other qualities which commonly, rightly or wrongly, are considered virtues in humanity.

Through weeks and months of nightly following Andy made a friend. He had long liked and admired Officer Breck from a respectful distance, but Mike Breck was already surrounded by friends wherever he went. As he rode or strode into the night, the dark seemed to retreat and the light begin to break in the east. He was a burly man in his late thirties, the son and grandson of local officers of the law, with a shock of red hair, keen gray eyes, a big hook nose, a broad warm grin, huge warm hands. Everything about Mike Breck was big and warm, and wherever he went he had stories to tell in his rich brogue — stories for fellow officers at the station, stories to bring smiles where there had been tears, stories for the rare criminal with whom he caught up. By no means always a new story, but always worth hearing again. There was no home in his district where he was not known and welcome. Even a drunkard abusing his family often turned to Mike with half-sensed relief and gratitude that he was now to be saved from himself and his loved ones from him. Andy, waiting outside to follow Mike back to the station, often saw him through a lighted window drinking coffee at a littered kitchen table with an old woman in a bathrobe or a young one in curlers, and telling her a story to cheer her up, while her husband snored on a blanket in the back of the wagon. Through it all, night after night after night, Mike Breck loved life as he found it, with every breath he drew. He had a secret, and month in, month out Andy followed him, hoping to find out what it was. But Andy was a newspaperman and he had heard Mike say that it was best to fight shy of them fellers.

So it was a long time before he got near to Mike and when he did it was by a strange turn of events.

The boy did not climb to the flat roof of the nine-story, third-class Baker Hotel and stand on the edge of it in the nighttime when Mike and Andy would have been on duty. Even if he had, no one would have been likely to see him before he plunged. Anyhow, the Baker was not in Mike's district. Instead, he did it about three o'clock in the afternoon, the hour when Andy was always sleeping his soundest after turning in around ten in the morning, having left his copy on his superior's desk and eaten breakfast. He did it at a time when the street was crowded with shoppers, people returning from late or long lunches, women pushing baby carriages, and pupils just released from school. So there were shouts and shrieks, alarms were sounded, sirens blew, police and firemen rushed to the scene, a net was spread; and the boy kept swaying there, bewildered by the uproar. This gave the hotel management time to find out that he was registered

for Room 203 and to try to contact someone at the
address he had given, while police unlocked his door
and found a note he had written to someone he called
Gretchen, telling her that he was glad she had made
the decision she had, for if she could be happy, she
ought to be. It was wrong to postpone being happy,
for then it might never happen. It would never happen to him. There was no future for a man who had
not graduated from college, and he could not even get
into college. He had just flunked out of preparatory
school. Even in the courses he was best in he was not
good enough. He wished Gretchen would say good-
bye to his mother for him when she came back from
Europe. "This is it, Beautiful. Good luck. Peter."

The note had no address. The room had been registered in the name of Robert Hartley, 1616 Padelford
Avenue, Waterbury, Connecticut. The handwriting
on the registration slip was the same as that in the
note. There were no Hartleys in Waterbury and there
was no Padelford Avenue.

The heads of policemen were through the skylight
now, and other police on the fire escape. The firemen
were putting up ladders.

"Listen, fella. Let's you and I have a little talk,
huh?"

"Stop! Don't come any nearer! If you do, I'll —"

"Look here, now, what do they call you, buddy?"

"Stay where you are! I'm going to jump —"

Down in the street an old woman was pleading,
"Step back a minute, honey! Just step back! A priest is
coming up! Talk to the priest!" while a girl with long

white hair yelled between cupped hands, "What's the matter? You crazy or somethin'? If you're gonna jump, jump." And men laid bets on whether he would or wouldn't.

By four o'clock, when Andy Pollister's alarm rang and he groaned and turned on his radio, every local station had a sound truck as close to the Baker as it could get.

". . . It's fantastic the show this boy is putting on! Lately he sits down every little while, sometimes with his legs dangling over the side — but his head twisted so he can keep his eye on the skylight and the fire escape — and sometimes with his back to the abyss, hugging his knees and rocking back and forth. Then the street is so quiet you can hear people around you breathing. But the instant he gets to his feet again a roar goes up and he just stands there swaying. Through my binoculars I can see his face, and he looks desperatedly tired. We have photographers at several points. It's fantastic the way he has kept everybody away from him. Everybody believes he will jump, as he says he will, at the first step on the roof, or if a fireman on the ladder passes the row of windows below him."

The contents of the boy's note were discussed, and the room registration. He had left only a few belongings in his room and none of them identified him. Private preparatory schools were being contacted as fast as possible, but there were a great many of them in the country. And of course a public high school was a preparatory school, though not usually so called . . .

By then the radio in Andy's room was running unheard, for Andy, unshowered and unshaven, without a tie, in the wrinkled slacks and jacket he had tossed on a chair that morning, was hailing a cab and saying, "The Baker."

Yesterday the cabby would very likely have asked, "Where's that?"

Today he said, "Can't get nearer than six blocks from it."

"Do that. I know the alleys of this town better than I know the main streets."

Once out of the cab his low, urgent, incessantly repeated, "I know the boy. Let me through. I know the boy. Let me by. Quick. I know the boy . . ." got him through the crowds, onto the stairway, and up the eight flights to the skylight. Only some of his fellow reporters and photographers had tried to hold their ground, all asking, "Who is he? Who is he?" and all but one of these had yielded to shoving. The one had gone down before the punch so long ready for delivery. "He's your brother, damn you," Andy had said then. "The one you talk about all the time. Remember?"

Now, to the three policemen and two priests he had joined, he said, "Stop trying for a minute, will you? Give me a break. I tell you I know him. Bend over. Out of sight."

The boy had just lunged to his feet, and the uproar

below began, but there was silence on the rooftop. After a minute Andy said, "Peter? I don't know whether your name is Peter or not, and I'm not going to ask you. I'm not going to ask you anything. It doesn't matter. Nothing matters. Only I've been right where you are. I know how it feels. I'm not far from there now. I want to be beside you. You have my word I won't try to stop you. I won't even touch you. I just want to be with you. If you go over, I may go, too. The trouble is being alone. I'm alone. Okay if I come where you are?"

The boy looked at him and did not answer.

Andy's shoulders rose slowly from the skylight. He got one knee over, and hung there.

"Okay?" he asked the boy.

The boy looked at him and made no answer.

The other knee. There Andy knelt.

"I don't want to stand up. They're waiting to take pictures. I hate having my picture taken. Let's crawl. I'll crawl toward you, and you crawl toward me. I'll stop before I quite get to you. On my word. I won't touch you."

He waited until the boy was down and moving toward him. Then, as he had promised, he stopped before they met, but the boy kept on until his disheveled hair brushed Andy's disheveled hair. Both turned wearily to sit on their feet, shoulder to shoulder, and Andy began to talk in a voice only the boy could hear. He talked about Kathy but he called her "a girl." He talked about the university but he called it "school."

"You can't count on a girl, can you? She says she'll wait for you but she won't wait for you. It's too long to tomorrow. She has to have today. And her hair smells so sweet and her mouth tastes so sweet, you want her to have today, too. You want her to have whatever she wants, if you're that way about her. Only it hurts like hell that she won't wait, man, because a guy has to wait. He has to wait for everything and nothing waits for him. All that waiting and never getting hold of anything gets to be too much. You figure it's all pay in and no take out here, and you better be going. That's how I figured. I guess it's how you figure. Right?"

The boy bobbed his head once. A man began pulling himself through the skylight.

"Get down!" Andy roared. "Get down or we'll both jump. I'm sticking with Peter."

He said to the boy, "I just called you that. I don't know what your name is."

The boy muttered, "It's Peter."

"Then maybe Gretchen was your girl's name. Mine was Kathy. She married another guy and went to live in Germany. I was in school then, but I didn't finish the year. You can't. You're down and they keep pushing you deeper. It's like as if you were going to drown. You have to get out, and then you have to find somebody to talk to. If you can't find somebody to talk to, that does it . . . It's helped me a lot to talk to you. If you want to talk to me, go ahead. If you don't, that's okay."

The boy didn't say anything.

"Okay if I keep on talking? It's helping me a lot. I'm seeing things I didn't see before. I see it's getting dark, and there are some stars up there. I come from a little town where you can see a million stars every fair night. But I don't go back there much, because Kathy isn't there. In a city like this, you don't see the stars very often. There are too many lights. But it's fine they're up there, — you know? In case the lights go out. Stars never go out. They're always there, even if nobody looks at them, even if they're covered over. They're like magic. There is magic, I'm sure of that. Something that any minute might make a great thing happen. I don't know what. I won't either, until it happens. Then I won't know what made it. Only that it was magic . . ."

Andy did not talk constantly. Sometimes there was a long pause.

In one of them the boy shivered and said, "It's cold here."

"Right. A cold wind has sprung up. How about coming over to my room? I've got a room with a fireplace, and some wood. We can pick up sandwiches and coffee at the corner and go home and build a fire. There's a rollaway bed we can pull out of the closet, when you're ready to sleep."

"I don't sleep much."

"You may tonight. Being out in a wind like this makes anybody sleepy." Andy yawned and began slowly getting to his feet. "Huh! We're getting stiff here, man. Let's go build our fire and get warm. Okay?"

The boy began getting up. He was stiff, too. He swayed, looking around as if for a path out of a thicket.

"Guess it will have to be single file, to start," Andy said. "This way. Just follow me."

He moved toward the skylight. When he reached it he gestured at the turned-up faces below.

"Go on down," he growled. "Leave us alone. He's okay. He's going home with me."

He glanced back, and the boy was close behind him.

"It's a bit of a trick getting in here," Andy said. "Watch me. Do what I do."

He sat on the edge of the opening with his body twisted so that his left hand gripped the edge to the right of him and he could grin at the boy, who by doing as Andy had done, turned his back on those below, if they were still there.

"Now a quick flop and grab on with your right, and our feet will touch in a minute . . . Man, here we are! Now let's head for the sandwiches —"

But before they could turn they were surrounded, the boy by one group and Andy by another, separated from each other by massed bodies and voices.

"What did you say to him? What did you find out? What's his real name? Who are you? Where do you come from? Did you know him before? What did you say to him? What did you find out? What's his real —"

"None of your business," Andy yelled. "Shut up, will you? Let me through. I'm taking him home."

"Whose home? His? Where? That was quite a stunt

you pulled. What's his name? Did he tell you about the girl? Did he get a Dear John? Who are you?"

"If you don't let me through, I'm going to knock somebody down."

"He's getting mean. Look here, buddy, how about a drink? We'll all go round to Harry's Bar. Drinks on us. All you want, if you'll give us the story —"

"Can't you hear me? I told you I'm taking the kid home. So make way, because *I'm coming through* —"

They shrugged, and made an opening; but by then the boy was nowhere to be seen.

Andy swore and started at a run toward the stairway, but was stopped by a familiar voice at the end of the shadowy, low-ceilinged hall.

"Kid! Don't break your neck. The medics and the priest took the boy down in the elevator. He's on his way to the hospital by now. They'll look after him. But if it hadn't been for you —"

It was Mike Breck, in civilian clothes. He did not go on duty until nine o'clock.

"Oh, God!" Andy groaned. "What hospital, Mike? You know what hospital? I've got to find him. I told him we were in this together —"

The massed bodies surged back.

"You know this man of the hour, Mike? What's his name? Is he on the force? Where does he —"

"No, he ain't on the force," Mike told them, "and that's all you're going to find out from me. If he won't talk to you, why the hell should I? Come on, kid. Let's get out of this mob. I'll help you any way I can."

With Mike's arm across his shoulders, Andy found

himself propelled into a small room off a landing, and a bolt pulled in the door. The only other person there was an old woman stitching up rents in sheets.

Mike said, "Hiya, Mary," she answered cheerfully, "The best, Mike, bless yer inquirin' heart," and went on with her stitching.

"Deaf as a post, Mary is," Mike told Andy. "Don't have a notion what's been going on. Good thing, too. Be breaking her poor old heart over it. Take the weight off your feet a minute, boy. You look done in, and no wonder at all."

"I'm all right. I just want to get where the kid is. I told him I was with him and I was, until that flock of vultures got between —"

"You've been hanging around the station a lot, so you may've heard me say time and again it's best to fight shy of you writer fellers. Now you see what I mean. Because that's who jammed you in, of course. A gang that'll spear anybody to the very soul to suck it out and make a headline. But you done something more for the kid by taking 'em on, you know. Kept them off him and give the medics a chance to sneak him into the elevator . . ."

"Where were they taking him, Mike? What hospital?"

"God knows. Any one of several. Makes no difference. The medics won't let anybody near him tonight. First thing they'll do, they'll put him to sleep. It happens every time. They won't let anybody bother him."

"I wouldn't bother him. I was getting to him. He was coming home with me. I *promised* him —"

"Yeah, but he's out of your hands. He's with specialists now."

"The kid doesn't need specialists. Not tonight, anyway. I'm what he needs."

"You may be right. You had something for him, that's for sure. But specialists is what he's got, and there's no getting by them tonight. Maybe tomorrow. You've done quite a thing and you ought to feel good about it. As soon as you can feel anything."

Mike opened the door a crack and put his eye to it.

"All clear, boy," he said. "My car's down in the alley. Let's make a run for it. We'll go to my house and eat before I get into my working clothes. Looks to me like we ought to start getting better acquainted, Pollister. You're no run-of-the-mill writer-feller, I see now."

That evening Andy saw Mike and his big family through shadows. Their number, their noise, their laughter, their hunger and their frank delight in satisfying it seemed unlikely, beyond belief at the time. He could think only of getting away, once he was there, back to the streets and the search for Peter. He sat at the table morose and uneasy, darkly resentful of being detained. At the curb in front of the house, he and Mike separated and he caught a cab to make the round of the hospitals. But it was as Mike had said; he could not get farther than the waiting room of any of them. So at midnight he returned, still unshaven, to the station and spent the rest of the night with Mike, refusing even to call in to the *Sun*. They talked a great deal, but Andy could never remember afterward what they had talked about.

When the morning papers reached the stands, every one had a front-page story on the boy, with a carry-over to the inside, where the pictures appeared. The papers named the hospital he was in, and said he had been identified by his school and by his father, who was flying east from the Coast. The boy's name was Peter Lockheed, he was an only child, his parents were divorced, his mother was abroad . . .

Andy made one more try. He returned to the hospital named in the papers and told the nurse that he had brought Peter off the roof and had made promises to him which he felt obligated to keep. The nurse was very sympathetic and consulted a doctor who came and expressed his appreciation to Andy, but said it was impossible at present; no one could see Peter until he was released to his father, who was expected about noon. The doctor said he would mention Andy to Peter's father, who certainly would be deeply grateful and would want to contact him. The doctor took down Andy's address and telephone number, and Andy went home to wait for the call.

None came. In midafternoon a news flash interrupted a soap opera. Peter Lockheed had jumped out of the cab in which he was riding with his father toward the airport, climbed over the railing of a bridge, and gone down to his death.

Andy went out and walked. He walked for hours

without knowing where he was, and found himself turning in at the gate of the uneven brick walk leading to the Breck house. Mike's wife said he was still asleep. Andy said, "Don't call him." She called him. He came downstairs in his undershirt, a wrinkled pair of cotton pants, and big bare feet, stood in the middle of his crowded kitchen with his hands on his hips.

"What's up now, Pollister? You've had another jolt."

"The kid . . . It's all in tonight's papers . . . He went over a bridge."

"He — well, of all the —" After an instant's silence Mike heaved a long, whistling sigh and began again. "He was bound to go. When they're bound to, nobody can stop 'em long."

Andy said savagely, "I could have. I was going to."

Mike shook his head.

"I don't know, Pollister. I don't know. You sure tried . . . You called your paper yet today?"

Andy shook his head. Mike's wife put a cup of coffee beside him. He sat looking at it.

"Better call 'em."

"I'm not going to. I'm through."

"You're no such fool. You're not through. That may not be much of a job you've got but it's the only one you've got, and you keep it until you get another one, you hear me? What's the matter with you kids? Can't you ever think of anything to do when you get a punch in the jaw but fall flat and wait for the countdown? There's plenty of trouble in this old world and if more of you don't work up the spunk to look it in the eye, a fine mess you're going to be in and the world with you. What if you had nine mouths to feed besides your own, like me? Think then you could throw up your job every time you felt low in your mind? I bet I had four to feed by the time I was your age, and I can tell you —"

It went on and on. There seemed no end to it, and gradually Andy passed from shock through fury to understanding that Mike Breck was fighting first to pull them both out of a slough of despondency, and then to drive back from everyone in the room but especially from his young brother Padraic, and from Andy, and from his own five boys between the ages of seven and fifteen, the bodiless shadows in which he had known so many young people to become helplessly and hopelessly entangled and which had carried more of them than Peter to what Mike considered a totally unnecessary and inexplicable early death.

"What would you say the good Lord put you on this earth for? To take one scared-rabbit look-see and then turn your back and cover up your eyes and get a steamroller to do you the favor of running over you? If that's what you think, little use you are to yourself or anybody else. I say we're here to *do* what we can about it. If you don't like what you see, set out to change it. A little piece of it, that is. If you can't, tackle another piece. Whatever you do, never give up altogether, or you're a weak, yellow, low-down, good-for-nothing, chickenhearted waster of everything the Holy Father stirred into the dough he made you of and not only that but all the good stuff He left laying

around for you to work with if you could just manage
to get down there where it is and up again. Use the
spring that's built into your legs! You listen to me
now. There's just one thing to do when everything
goes wrong today and that's make up your mind what
the first thing is you're going to do tomorrer —"

When at last Mike ran down and stopped, his sons
continued to stare at him without moving, but Andy
and Padraic exchanged quick glances.

Andy said, "You're right, Mike, I'll call in."

"No," Mike told him in a completely changed
voice, a deep but gentle voice. "I'll call in for you.
What's the number?"

He strode to the telephone, dialed with a blunt
forefinger, and told the news desk that their man Pollister had been too busy to call in for twenty-four
hours, being on the Peter Lockheed story but not
writing it, living it. He said he was Officer Breck of
the fourth district, had seen a good deal of their man
Pollister during the last few months, but especially
during the last twenty-four hours, and wanted the
paper to know he was much respected at the station,
"which as I guess you know can't be said of all reporters, and we'll give him any lead we can any time."
But he asked that Pollister be sent home for a night's
sleep. "He's bushed, and he's got to sleep or he won't
be any good tomorrow night," said Mike, scratching
between his shoulderblades with his thumbnail.

When he turned away from the telephone he said,
"It's okay. He says for you to call there when you
wake up tomorrow. Dish up your corned beef and

cabbage, Eileen. After we eat, I'll drop Andy off at his place on my way to work."

When Andy called his editor early the next afternoon, he was asked if he had seen the morning paper, and, since he had not, was advised to pick up one. "Gus has scooped you." It was Gus Harrington, then, who had written the story Andy found there about the anonymous *Sun* reporter who had brought Peter Lockheed off the Baker roof with the intent of taking him to his own home for the night when the two were separated by medical men and overzealous reporters, and never saw each other again, with the chilling result already familiar to all who followed the news. The story closed with quotations from police officers who strongly protested the drive for a human-interest story at any cost, including even human life. Questions were raised as to whether it should be assumed that the professional, institutional approach was always the safest and most constructive, and also that a member of his family was the best or only personal contact for a deeply troubled person to be permitted at a critical time.

Andy, reading, had no doubt that Gus had gone to the police station of the fourth district and talked with Mike Breck. He was grateful for anonymity. Neither the news story nor the death of Peter Lockheed was ever mentioned thereafter between Andy and Mike. But nearly every other subject which stayed long in the mind of either was talked over in considerable detail during the next few months. They talked in the station, in patrol cars, in paddy wagons,

on park benches, at Mike's house while his young
people listened and Eileen waited on them or sat
hunched over her heaped mending basket, and alone
together in Andy's room. They talked, too, with other
men, while riding with them, bowling or shooting
pool with them, drinking Coke with them; but afterward they talked alone of what they had seen and
heard.

Mike Breck was a born optimist, convinced that
there was good in every person and every situation
and all a man had to do was look for it until he found
it. He even believed that most of it would be found
and developed and all humanity's worrisome problems eventually solved. He lived unquestioning by
what his church taught him and by what his parents
and others he had respected when he was a boy had
taught him. There was no doubt in him that whatever
was not clearly right was wrong. Honesty was right.
Marriage and monogamy were right. Hard work and
hard play were right. Taking responsibility was right.
Helping others to help themselves was right. Respect
for property was right. Body cleanliness was right.
Keeping the laws of church and nation was right.
Cheerfully doing without what one did not have,
until he could get it, was right. Meeting trouble with
the chin up was right. All the opposites were wrong.
These rules of living Mike was grateful for having
been taught and proud of having learned, and his goal
was to spread the word wherever he went and as far as
he could. In all the hours of questioning and discussion Andy never saw him shaken in his conviction that

the principles by which he lived were essential to human life, if it was to be good, and that those who did not have them were consciously or unconsciously seeking them, therefore would surely find them if they did not stop seeking. It became clear early in the friendship of these two that the taking of one's own life, whatever the provocation, was to Mike Breck the most irrational and inexplicable and tragic of all human acts, since it consigned a person to irretrievable and total defeat. The taking of the life of another might be in part explained, however unacceptably, and was less tragic in that only chosen defeat was total — perhaps the murdered man was already a victor — and to the degree that the killer later found what he had so long sought in vain. Mike's overall rule was *keep on;* keep on living, keep on searching, keep on working, keep on moving, keep on loving, keep on laughing, keep on praying . . . *keep on,* however long and dark the tunnel, for it would end in sunshine . . . *keep on* . . . *keep on* . . . *keep on.*

And Andy Pollister could at least agree that if there was hope for civilization it depended on men like Mike Breck keeping on and retaining and gaining followers from the sphere of influence of those false prophets who so cleverly taught that men should be relieved by agencies of all the burdens which alone raised them above the level of animals; freed of ropes they were capable of untying and placed in indestructible webs, there to swing as in soft hammocks until their captors grew hungry; cut off from knowledge of their duty to God and therefore of their own potential; reduced in courage and narrowed in vision until each lost all value in his own sight and thus, perhaps, in God's, having become only an infinitesimal, weakly pulsating cell in a mass of worthlessness.

It was something — in fact, it was a great deal — all those months to know that big Mike Breck was out there, pushing back the world to make room for God, even when Andy was not with him.

But then came the summer night of a call from a police alarm box in Westover Square. A riot had broken out in a dance hall there. A paddy wagon roared out of the station, and Andy followed it in a cab. He was there in time to see Mike run up the steps, put a shoulder between two boys who were struggling with each other, and stand with one in the curve of each arm, looking down at them, talking to them. That was when another boy hunched between two marble pillars at the side of the doorway raised a revolver and shot him . . . Mike.

Mike Breck fell headlong down the stone steps and lay in a heap on the sidewalk under a blazing streetlight with his blood running out and filling depressions in the cement, while fellow officers packed the wagon with ringleaders, dispersed the onlookers, cleared a space in which an ambulance could be brought close to where Mike lay and Mike's body could be lifted in. But he had been dead before he fell.

Andy followed in the cab to the hospital. He went with Mike's two closest friends on the force to take the news to Eileen, Padraic, and the children. He wrote the story of Mike's death at Mike's kitchen table and telephoned it in to the *Sun,* together with his resignation from the paper. He stayed with the Brecks until after the funeral, and then he took a bus to the mountain town where he was born. He had been there, working on the *Clarion,* ever since.

Perhaps Mike would not have thought this was what he should do. Perhaps Mike would have thought there was more he could do. But, if so, Andy had not yet been able to discover what it was.

He stood in the office doorway, feeling the heat roll up from the still village street, and thought of Mike bowling, Mike eating Eileen's corned beef and cabbage, Mike joking with a woman he had just rescued from the corner of a dingy room, Mike carrying a child on his shoulder, Mike spouting righteous rage . . . Mike dead in a pool of blood . . .

That Indian-summer day Susan Wentworth Norris lay in a Midwestern hospital listening to the rapidly tripping feet of visitors along the corridor outside her door, and wondering with faint interest whether her daughter Mrs. Maxwell Frome or one of her granddaughters would be in to see her that afternoon. X-rays showed that the silver pin in her hip was doing its work well and she no longer had a temperature in the afternoons, but she was not a model patient. It was three weeks since her accident and surgery, and the nurses kept telling her how other old people had been flying around in wheelchairs and trying out walkers much sooner than this. But Suse knew of no place

where she wanted to go, or wanted to be, so she flew
nowhere and tried out nothing, rose only if lifted. She
lay, staring at the ceiling, and waited. Even when
spoken to, she rarely spoke.

It was one of Mrs. Maxwell Frome's afternoons at
the Settlement House. She went there to sit in the
music room and play the piano, as she had twice a
week for many years. It was good for the piano, the
sound was pleasant throughout the building and beyond the windows, and in the years past she had
taught many to play. Now there seemed to be little
interest in studying piano. Children who wanted a
musical instrument wanted one small enough to go
with them to the park, to school, on the bus, to the
soda fountain. These were difficult to keep available, as when they were taken from the House they
often did not come back; worse, children reprimanded
for not returning them often did not come back. So
Maida sat by herself that afternoon and played, thinking of many things. She thought of her mother,
feeling guilty that she was not with her, but knowing that she would be little or no comfort to her if
she had gone to the hospital. Her mother had been
slowly turning inward for a year or more, and breaking her hip had all but closed the door. She might
never be able to come home again; Maida must discuss nursing homes with the doctor . . . She thought
of her daughters — of Suzanne who had left by bus
for Florida that morning to keep a vigil outside a jail,
Suzanne who was always keeping a vigil or on her way
to keep a vigil, and whose eyes grew tireder and more

angry every day; of Kim who seemed enclosed in a
world of paper; of Maisie, the hunted, hollow child —
and she blinked back tears . . . She thought of her
husband and shook her head. She no longer knew
Max. He went to the office and he went to the club
and he went to the lake to fish.

There was no choice but the familiar one. From
habit, she took a grip on her mind and turned it by
main force, as the man on the bridge once turned the
wheel of his ship, to the only possible course. She
thought of her next meeting, the note on which it
would open, the member who should be called on to
present which first topic for discussion, the amount of
time to be spent on each of how many topics and on
the various committee reports.

Rick Tucker was in Saigon that day, on a forty-
eight hour leave just ahead of the monsoons and the
enemy offensive they always brought. He had all but
scrubbed off his outer layer of skin in the shower and
with the startlingly white Vietnamese towels, and
gone to sleep bare between startlingly white Vietnamese sheets. When he waked he had dressed in new
white sport shirt, tan chinos, and white canvas shoes,
and gone out to stand on a busy corner and be
brushed by the hurrying crowd of small, dark people
of all ages, all in shirts of the inevitable startling
white, crisp and smooth as if not more than a minute
ago they had been taken from a rack where they had
been hung to air after ironing. It was personal cleanliness he needed above all else when he came in from
the field, and it was in Saigon in abundance. He stood

in the sunshine, surrounded by cleanliness and life
and simple enjoyment of the moment, drinking it in
gratefully, like a thirsty horse, and thought of nothing
which had been before or would be later; nothing but
now . . . And at the edge of the city a man passing at
high speed on a motorcycle lobbed a shell into a
group of waiting bus passengers. Three of them were
U.S. Marines; the name of one was Walter Ross. He
had reached Saigon from the States only that morning.

Audrey Mason did not know where Walt was, only
that by then he had probably left Parris Island. She
had waited for her bus and boarded it and gone into
town to begin a six-week period of teaching observation, one morning and one afternoon each week. She
was allowed to make this observation in the grade of
her choice and the school of her choice, and to change
as often as she wished. Perhaps in part because it was
the first school she came to after leaving the bus, but
more because she had from time to time wondered
about the approach of Catholic Sisters to teaching and
the effect of their dress upon the atmosphere of a
classroom, she had followed a line of children into
a parochial school and been cheerfully welcomed by a
merry-faced nun who scarcely listened to her self-
introduction but kept nodding brightly as if that were
all very nice but did not matter.

"Oh, yes . . . Yes . . . Well, now, the children
will be very happy. We are going to have a spelling
match this morning, and a guest will add to the spirit
of competition, which is always very keen. Would you

prefer to sit in front, facing the children, or in the back?"

Audrey took a chair in the back of the sunny room and watched a seventh-grade class called to order and led in devotions by an elderly Sister with paper-white skin and intense dark eyes whom the children regarded in silent awe. After her last amen she vanished without a sound through a door which closed behind her, and the merry-faced little nun trotted to the piano saying, "What would you like to sing? Call out the number. Quick! Quick! The first number I hear is the one I'll play!" After several songs in such rapid succession that they were almost a medley, she whirled on the stool and said, "Now tell me! Tell me something interesting! Nothing personal. Nothing about anybody at home, remember. Something you read? Something you heard on radio or television? It could be something you saw or heard outdoors, but if it is about a person don't tell us what person, you know. We may need industry in this town but we don't need a gossip factory, do we? Without invading anybody's privacy, tell me something interesting you didn't know when you left school yesterday. Oh, good — four hands up! More coming up! Well, who would believe so much had happened overnight? Teresa?"

A dinner had been given in honor of the pastor of the Congregational church who had been in the ministry for forty years, and he and his wife had been presented with a Paul Revere bowl. There had been a picture of them in the paper last night, holding the bowl, which was a perfect copy of one made long ago by the man who rode the horse through every Middlesex village and town to warn the Americans that the Redcoats were coming . . . At Roberts's Market yesterday afternoon a man was shaking hands with everybody and saying he was running for the state legislature, and he hoped people would vote for him. The meatcutter asked him, "Why should I?" and he didn't smile when he said it. He looked quite mad. But the candidate said, "I'm glad you asked that question," and then he went on to say he thought people should vote for him because he wanted senior citizens not to have to worry and all young people to go to college and all children to have hot lunches, and he would work for wide, straight roads and against the war and against high prices and for better homes and more police protection . . . A girl was on television saying she was studying karate and she showed what karate was. It was lying on your back on the floor and pounding your stomach, and when you got up if somebody put his arms around you from the back you gave him an elbow to the gut that made him double up. It was also breaking a board in two with the side of your hand. It made you very strong and then you didn't have to be afraid of anybody . . . A professor from the University was having a class in writing every Thursday night at the high school. What he did, he brought in a painting one night, or several pieces of different kinds of cloth another night, and spread and bunched them up on a table. Or he brought a record and played it. Then everybody wrote what it made him think of, or how he felt when he looked at it or listened to it. You could write a poem or a short essay, whatever you wanted to write about it in twenty minutes. Then everybody read aloud what he had written, and they took notes and discussed what was best and most original and separated out those parts and helped the professor put together just what they decided was best. People who went said it was wonderful what came out of it every Thursday night. Always something so much better than what anyone in the class had thought of by himself that you could hardly believe it . . . And much else had happened since yesterday afternoon in Dewey . . .

The merry-faced little nun passed from one event to the next with no more comment, if any, than, "*How* interesting!" or "Remember that now, for Miss Sheaffer is going to want to talk with you about it, you know." But she listened to each with a lively expression and eager bobbing of her head and then triumphantly wrote an identifying word on the blackboard. BOWL. CAMPAIGN. KARATE. COMPOSITION . . . There were still hands raised when she gestured toward the clock with obvious regret and said the time was up, but she was jotting down the names of the remaining volunteers and they would be the first to be called on the next day. Now it was time for the spelling match, and Thomas and Gerald, whom they had elected as captains yesterday morning, would stand and choose sides.

At this point a girl rose and left the room. Audrey, who had not noticed her before, had the fleeting impression that she was older than the others — perhaps over from St. Mary's Academy to take attendance or on some other assignment — and forgot about her in watching the lineup for the match.

"This is our monthly examination in spelling," the little nun explained at Audrey's shoulder, bending to her ear to be heard through the noise. "Much more fun than sitting still and taking dictation! Isn't it *hard* to sit still? Please feel free to move about now, if you like. We're so pleased you're here. An audience adds so much!"

The spelling down took an hour and Gerald's side won, which seemed to please everyone except Thomas, who, the little nun whispered to Audrey, had to learn that fellow members on the champion baseball team were not necessarily champions at everything.

"Notice Gerald chose many more girls for his side than Thomas did," she said to the class. "Do you think that had any significance?"

Several girls giggled and one of them said, "Means Tom doesn't like girls, Sister. Everybody knows that."

"And Gerald?" asked the Sister demurely.

Gerald answered for himself.

"For a spelling match," he said in a voice which broke, "I choose spellers. I'd better, because I can't spell very well myself."

The Sister's eyebrows went up in delight. She whirled to the blackboard and wrote across the top of it in a big, round hand exactly what Gerald had said, within quotation marks.

"*That* is our 'Thought for Today,'" she said. "There is real wisdom in what Gerald said, and all of us should keep it in mind. I expect Miss Sheaffer will want to discuss it with you, along with your Events, after recess. Position, please. Turn. Rise. March . . . Will you come out with us, Miss —"

"Mason. Audrey Mason. Oh, Sister, I'm having such a good time!"

"Children make everything fun, don't they?" the Sister agreed. Her head seemed always to be bobbing as if it were as free as a bird's and its starched white and rippling dark cover no restriction at all. "Each day they come in they seem as new as the morning itself. You say you are going to be a teacher? That's fine. Children so need teachers, and it is the happiest work in the world."

On following the seventh-graders in from recess Audrey was surprised to find that the merry-faced little nun had not come in, that there were no dark robes in sight, and that the girl she had first supposed to be an older pupil had returned and stood behind the desk.

The girl said in a clear, carrying voice, "Good morning, seventh grade."

The pupils answered, "Good morning, Miss Sheaffer."

So *this* was Miss Sheaffer! Surely she was not more than seventeen. She was slight and not tall, had short, softly curling dark hair and round blue eyes, wore a straight gray tweed skirt, a white cotton shirt, and a red cable-knit sweater with pushed-up sleeves.

She said, "I'm always glad to get to the seventh. I'm with the sixth before recess, and I find that something quite amazing happens between sixth and seventh. You seem *much* more than a year older . . . I see we have a guest today. That is very nice. Will you tell us your name, please?"

Audrey was surprised that she was not embarrassed.

"I'm Audrey Mason, a student at the Teachers College, observing teaching techniques."

"Well, I'm Margaret Sheaffer, and I'm not sure I know any teaching techniques, but at least you will see a class in action, Audrey, because this is a very active class. It *thinks*. Every minute we're thinking we're learning. Anyway, that is what it seems like to us. I always go out of this class feeling I know *so* much more than I did when I came in. Don't you — all of you?"

The pupils responded with nods and smiles, but this was less convincing than their air of repressed impatience with the delay of introductions and explanations, the faint and growing expectancy which was filling the room, something electric, almost audible and visible — though Margaret Sheaffer had not a merry or even a particularly expressive face, showed none of the little nun's lively enthusiasm, and spoke almost in a monotone. The expectancy was not of what she or anyone in the room would *do*, but of what was now going to happen to everyone here. A kind of miracle.

Margaret turned briefly to the board and underscored BOWL.

She began talking as if no time had elapsed since the account had been given of the presentation of a Paul Revere bowl to a man and woman who had spent the forty years of their married life in the Christian ministry. She said no doubt they had heard of other similar occasions. A Paul Revere bowl was frequently the gift chosen at such a time. Why? Someone thought because Paul Revere made beautiful bowls. So he did. Did he make all these bowls? No, they must be copies. His bowls must be very beautiful indeed to be so much copied. Someone had seen one of the copies and would try to bring it to class tomorrow. That would be fine. Was it possible that any of the bowls Paul Revere actually made were still in existence? If so, would it be easy to borrow one of them to bring to a classroom? Why not? Why were the ones he made so much more valuable than the copies? Now the pupils were asking at least as many of the questions as Margaret. How much difference did it make that Paul Revere was Paul Revere? How had Paul Revere made such a secure place for himself in American history? Was it because he had performed his heroism alone? How much had an American poet contributed to Paul Revere's fame, and how much had Paul Revere contributed to the poet's? Had the writing of "The Midnight Ride" accomplished much more than all the reading and recitation of it through the years? Well, that had to come first. Ah, then, how dependent we are on those creatively gifted enough to design a beau-

tiful silver bowl for others to copy, to compose the
music for others to play and the literature for others
to read, to paint pictures for others to see! But how
dependent the creative are on others to see the beauty
in the original design and copy it honestly for later
generations, to be worthy of the gift of such beauty or
to have the spirit which leads to the making of such a
tribute; to perform creatively the music composed
or to listen to it, really hear it; to recognize and appreciate literature; to see what is in great paintings.
And isn't there something else? Aren't even creative
geniuses dependent on their fellow men, their environment, their present as well as their past, for the
material of which great designs, great literature, great
paintings, great music are made? The peculiar gift of
the artist is in selection and arrangement. His basic
material, from which he selects and which he arranges
and combines, is no more and no less than what sur-
rounds us all, flows in and out through us all, is constantly being affected, altered, added to, diminished,
or changed by what each of us is, what each of us does,
by our thinking or unthinking, feeling or unfeeling,
by the rules we make for ourselves to live by and by
the extent to which and the spirit in which we keep
them.

"No human genius," said Margaret, "can create
greatness in a character — or in a people — though
often he can reveal it where it was not known to exist.
We might never have heard of Paul Revere, even as a
silversmith, if the poet Longfellow had not immortalized him for us. But if Paul Revere had not been a

hero, the poet would have lacked the material from which to immortalize him. And if in Paul Revere's day heroism had not been admired, appreciated, and striven for by the citizenry, would Paul Revere have been as likely to provide heroism to be written about? Perhaps. Just possibly. Once in a while there comes a man whose goals for himself are much higher than those of his comrades for him or for themselves. But if in Longfellow's day heroism had not been admired, valued, and striven for where would have been the public for 'The Midnight Ride,' and so how could the poet have immortalized Paul Revere? For that matter, if in Paul Revere's day, beauty had not been admired, appreciated, and striven for, would Paul have been inspired to design beautiful containers? . . . Oh, I'm talking too much. But there are so *many* possible ties in this, aren't there? It shows how important we all are. Every one of us."

She took another quick glance at the board.

"I'm sure we could spend all the rest of our time on CAMPAIGN. Whether those reasons the candidate was said to have given are good reasons for choosing him as our representative. But the election is a week away. Maybe we can get to that another day, if not too much else happens. And KARATE would be exciting. I'd especially like to figure out just why that girl feels the need to be so strong physically. Remember the girls we've read about, a hundred years ago, who took pride in being or being thought to be very delicate, even weak? We didn't think much of that attitude, or of the reasoning we thought was behind it. But if they felt safe that way, why don't girls feel safe that way now? Should everybody be afraid of *them,* if they have studied karate? Assuming it is men *they* are afraid of, why? Are men so much stronger than they used to be? Or are they meaner? And what does a girl who studies karate do about a man who has studied karate? Please do think this over by yourselves. It's too good to skip . . . But after all this is supposed to be an English lesson, so let's get on to COMPOSITION. Remember how that writing class is organized? Every member writes on the same topic, and the compositions are read aloud and analyzed and the best bits are taken out and combined and added to in the course of the discussion until a single poem or essay, a joint effort, is composed. The result is said to be far superior to anything one member ever does. How many of you would like to try that approach to composition?"

Many hands flew up.

"Lisa did not vote in favor. Why not, Lisa?"

Lisa was a tall Negro girl with narrow shoulders. Rolling her pen between long, thin hands, she said low, with dark eyes fixed on Margaret, "Because it — it frightens me."

"That's important," Margaret responded. She asked the rest of the class, "Did you hear what Lisa said? She said that approach to composition frightens her. This is very important, because Lisa is the most creative of all of us. No one can create if the process frightens him. If it hurts him, yes. If it exhausts him, yes. But not if it frightens him. Can you tell us why it frightens you, Lisa?"

Lisa said it would not matter, it might even be a good idea, for writing a newspaper story, or explaining exactly how to do something like making a garden or building a house.

But in this composition class they were writing poems and essays on impressions of art objects, reactions to color, lighting, texture.

Lisa said uneasily, "I couldn't."

"Can you tell us why? We all need to know why."

She said well, to begin with, you couldn't see or hear quite as well when other people were there. They made a little haze. It was hard to explain. It was not that you couldn't concentrate. Maybe you couldn't, but even if you could the haze was still there. That is, if they were looking at or listening to what you were. It was funny, but if nobody else was reacting to what you were reacting to it made no difference how many were there; you were still alone with it.

"I didn't know that. What else, Lisa?"

Then when you had put down as well as you could what you did see or hear, it would be frightening to know it was going to be snatched away from you the next instant and chopped up. You needed to feel it was going to be all yours until you were ready to let people see it. Maybe you could never bear to let anyone see it. You needed time to get acquainted with it — to find out if it was alive and strong enough to go on living separate from you.

Someone said that if it was not very good, the others would think of ways to make it better.

"Nobody else can make what I see better," Lisa said painfully. "Don't you understand? I'm the only one who sees just what I see, and if it's different it's something else. If what I do is dead and they snatch it away and chop it up and stitch things onto it, it's still dead, no matter how pretty it looks, and it's been — been mutilated. That's awful enough. But if it's alive, if I know it's alive, never mind what anybody else thinks, if I know it's alive —"

Lisa turned her head and looked out of the window.

"She means," said another girl, awed, "it isn't like a dress. It's like a — a baby!"

Nobody laughed. The room was hushed. A bell rang.

Margaret said, "Lisa has told us something nobody we know but Lisa could have told us. I'll never forget this, will you? Group composition may be fine for people like me. When I write I'm just making a dress. But never, never for people like Lisa, who sees what nobody else sees unless she can make it come alive and strong and show it to them. I think we do understand now. Aren't we lucky to have Lisa? And isn't she lucky to have us? . . . Class dismissed."

She moved into the group of pupils hurrying toward the hall, as if she were one of them, but then remembered Audrey and flattened herself against the wall to wait for her.

"Is this fun — observing? I never did that. I don't know. I doubt if I'd be able to keep out of it."

"After observing you I doubt it, too. But I've been

completely absorbed in observing. That probably means I'm not a born teacher like you."

Margaret laughed. "Oh, I'm not a born teacher at all. I may be a born learner. In fact, I believe everyone is. Somehow it never got taught out of me, and I'm so grateful for that that I'm dedicated to keeping it in as many people as possible. The world is so jampacked with the most fascinating possibilities I absolutely begrudge the time I spend sleeping. Don't you?"

Audrey wondered how she could ever have thought this girl did not have an expressive face. And had she really spoken to the class in a monotone? Now it seemed that Miss Sheaffer had been a disembodied mind, or a spirit hand leaving messages on a blackboard. Margaret was suddenly the girl with whom, above all others, you would like to share a dormitory room.

"I think I'm going to," Audrey said. "Aren't you awfully young to be teaching?"

"I don't think so. This is my first year. I was graduated from Oberlin in June."

"I would have said you couldn't be over seventeen."

"I'm twenty-one. I'm so lucky to be here. Because no public school system would employ me. I've never had a course in education, and I never would. Not that I would want to teach in a public school anyway."

"Why not?"

"Oh, Audrey! Don't you *know* how stultifying they've become? You not only have to take those horrible State Department courses to get into them, but then you have to do the silly, deadly things they teach you to do! You're absolutely *trapped*. Look, can we have lunch together, or do you have to —"

"I can if you can. I'd love to."

"Oh, I can. I can do whatever I want to, all the time. I'm free. I've always been freer than most, I guess, but now I'm completely free. I was determined it was going to be that way. I planned it that way. But still I was lucky. Because I so wanted to teach, and I wouldn't have if I couldn't do it in a school like this, where nobody interferes with me. It's marvelous. Really marvelous."

They were on the street now. Audrey said she had no idea parochial schools allowed their teachers such freedom, and she had always supposed all parochial school teachers were nuns; but she was not a Catholic.

Margaret said she was not a Catholic either, but all her closest friends when she lived at home had been Catholic and she had visited them at their schools and gone with them to talk things over with their priests, as well as to special masses, especially the midnight mass on Christmas Eve. So it seemed she had always known that many Catholic school principals were chiefly interested in finding the best possible teachers for their pupils, and not restricted to making their selections from among those who had a great many credits from a college of education.

"But there my problem was how to convince anybody I was a good teacher until I could prove it. I didn't even know myself. I only knew what I wished I could have had, instead of so many dragging hours and deadly days. My mother still tells about the time when I was in first grade and my grandfather came to dinner and asked me, 'What did you learn today, Meg?' and I looked at him in surprise that he didn't know what day of the week it was and answered politely, 'Nothing, Grandpa,' adding as a nudge to his memory, 'I've been to school.' . . . So it was sheer luck — shall we say?— that one of my high school friends had a sister in the convent here who knew that Sister Agnes — the principal of St. Dominic's — was looking for someone to relieve Sister Mary Grace half-time so that she could study at the Conservatory of Music. My friend and I drove up and had interviews and Sister Agnes asked me if I would come on trial until Christmas. Would I! So here I am, teaching mornings, working in the library as much of the afternoons as I want to, and writing nights. I'm doing a biography of a man very few people but art connoisseurs ever heard of. Not that I expect it to be published but it may. Anyway, he absolutely fascinates me. I save my pennies to spend the Christmas holidays in metropolitan museums and libraries, tracking him down. Except for five mornings a week, right now I eat, drink, and sleep a bearded, threadbare, exquisite little guy named Algernon Montrose. I call him Algie."

They were now at a counter, their dark heads close together. Margaret had ordered a cup of vegetable soup and Audrey had told the counterman, "Same here."

"So enough of me, more than enough, Audrey. I've been dreadfully frank about my idea of teacher training courses. Now you be just as frank and tell me how wrong I am. Because you're taking them, and you must have reasons."

Audrey said her reasons were not very good ones. She had always wanted to go to college, maybe because she did not know of anything else she wanted to do when she finished high school. And she had chosen a teachers college because the cost was less for her parents than it would have been at the University, and she thought that she could earn her living by teaching as well as any other way and perhaps better.

"To be honest," she said, "I suppose it was the path of least resistance. I'd been in school almost ever since I could remember and I was used to it. Or I thought I was."

Margaret's eyes were warm with sympathy. It was clear that such an attitude toward life and the future seemed to her infinitely sad, as if Audrey were enclosed in a cell with barred windows.

So Audrey hurried on, saying what she had never put into words before: that by the time she went to college she had been so puzzled about everything, so afraid of everything, so hopeless for so long that she took this state of mind for granted, as the only way she could be or would ever be. It did not much matter where she was, or what she did; she would always be miserable. But then something extraordinary had happened. She told about the Hare and Hound Chase to the riverbank, and that she had been the Hare, and who the Hound was, and the succeeding events and their effect on her.

"The truth is," said Audrey, "that until today I've been living so much in myself, and lately in Walt, too — I can even call him Walt, since Philadelphia, and do, without a twinge — that I haven't given a serious thought to where my courses were leading me. I think now I was assuming unconsciously that I would never teach, that I was only going through motions, following a routine, keeping occupied until Walt comes home to marry me."

"Of course!" Margaret exclaimed. "I can see just how that would be. I think everyone must have to learn to live — really, fully live — in himself first — as I did — or maybe in himself and one other, as apparently you and Walt did. And while you're doing that or until you've done it, how can anything outside that circle have any meaning? Like that little old pebble dropped in a pool. Until it's dropped there's no stirring, no motion. Then comes one circle, and unless it was an infinitesimal pebble there comes a second *growing out of the first* and a third growing out of the second, and more and more according to the size of the pebble and the force of its contact with the pool. See how full of surprises life is? The light of that sunset over the river which picked out you for Walt and Walt for you was the beginning of something much bigger than you have any idea even yet!"

"I think I've been suspecting that all morning. Do

you mind if I do most of my observing in your classes at St. Dominic's for a while? Will it disrupt anything if I turn up there two mornings a week?"

"Disrupt? Of coure not. We'll love to have you. And don't hesitate about coming into the discussions if you can get in. I like 'em lively. And listen now, before you go — can't we get together again where just the two of us can talk?"

Audrey said she would like that, she surely would.

"Do you have afternoon classes?" Margaret asked.

"Every afternoon this semester."

"If I went out to the college with you after your next morning here, could I go to them with you?"

"Of course. Would you? Then come to my room. I have a single."

"Great!"

There was something happily conspiratorial in the smiles they exchanged as they separated, Margaret to hurry off up the street toward the library and Audrey to catch her bus.

Ellen Dockham was in her lower meadow picking wild cranberries for Thanksgiving. They had always come in thick along the ditches there, and she, as her mother before her, had watched them and picked every one as it ripened to use for sauce, for mock cherry pies, for a relish of chopped cranberries and carrots made and canned in great quantities when the family was large, and to dry for sauce all winter. For a while she had grieved that she had to throw away most of what she picked, since she could not use them and

her neighbors would take only what they could eat
fresh, but still she had picked them all, knowing it was
better for the vines and for the next season. But beginning the year the commercial cranberry crop was
found to be contaminated by the chemicals with
which it was sprayed, Chet Morrison had been able to
sell for her at the stores in town every quart she
picked, and every year there were several bushels,
bringing in enough to pay for whatever she had to
buy at the stores during the cold weather — her corn-
meal, flour, and molasses, maybe a little white sugar
(she sweetened mostly with the soft maple sugar she
boiled down from sap in the spring), a bottle of va-
nilla once in a while, a piece of stewbeef now and
then, the yarn from which she knit her stockings.
When she needed boots or shoes, warm underwear,
cloth for a dress, a petticoat, or a nightgown, she ordered them from a catalog; but that was rare. She had
not bought a coat or hat since sometime before her
husband died, but wore those he had left, and later
her sons'. She needed coats only for warmth, and hats
for shade.

She squatted on the grass to pick — this position
had become easier for her than kneeling — and
thought of her first picking, when she had come here
as a child of three or four, with her mother. She remembered when her hand was so small that she could
not hold even one berry in it while she picked another. It was partly, too that she had not yet got the
knack of holding with her palm while reaching with
her fingers. She picked a berry and dropped it in the

tin cup, waited for the sound, watched it bounce. She
and her mother rarely spoke in the field. They were
just picking. Except for the pop of Ellie's berries until
the bottom of her cup was covered, it was very still.
Sometimes a crow cawed. Once in a while a flock of
geese flew over in a wedge. That was as sad a sight as
seeing them coming back in the spring was happy and
exciting. Even a three- or four-year-old knew that,
could feel the difference their direction made. You
knew they were leaving you behind, to make out as
best you could through the cold months, the hard
months, the nights when the nails snapped in the
walls of the house, the wind howled like banshees
around the chimney, there was frost on the door-
latches and ice in the waterpail in the morning. There
would surely be sickness. There might be death. But
there would also be the crackle of the fire, the light of
the flames showing through the cracks of the wood-
stove, the hiss when her grandfather dropped into the
ashes the icicles broken from his whiskers. There
would be warm milk from the pail, the smell of gin-
gerbread in the oven, raspberry shrub to drink if your
throat was sore. There would be catalogs to color in
and cut families of paper dolls from, toothpicks to
make letters with on the windowsill, smooth warm
beach rocks in flannel bags in the beds, maybe a new
hood for Christmas. And there was still warmth in the
pale sun, the berries were hard and bright, and when
Ellie went to pour her cupful of cranberries into her
mother's basket, if she leaned against her mother for
an instant, she would fit her mother's body as if it

were part of her own and her mother would smell like her mother as nothing else in the world did.

It was easy to believe, as Ellen Dockham picked alone, that her mother was only a little way behind her. Ellie had always gone ahead, as a child, eager to see what she would find farther on, while her mother picked steadily and clean, as Ellen did now, leaving not one ripe berry where she had been.

And she thought of Suse Wentworth, who had written her two letters which were still behind the clock in the kitchen. Ellen had managed to answer them both, though it had taken her a long time. And now there was another letter tucked in with Suse's. It was from Suse's granddaughter Kimberly, and had been written on a typewriter, which made it very easy to read. The new letter said Suse had broken her hip and was in the hospital. Kimberly told the name of the hospital and what street it was on, and said she hoped Ellen would write to Suse there because Suse needed to be interested; she seemed to have lost the will to get better. Ellen had heard of that happening to other people, but she had never seen it happen. Death had always struck suddenly in her family, long before it was desired or even accepted as a possibility. It was a pity that it should happen to Suse, who had been such an alive little girl, with her red hair and pretty dresses, so quick in school, and could play the church organ like an angel before she was ten years old; had been a doctor's wife and still had quite a family that she lived with. But you had to admit both her letters sounded as if it was beginning to happen to her even before she broke her hip, which was a dreadful thing to happen to anybody. Old folks always used to die a week or so after that happened; but now doctors kept them alive whether they wanted to be or not.

It was better thinking of Suse as a little girl at the church organ or at a front desk at the district school.

When Suse started school the desk and benches were the same ones put there when the building went up and free public education in the state was begun; long desks, slightly sloping, with an indentation for slate pencils and a shelf underneath for books and slates, and each bench seating six or eight little ones, four or five older pupils. The slender wooden legs of desks and benches grew markedly in height from in front of the teacher's desk to the back of the room. When Ellie first went to school there had been a fireplace beside the teacher. By the time Suse came it had been bricked up and a new chimney placed at the rear of the building from which two long black smoke-pipes ran along the ceiling to connect with two stoves set on platforms in the spare floor between the teacher and the first row of pupils. So the teacher and the children looked at each other between the stoves. The stoves were very important, being all that kept off the icy blasts of winter which rattled the single windows and doors, pulled off clapboards, and came up through the wide cracks in the floors. The stoves had big flat tops which could be raised for putting in two-foot logs, and a cover with a lifter which admitted split wood, small round sticks, and kindling chips. They had shelves, too, on and under which wet boots could be dried in spring and fall and lunch pails set in winter to keep the food from freezing. There was a water bucket on a corner shelf, and a tin cup hanging by its handle from a nail. There were blackboards and maps, a globe standing on the green wooden box in which it was kept during vacation time, and a canvas flag bag hanging from the corner of a windowframe — an empty bag during every school day while the flag flew from the top of a peeled pine pole held by iron bars to the front of the building.

That was all. Just books and slates and maps and blackboards, desks and benches; wood fires, water, and lunch pails; teacher and pupils, ranging in age from four to eighteen (sometimes the teacher was no older than her oldest pupils), dressed in as heavy underwear, stockings, boots, jackets, shawls, hoods or caps as they needed for the season if they owned that many of that weight. Those who shivered were allowed to bring their benches as near as possible to the stoves and write with their slates on their knees.

When Ellie first went to school the town did not supply books. The parents bought them for beginners, and older pupils took a term off from time to time to earn the cost of theirs. But perhaps by the time Suse went the teacher had books to pass out to the classes; Ellen was not sure now. She knew that when her children went to school she had not bought their books.

Mothers usually asked an older girl to look out for a little one just starting, and as Suse had no older sister her mother had asked Ellie, who was very proud of this trust. Suse was a beauty, and had such pretty manners and such pretty clothes, and, Lord, how smart she was! She could read the primer straight through the very first day, and say her alphabet and print every letter of it nice and plain, and count to fifty. So she was put in the class with those who had already been to school a year, and by Christmas time she went into the second reader, still only five years old. It was almost more than anybody could believe! Everybody loved Suse. She always played with the youngest ones at recess and noontime, when they went outside, but on stormy days when the older ones played map games or blackboard games she would watch, and lots of times she could find a river or spell a word or add a sum some of the older ones couldn't. Walking home from school, she was always full of questions about what she had heard Ellie and the boy who was in her class recite on that day, especially in history and the poems the teacher had had them read aloud. Suse was curious about geography, too. Ellen could remember how pleased Suse was to get her first geography book. By then Ellie had left school, first to take care of her mother in her last brief sickness (from blood poisoning, after getting a nail in her foot in the barn cellar) and then to keep house for Ethan Dockham's crippled mother while Ethan tried to keep both his own and the Foye farm going. That was the fall before Ellie and Ethan were married and moved onto the Foye farm, taking his mother with them and selling the Dockham place, which was near the school-house and on Suse's way home, so she often stopped in there afternoons and had cambric tea and cookies with Ellie and Ethan's mother.

How her eyes shone when she showed Ellie that little geography book! That is, it was little compared to the big geography books, but it was the biggest schoolbook Suse had had yet. It was almost like new, for it had never been left out in the rain and nobody had written inside it, only on its cover made from a brown paper bag.

"I'm going to ask my mother to make it a cloth dress," Suse said. "I know she will, because she has for all my other schoolbooks. She sews flowered calico over the covers. I have three and I know which is which by their dresses. Of course I'll know my geography by its shape. Still I want it to have the prettiest dress of all because it's my favorite book. It tells about *the whole world.*"

She talked about it as if it were a doll, and she held it, picked it up and put it down as if it were a china doll and easily broken.

"Oh, Ellie," she said, "I wish you hadn't stopped coming to school. How could you bear to? I never could."

"You can when it comes time," Ellie told her. "When you want more to do other things."

Ellen could still remember Ethan's mother's little chuckle when she said that.

But it had not come time for Suse to stop going to school for a long while. When she had been through all the readers in the district school, her parents had sold their farm and moved into the village so that Suse could live at home while she went to the Academy. From there she went away to another academy which people said was a finishing school, and then to a conservatory of music, and after that taught music at the finishing school until the boy she was going to marry had his medical degree. Then the little girl they had was their only child.

As Suse had been an only child. But at least as long as Suse lived on the farm she had been everybody's darling and everyone she went to school with or ever had been to school with was like a sister or brother to her. Long after she left they wondered about her, often talked about her, and hoped she was happy up there in Boston and out there in Philadelphia.

But they were all gone now. All but Ellie.

Ellen, picking up her two peck baskets, heaped with cranberries, and trudging up the hill toward home, hoped they came to Suse in dreams on her hospital bed and told her not to worry, not to be afraid, but be a good girl and try to get better so she could look at her books and write her letters and maybe take a trip home next summer.

5

YOU read in the newspaper that a predominantly Negro area of a great city was a ghetto and about to burst into rioting because the schools were poor and the homes rat-infested and the people there hated the people of other races and other areas because the people of other races and other areas hated them. A speaker at your club — which had several Negro members, but was admittedly predominantly white — told of these conditions and a committee was immediately named to arrange for a bus to take club members to see them for themselves. But the Negro members protested that they had relatives in that section who had fine homes and would live nowhere else, though it had its slum sections like most large city areas. You saw on television a private school recently established there, with clean and pleasant classrooms, and with a faculty composed of both Negroes and Caucasians, all highly intelligent, experienced, and dedicated teachers, happy in their association and proud of their achievement and its challenge. Also on television you saw and heard the manager of an outdoor art festival there say that every picture in the show had been painted by a resident of the community; hundreds of residents had brought their paintings, all of which were interesting and some very fine, selling in three figures. He was a Negro and he was asked if any whites had "tried to crash the show." He looked startled and replied with dignity that he was not sure what the questioner had in mind, that the festival competition was open to everyone in the community, that the complexion of the artists was neither here nor there, only the quality of their work mattered; and, yes, come to think of it, quite a number of them were white.

Your married daughter lived in this community, in an apartment building of which, along with others on that street, a Negro was the superintendent. He and his family lived in the apartment adjoining hers and a twin to it. They were good neighbors. He had a car and she didn't. He had a fine vegetable garden in the outskirts of the city and often brought her produce far superior to any in the market. Their children played together and with many other small children in a park across the street. You walked there one sunny day and a dark little boy, perhaps eight or ten years old, seeing you approach, suddenly threw himself flat on a footbridge over a winding brook into which he had been tossing stones. He squeezed his head and shoulders under the railing, shouting, "I'm going to fall in, lady!" You said with pretended anxiety, "Oh, don't do that!" and looked down at him over the railing. He was nearly twisting his head off to grin at you, to threaten and enjoy your response. "Yes, ma'am. Here I go!" You said, "No, no. Please don't. Please, please don't. You would get wet. You might hurt your head, or break your arm." He pretended to consider these possibilities, and then wriggled back under the railing, stood up, brushed off his sweater, said reassuringly, "Okay, ma'am. I won't" and raced off. Your daughter went to the hospital to have a new baby, and as you paced the corridor, waiting for word from her doctor, a Negro nurse rose from her desk, came to you, put her arm around you, and walked with you up and down, up and down, saying nothing in words. Later when all was well, and you could thank her and ask, "How did you know how much I needed that?" she said, "I thought my mother would if I were up in the delivery room." You took a taxi and the driver was a Negro. He said he had nine children, five girls and four boys between the ages of two and seventeen; all the oldest were girls, and wasn't it a funny thing how girls of that age never have enough clothes? "You think they have," he said. "They've each got a party dress and party shoes, and a suit and shoes for church, and two pairs of shoes and a lot of skirts and blouses and sweaters for school, and a raincoat with a zip-out wool lining. Sounds like enough clothes. But they never think it is, do they? You got daughters, ma'am?" You said, "Yes. And I know exactly how it is. But you're lucky to have it, you know. Mine are grown now, away from home, and buying their own clothes." He gave you a quick, compassionate look over his shoulder. "Gee, ma'am, I bet you miss 'em. My wife wants at least one more baby and hopes it'll be a girl, to kind of help us out when Docie gets married. Docie's the oldest, so we figure she'll be the first to go. Name's Dorothy but she called herself Docie when she began to talk and it's stuck." Another day you took another taxi with a Negro driver, and he told you that until a few years ago he had been a Pullman porter and would be still but that his home had always been near Boston and he wanted to stay there and there weren't many Pullman cars out of Boston these days. He said he couldn't get used to the change, people getting so they didn't enjoy travel any more, just wanted to get wherever they were going as soon as they started. He remembered, he said, when some of the people he took care of on the trains came, over the years, to be old friends, almost own folks. They would wave to him as they hurried down the station platform, and the children would run ahead and hug him, and there would be quite a reunion before any of them set foot on the portable step he always had ready. Then when they were settled in their sections, they would hear his family news and he would hear theirs — about the wedding, the new babies, who was away at school, sometimes who had died — and he would fix the baby's bottle, keep an eye on the baby while the rest went into the diner, where the table-cloths were white linen and there were fresh flowers in vases and good Southern cooking and their special waiter was as glad to see them as he was. When they came back the berths would be made up and he used to tell the children stories or sing to them while the parents went down to the club car to visit. Sometimes just one of the children would make an overnight trip and be put in his care. He liked that. He never had any trouble with children. But you didn't see enough of any child or anybody else to get acquainted in a cab. You had to feel you kind of belonged to some-body and they kind of belonged to you, at least for a few hours, to get to know them. There was barely time to say hello and good-bye in a taxi ride, so you didn't say it; a good many times you didn't say any-thing except to repeat the address they gave you. You didn't even tell them what the fare was; they read it on the meter. He said times had certainly changed, and not for the better. Something had gone wrong. Somehow people had learned not to want to do any-thing for anybody except give them money, and not to want anything but money of anybody. And nobody had much respect even for that any more. It was just something you were supposed to have. "I don't un-derstand it," he said. "Don't understand it at all. Didn't use to be like this. I think a lot about people I took care of on the Pullmans and wonder where they are now, and if they like things this way."

You were driving south and went into a city hotel

where you had stayed on trips south years ago, a hotel
with a fairy tale staircase which many a Southern bride
and many a debutante had floated up and down between dressing rooms and ballrooms; and with, over-
looking the grand lobby, a mezzanine balcony, where
you had been served spoon bread, deviled crabs, hom-
iny grits, black-eyed peas, and fried chicken by Negro
gentlemen as elegant as royalty was then, handsome,
gracious, and dignified in their fine uniforms. This
time the hotel was the same as in other years except
that you felt haunted. No one else was there except
the room clerk. You were apparently the only overnight guest. At dinner on the mezzanine the food was
as delicious as before, and the waiters were as royal
but there were far fewer of them and they were all
very old. The only other dinner guests were a party of
elderly local residents celebrating a birthday. Before
going to bed you expressed to the room clerk your appreciation of the hospitality, and asked if it was usual
for so few to avail themselves of it.

He said sadly, "Yes, madam. I don't know how
much longer we can keep open. So many people fly
direct to Florida these days, and those who drive don't
care to take time to come off the parkways. They seem
to like the big new motels out there, and the roadside
restaurants where they get typical roadside meals —
hamburgers, french fries, and so on. They're getting
so accustomed to hamburgers and french fries and
being on the same level with the traffic that they're
homesick without it."

You and he looked at each other and shook your heads. You remembered the Pullman porter turned taxi driver who said, "They don't enjoy travel any more, just want to get wherever they are going as soon as they start." So when they arrive they have missed everything which led to journey's end, and when they get home again they do not know where they have been except that it was warmer there.

In the morning when you paid your bill you said, "I hope to come again before I die."

The room clerk answered, "I hope you will, madam, and that the doors will still be open. But don't wait too long."

You saw ease of transportation isolating people to their cars and their regimented, characterless accommodations at the same time it was replacing with dull sameness the once infinite variety in the regions of a great country and of the world as the numbers multiplied of those who strove to be like everyone else, eat like everyone else, speak like everyone else, dress like everyone else. The modern buildings going up in every population center from the ancient metropolises of the world to the smallest town made every skyline similar to every other, and contrived to paint QUAINT or AMUSING or OBSOLETE or SOON TO BE DEMOLISHED on every roof which had caught the rains of fifty years or five hundred or more and sheltered the aspirations, the fears, the daily delights, the triumphs, the defeats, the slow growth in wisdom of many generations.

It was strange that all the effort, all the pressures to

make every human being like every other, every aggregate of human beings like every other, and all the persuasions and forces in favor of togetherness actually served, to the extent that it was successful, to push people apart, to separate each human being, in his own transparent, plastic-like cell; alone on his stool at the counter with his hamburger, French fries, and mug of coffee; alone in his room just like those on either side, each with its tiled shower, television set, metal chair, glass-topped dresser, pink bedspread, mattress massage, heating and air-conditioning thermostats, electric hot water pot, package of powdered coffee, powdered cream, sugar, plastic cups and spoons . . . Or was it so strange? Is it not still the intriguing difference from one's self which attracts one to a member of the opposite sex, even in this era when both strive to look and act alike but have not yet overcome basic physiological and biological facts? Do we not find it easier and more rewarding to study and come to understand those who are unlike us than it is to try to understand ourselves? Don't we all long to escape, temporarily, into new personalities? Is it natural to be fascinated by our own reflections, as in a long hall lined with mirrors? Can we possibly be driven to love counterparts of ourselves? Or are we instead repelled by the suggestion, however disgraceful it would be to admit it? Is that why so many of us mouth tenderness, if we say anything at all, with blank, unsmiling eyes, from inside our plastic-like containers? Why those who are still individuals can scarcely fail to recognize other individuals on sight, and reach out to them as those parched with thirst reach toward a cup of water?

The day before Christmas Walt Ross went outside for the first time in six weeks. He took his latest letter from Audrey, stuffed it into his hospital-shirt front, picked up his crutches, and made his way among the beds to the door which opened onto the runway where the ambulances pulled up and the helicopters set down. Along the walls on either side of the door quite a few men stood smoking and some sat on benches. Walt stood for a minute blinking in the sun, trying to look at the sky of which he had had only glimpses for so long, then made his way slowly, awkwardly to an unoccupied bench where he took out his letter.

"Not a new one?" asked a passerby.

"No. Got it three days ago."

"Didn't think the mail was in yet today. Bound to be a big one."

No one else spoke to him as long as he appeared to be reading, but when he finally refolded the letter and tucked it away, the same stroller dropped down beside him. Walt did not know it was the same one until he spoke. He had not looked at him, but he recognized the voice, which was tenor and had a bright bounce in it.

"Where'd you get smashed up, mac?"

"At a *bus* stop," Walt answered. He was still disgusted about that. Disgust made him lean back against the hospital wall to feel the sun on his face, and the sun made him close his eyes. "Just landed that morning. Just got into town."

"Downright dirty," said the other. "How long they been patching you up?"

"Six weeks."

"Think you'll hold together?"

"Oh, sure."

"Good enough."

Walt, opening his eyes, rolled his head toward the other, a small but tough-looking boy with the mark of the shamrock all over him. He had bushy hair and eyebrows, a cleft in his chin, pockmarked cheeks, and a knowing, half-sad, half-merry glint in his eyes which made one want to inquire for things in Glocca Morra.

Instead Walt asked, "You been in here long?"

"Two days only. I'll be back patrolling my village in two or three days more. Some V.C. likes me, wanted to give me a Christmas leave."

"What did you get?"

"Nothing but a scalp wound." He knocked off his cap and showed the bandage. "Just deep enough to give me a concussion. I was out for fifteen hours, but no sweat."

"Lucky guy."

"Lucky Paddy, that's me."

"At least you've done what you came to do. You know where the war is and you've been there."

"Oh, you'll get there." Suddenly the Irishman laughed, a mischievous sound. "I sure bet you hated being picked off at a bus stop! But you're not the first one it's happened to . . . And you've got your own brand of luck. You've got a girl."

"Haven't you?"

"Nope. I'm a slow starter and never got around to it before I left. I enlisted on my seventeenth birthday. Just couldn't wait to get here."

"I was older than that before I had one. How did you know I had?"

"Easy, man. You're still reading a three-day-old letter. Course she may be your wife for all I know."

"Not yet."

"But going to be."

"I sure hope so."

"Got her picture?"

Walt slid it out of his wallet.

"Hey! She's a doll." The boy jerked his head admiringly and passed the picture back. "What's she doing while you're over here?"

"She's in college."

"That right? I knew a feller pretty well once who had been to college. He was older, a friend of my brother's. How old is she?"

"Nineteen."

"That's just my age. How old are you?"

"Twenty."

"You go to college?"

"Started, but I didn't stay."

"I bet I wouldn't. Only I never thought of starting."

"What did you think of doing? Before you enlisted."

"What I've always meant to do, and still do. Getting on a police force. Like my brother . . . How about you?"

"Never could get any idea. Still can't."

"A lot of guys like that."

"Yeah, but looks like Audrey's going to graduate from that college, with degrees, diplomas, certificates, and all the rest of it. Guy can't marry a girl like that without knowing how to do *something*. Something pretty good."

"It'll come to you. That her name — Audrey?"

"Uh-huh."

"Never happened to know anybody by that name. What's yours?"

"Walt Ross."

"Everybody over here calls me Paddy."

"That your name?"

"Padraic. My brother and his family always called me that. I grew up with them. My mother died when I was born and he and his wife was just married. My father had a houseful of older kids to look after. He got married again later on. I was never with them much. Seemed like I belonged to Mike as long as he lived. Last name is Breck."

"Your brother died, you say?"

"Two years ago. Shot trying to stop a teen-age rumble."

"Rough."

"That was why I signed up soon as Eileen and their kids got settled in the country near her folks. Felt as if

I had to get going. Figure I'll stay in the Army until I'm old enough for the force."

"What happened to him didn't change your mind about that?"

"Just the opposite. Mike was quite a guy. The greatest. I watched and listened to him by the hour, year on year. What he was doing, the way he did it can't stop, or it all goes to waste — what he did, and what's going on over here, and all the other wars beginning with the Revolution, and all the Constitutions and Federations and Declarations ever written to spell out what freedom is and how you get it and keep it or lose it. Way he saw it, and way I see it, where peaceful citizens don't feel safe on their streets and in their houses, civilization is trickling if not flooding down the drain."

Walt was swept by a wave of weakness.

"You're right there," he said. "Wish I'd known Mike. Glad to have met you, Padraic. Look, I guess I've got to get inside while I still can."

"Yeah. You're pale. Throw an arm across my shoulders. I'm handier than a crutch. Here we go. I know just how it hits you, after about so long up . . . There you are. It'll pass off in a few minutes now. So long. See you later."

The next day Padraic came around with Christmas wishes and a plum cake from Eileen. Walt was lying on a bed littered with cards and cookie crumbs, and Padraic perched on a stool, knees hunched up, elbows resting on them, jaw in hands.

"How are things in Glocca Morra," Walt asked, yielding to temptation.

"Sure and the little brook's still running there. They still go down to Donny cove, too. You got a card from Audrey, likely."

"Likely."

"Bet I could tell from the front which one it is. Says 'Merry Christmas to my Sweetheart.' Or is it 'To the Most Wonderful Man in the World'? Let's see —"

"Hands off this stuff!"

"Take it easy. I won't look inside."

"Hands off, I say."

They wrestled for a minute. It felt good. Then Padraic drew back.

"Okay. They're probably all from the hometown Red Cross anyway."

"Think what you like. Have a broken cookie. Or a spoonful of my mother's fudge . . . No. Audrey wouldn't send a card like that. Here's hers."

He pulled it out from under the pillow. It had no words at all on the cover. Just a picture of a partridge in a pear tree.

Padraic grinned and nodded, beginning to whistle the tune between lappings of the spoon Walt had brought back from breakfast.

"She sent a box of presents, too. Soap and magazines and a sweater she knit. But the letters were the best. I got three from her yesterday afternoon."

"Think of that now. Three."

"Mostly about a new friend she's got."

"Male or female?"

"Name's Margaret. See, Audrey's taking this course where she has to visit schools twice a week and observe teaching methods. This Margaret is one of the teachers she's observing. The only one yet, far as I know. Audrey seems to have a thing about her, and she comes out to the campus to see Audrey. Sounds like quite a girl. Well, here; wait a minute —"

He opened an envelope, scanned several pages and selected two which he offered to Padraic, who raised his bushy eyebrows.

"You mean I can read it?"

"Would I be pushing it at you if you couldn't?"

"It won't burn me? Remember I'm only nineteen, and I told you I'm a slow starter."

"Read it, you fool."

The two pages were from the letter Audrey had written the night after she met Margaret; bulky, as most of hers were, for she wanted to tell him everything and used the first paper which came to hand, often sheets pulled from her loose-leaf notebook. It was only occasionally that she wrote on a thin sheet and sent it by air.

"I guess I am what is known as excited, but I wouldn't swear that is the word for what I am, being so unaccustomed to it. The only time I can compare it with is that evening by the river two years ago, and if what I was then was excited, it isn't what I am now. All I can say is that those two are the two best feelings I've ever had when I was right with somebody, except for Philadelphia when I *know* I wasn't the least bit excited. Whatever that was was far, far better. But the riverbank feeling was great, just the same, and so is this, which is different. For one thing, that night was — *you* know — like a faint light appearing where there wasn't supposed to be any, so I thought it just wasn't there. It grew brighter and I thought it might be a UFO. So what? UFO's aren't there either. You don't get excited about what isn't there, if you have a grain of sense. Actually I didn't believe until quite a while afterwards that you were really there. Even your first letters — I read them as if I had made them up myself, and I felt embarrassed answering them. Did I ever tell you that? . . ."

"You sure you know what I'm reading here?" Padraic asked.

"Pretty sure." Walt was pawing through a cookie box.

"Well, I'm not. May be personal as the very devil for all I know. Can't make heads or tails of it. Looks real pretty, though."

"I guess this is advanced stuff for you, kid, but keep going. You may get yourself a blind pen pal, and then you can start at the beginning."

So Padraic plowed on through Audrey's description of her first morning of teacher-watching, of the merry-faced little nun, and of the girl who came in to take over the seventh-graders, as happenings in broad daylight, in three solid dimensions, so that she never doubted for a minute they were real. And since it was obviously all going on right before her eyes, and was so far ahead of anything she had ever seen in a classroom, and she began to realize she was having literally to hang onto her chair to keep from jumping up and telling this Miss Sheaffer the ideas that were flying off her mind like a Leonides meteor shower, probably what she was was excited. Anyway it was all great . . .

"And can you believe that afterwards I went to lunch with this Miss Sheaffer and we now call each other by first names — hers is Margaret — and —"

"Margaret *Sheaffer!*" Padraic exclaimed, letting both feet fall *slap* on the floor from the round of the stool. "Hey, that couldn't be the Peg Sheaffer who went to the same high school I did, could it? You don't think —"

Walt was cutting himself a second piece of Padraic's plum cake with the handle of the spoon.

"Not thinking," he said. "Your sister makes a good cake. What's for *me* to think about Margaret Sheaffer except what Audrey says? I don't know where she went to school, don't know where you went to school —"

Padraic had returned to the letter, running the tip of a forefinger under each line.

"See here now. Mmm — mmm; says she's not a Catholic, and Peg wasn't, fact her father was a bigwig in some other church, used to know the name of it, can't remember now. Mmm — mmm; most of her school friends were Catholic. Hey, Peg's sure were! All the kids she ran around with went to the church I did. Some of them had been altar boys when I was —"

"But you didn't run around with this Peg. Why not?"

"Oh, not a chance. She was older. Oh, maybe not

much older, but way ahead of me in school, and, man, was she smart! Just about every assembly, either she was up front taking some part in it, or getting her name read out for some honor, or at very least playing the piano or maybe a solo on some other instrument. Seemed like there wasn't anything Peg Sheaffer couldn't do, and every time you turned a corner there she was doing it for all she was worth. She never seemed to notice she was the one doing it, though, if you know what I mean."

"Must say all that sounds like the one Audrey's met. Be something if it is, wouldn't it? Tell you how we can find out. I'll have Audrey ask her. If she is, maybe she'll write to you. Maybe she will anyway. If Audrey has your address to give her."

"Aw, no. Peg Sheaffer would never remember me. No reason to . . . But it would be interesting to know if Peg's teaching in a Catholic school now. Eileen might know, if she still lived in the city. Maybe she still takes the *Sun* and might have seen something about it there. I can ask her. Got to write to her tonight. But no reason for her to remember, if she had read it. She never knew Peg."

"Best way is for me to ask Audrey to ask Margaret where she went to high school, what year she graduated from there, and so on. That'll pinpoint it. Audrey needn't mention you. But you'll have to give me an address that'll reach you after you leave here. So I can let you know what I find out. Put it on the back of this envelope."

While Padraic was writing the address, Walt sorted

out sheets from Audrey's two more recently written letters.

"Here's more on Margaret Sheaffer," he said. "Extra! Extra! Read all about it! Me for a little shut-eye."

He meant only to give Padraic what privacy he could, for the reading, but Padraic read slowly all a girl will tell her lover about the first close friend of her own sex, the first in-person companion she has ever had, and when he finished Walt was snoring. So Padraic smoothed out the pages from Audrey's letters, carefully put them in order, and slowly read them all through again. Then, as Walt was still asleep, he put the folded letters deep under Walt's pillow, and Walt still did not wake. Padraic went back to his own bed in the wing from which all patients were soon to be sent back on duty, and began a letter to Eileen. In the course of it he asked, "Do you still hear sometimes from that Andy Pollister that used to come home with Mike a lot? I got to thinking today I wondered where he is now and what's been happening to him lately. Maybe he's over here somewhere. I thought he was a real nice guy. I know Mike did, too."

Everywhere, everywhere, Christmas tonight.

In a spacious corner room of the convalescent home considered the best in one American city a small, perfectly symmetrical and tapering fir tree stood on the dresser, with tiny colored bulbs, strands of rainbow tinsel, paper icicles, and gaily wrapped gifts reflected softly in the mirror by the light which came through the open door from the hall. The tree lights were not turned on, for the occupant of the room was not convalescent and was thought by the nurses to be sleeping. Kim Tucker entered quietly, but her tweed suit and flowing hair gave off the breath of the outdoors so electrifying to those confined, and her grandmother opened her eyes.

"I was just thinking about Ellie Foye," she said.

"That's good," Kim answered, sitting down by the bed. "What did you think, Gramma?"

"I think I'd better go to see her."

"I do, too. You know I said so when you showed me the last letter you had from her."

"You sure you and Rick can get me there?"

"Of course we can. Why not? That's the first thing we'll do after he gets home."

"Well, I hope he gets here before Christmas. Ellie called me up today. She wants me there before Christmas. They're going to have a Christmas party at the schoolhouse and they want me to sing . . . Either speak a piece or sing, she said. I was thinking I'd rather sing . . ."

When after a minute she did not go on, Kim said, "That would be lovely. I remember your singing 'Bring a Torch, Jeannette Isabella' to us on Christmas Eve when we were little."

". . . She wants me to sing 'Hark the Herald Angels.' My mother does . . . I guess the Foyes don't have a telephone. Ellie must have been calling from Mother's. Because after Ellie talked, Mother talked . . . She's making me something. Something to sing

in. She called it . . . She called it . . . I think —
she called it a robe . . ."

Suse's eyes closed. She did not speak again, even
when, after a while, Kim rose and bent over her,
touched her hand and whispered, "Good night, dear
Gramma." She did not open her eyes when Kim
kissed her. Her breathing was very soft.

In the corridor Kim asked the nurse at the desk,
"Would you see if you think my grandmother is all
right, before I go?"

The nurse nodded and went into the corner room,
while Kim waited by the desk. When she came back,
she told Kim quietly, "There is no emergency. Mrs.
Norris fails a little every day. We told your mother
when she brought the tree this afternoon that she
must expect the end soon, but I don't think it will be
tonight. Don't let it spoil your family holiday. I'm
sure Mrs. Norris wouldn't want that, if she knew. She
is comfortable, and sleeps nearly all the time."

At the Max Frome house on High Street there was
a wreath on every door, an electric candle in every
window, and a huge blue spruce by the garden gate
illuminated to the tip. Inside there was holly on every
mantel, mistletoe above every archway, logs burning
in the fireplace, a candlelit dinner table with places
laid for seven, and a tree blazing at the far end of the
double living room with gifts stacked below it. At
dusk only Maida and Kirsti the maid were there, but
Max came from the club at six, finished making the
eggnog in the silver punch bowl and was setting it on

the tray Maida had ready on the console table when Kim came in.

"Hi, Daddy. Hi, Mom."

"Hi, Kim."

"The others aren't here yet? I'll run up and change."

When she came downstairs in a sleeveless yellow linen dress Rick had loved to see her in in the summer — wearing it so that she could write him she had worn it when she opened his gift — Maisie was there. She had returned from the ski lodge up north where she had been for Christmas Eve with college friends, had dropped her sleeping bag in the hall, and now was seated in her favorite, cross-legged position on the floor near the tree, strumming and humming. The tune, such as there was, was vaguely familiar, some medley of old-fashioned Christmas songs with a new rhythm. When Kim approached she dropped the guitar to her knees and called, "Mom? Daddy? Kim's down. Let's have at the eggnog. I sniffed it and it smells absolutely divine. Let's *not* wait for Sue and Nat. We don't have any idea when they'll get here, if they get here."

Max and Maida opened the library door and came out together, Maida wearing a new bracelet with diamonds and jade, pleased and tearful, Max pleased and embarrassed in a new plaid waistcoat and black velvet jacket. So Max in plaid and velvet, Maida in jewels and a floor-length crimson hostess gown, Kim in yellow linen, and Maisie in an oyster-gray wool shirt, black bell-bottom slacks belted with hemp rope, and thick white wool socks gathered around the wassail and somewhat later went in to dinner. But Sue and Nat did get home before they had finished; ate hungrily; and asked for time to shower and change before going to the tree. There *is* something about Christmas . . . Nat came down in slacks, but they were new — her gift from Sue — of checked flannel and with them she wore the blouse of heavy dark green crepe which Maida had left gift-wrapped on her bed. And Sue had found a brown velvet jumper in the back of her closet, to wear with the tan silk blouse and big black bow her mother had left for her. In these she took on a little-girl look she had not had for years. When she took her first sip of the eggnog she smiled and said, "This is *good*. You make it, Daddy?"

Among the gifts under the tree there were jackets of man-made fur with hoods for all the girls, a chinchilla evening wrap for Maida, cashmere sweaters, sterling, gold earrings, handsome luggage, an electric typewriter, neckties from Scotland . . .

Margaret Sheaffer, having been at home for a week with her family, which traditionally gathered for its reunion and celebration on Christmas Eve, had flown that afternoon to the airport nearest Audrey's home and was with the Mason family, which had opened its gifts that morning and had a turkey dinner at noon. The Masons were Audrey's father and mother, her father's unmarried sister, her maternal grandmother, and Audrey herself. There had been no tree, as Mr. Mason was no longer able to go into the woods to cut one and felt that to buy a tree which must be sent to the dump for burning in a few days was an absurd waste of money. The women of the family were content with his decision because they were extremely neat housekeepers and liked the furnishings to stay in their accustomed places, were made uneasy by the danger of scratches on wallpaper, dark marks on the white ceiling, sticky needles littering the waxed floors and working into the naps of rugs. It had not mattered to Audrey that she did not have a tree. Between breakfast and dinner, after making a balanced arrangement of her gifts on the desk in the den where she had done her homework while in grade and high school, she had gone to her room and written a long letter to Walt. She had told him that the best present she could possibly have had was his airmail letter saying he was now getting around easily on crutches and expected soon to be graduated to a cane; that it was absurd of him to worry about not being able to send her a package from Saigon when he knew that all she wanted was to keep hearing that he was improving every day . . .

But because of his letters coming almost daily to the house (she had asked him to send them there on carefully figured dates, knowing that this time she could not endure letting them accumulate in her box at the college as they had the Christmas before) it had been necessary to tell her family of her friendship with Walt Ross. This had cast a cloud over the holiday in the Mason household, since her family knew him only by an unfortunate local reputation. Though little had been said about it, for the Masons were not articulate people, their concern had shown itself in narrowed eyes, compressed lips, and less conversation even than usual.

It could not be denied that Christmas had begun for Audrey when she met Margaret's plane. To see Margaret coming down the steps and waving as she ran through a snow flurry which frosted her dark hair, in a navy pea jacket and brief red skirt, suitcase bumping against one bare knee, the strap of her handbag slipping off the other shoulder and sliding down her arm — "Oh, *Audrey!* There you are!" . . . To hug and be hugged, as if they had been separated for months, with case and bag getting in the way and Margaret asking breathlessly, "What's the latest from Walt?" . . . To drive her father's delivery truck home along the familiar streets with Margaret beside her exclaiming about what the falling snow was doing to roofs, fence posts, leafless branches . . . To take her into the quiet, orderly house — so neat, so quiet it had seemed almost unoccupied — and see it come alive, however reluctantly and stiffly, like a wooden doll or a tin soldier, in response to her interest and spontaneous enthusiasm . . . To have her at last in Audrey's own room with the door closed after them, this room where for so long Audrey had wrestled alone and fruitlessly with the gremlins of adolescence and the ogres of a place and time even the mature lacked weapons against. Now Margaret's jacket was tossed over the plastic-covered arm of the rocker, her bag open on the cane-seated straight chair and her boots under it, and she sat in the middle of the tufted white spread shaking the snow out of her hair and beaming.

"Oh, Margaret, I know now I didn't believe it."

"Believe what?"

"That you really would come."

"Silly. I jumped at the chance the minute you asked me. I know I'm going to have a marvelous time. I've never stayed in such a little town. With you to lead me around and answer my questions, I ought to be able to find out everything about such a little town in a week . . . But, first, have you things you want to tell me about what has been happening to you since we left Dewey? Because if you have, I want to hear them, and then I want to tell you about *my* pre-Christmas week."

"Oh, tell me about yours now. Please."

"First? You sure?"

"Sure I'm sure." Audrey threw herself across the foot of the bed, lying on her side with her head propped on her arm, looking at Margaret expectantly. "Nothing has happened here. Really. And I can tell that something has happened to you."

"Well, it has," Margaret said. "It sure as heck has. Whether I can tell it so you can see it, I don't know. But I'll try, because it just has to be passed on. If I can make you see it, you'll have to pass it on, too. It's that kind of thing. Like what I imagine orchestra players feel with a director who's a real genius. If he asks for

something, you give it to him if it's in you. You
couldn't hold it back even if you wanted to . . .
Well, here goes —"

She said she had had a revelation. Or a vision. Actually a series of revelations. Or visions. If it was permis-
sible to apply those words to what did not emanate
from another and better world, but was wholly in and
of this one and thus was — at least to Margaret —
all the more spectacular, earthshaking, and all but incredible.

"I assure you I am shaken up," said Margaret.
"From end to end."

It had begun ordinarily enough, for the holiday
season. Margaret had been the first of her parents' six
children (the three older and one younger than she
married and the youngest in college) to reach home,
and she and her parents had been pleased about that
because they had common interests the others did not
share. For one thing, Margaret loved the Christmas
preparations — last-minute shopping, wrapping, dec-
orating, baking — and the others would be glad to
find them finished when they arrived. The first
evening she was there her father popped corn to fill
huge yellow bowls and strung a lot of it into chains
for the tree, while she and her mother cooked syrup
and made cornballs. When they had set up the tree in
the corner where the Christmas tree always stood,
they brought out of storage the decorations for it
which had been used many times. She searched eagerly through the boxes for her favorites — the blue
cones, the silver birds with rosy silk tails spread like

fans, the gilded lanterns. The next morning her
mother had tied an apron around her, and they had
made and iced star-shaped cookies.

"Your father's going to try to get home for lunch,"
her mother said, "and take us into town this afternoon to finish the shopping. Deborah wants matching
green velvet dresses for the girls and I haven't yet
found a style that seems to me suitable for both a
seven-year-old and a three-year-old."

"It's about a fifty-mile run to the city from where
we live now," Margaret told Audrey, "and the traffic
was ghastly. But Daddy got us there about three
o'clock and left the car where they're driven up on
ramps to sixth and seventh floors. He says he won't
take a chance on leaving it outside anywhere in the
city now. He had to go ahead to make a way for us
through the crowds in the stores and several times we
almost lost him, but when we were conscious of cold
air on our faces again we somehow had everything on
Mommy's list, though she had had to settle for green
velvet jumpers and white silk blouses for the girls and
was afraid Deborah wanted dresses with sleeves. Then
Daddy said, 'Praise the Lord and pass the ice cream.
We're going to Driscoll's.' "

She had known they would; though she could remember years of early childhood, before she had made
the connection between Driscoll's and the traditional
last-trip-into-town-before-Christmas, when this announcement had come as a delicious surprise at the
end of a bewildering sequence of cascading colored
lights, flaming torches, illuminated nativity scenes,

costumed carolers, automated-fairly-tale store windows, Santa's ear to whisper into, bell-ringing, foot-
stamping Santas, and giant Santas laughing over loud-
speakers. After so much that was so wondrous it was
almost completely incomprehensible, it had been like
waking from a dream so exciting and confusing that it
had some of the elements of a nightmare to hear her
father saying, "Okay, kids. Now we're going to Driscoll's." Almost instantly, it seemed, her mother would
turn into a narrow alley, leading the next-to-youngest
by the hand, the other children following her in single
file, and their father bringing up the rear with the
youngest on his shoulder. The lights, the crowds, the
noise, the Santas were left behind. The Sheaffer family was alone in a dim, quiet, friendly passageway to a
heavenly parlor come to earth for Christmas.

A corner turned — and there were its gates, suddenly familiar from last Christmas. They passed
through, and there it was again! The polished dark
wood panels framing gilded angels, all around the
walls; the glass-fronted cupboards padded inside with
tufted dark red satin and their glass shelves displaying
star-shaped candy boxes in red and silver with contrast-
ing red and silver ribbon bows; the glittering chandeliers swinging from the high vaulted ceiling; the long,
long white marble counters with their rows of tall
stools with heart-shaped backs, and the many round
tables with marble tops and chairs with heart-shaped
backs. The heavenly parlor, warm, softly lighted, and
smelling of chocolate! Just inside, a small child stood
still, immobilized by awe, until she was propelled to a

table by older hands, her cap, scarf, muff or mittens removed and her coat unbuttoned, before she was lifted, blinking, into her chair.

By then her father was at the counter ordering, according to tastes he knew, so many ice cream sodas of this and that flavor, so many sundaes with so-and-so sauces, with or without marshmallow, with or without nuts. Her mother and the older children went to help him bring back the laden silver trays, and then they were all sitting together, each with the best taste he knew flowing over his tongue from straw or spoon. They smiled around the circle at one another in silent delight. Ecstasy! Christmas ecstasy in the heavenly parlor!

Sometime later, at the point of eating and drinking very slowly to make the contents of tall glasses and silver dishes last, the parents would begin to tell the children in low voices of how Daddy used to come to Driscoll's with his parents and brothers and sisters when he was a little boy. That family had had a house in a place which was now considered part of the city center and had no houses, only apartment buildings and shops; but then it was like a village, with big elm trees, and empty lots where the children played. Daddy's family had come into this part of the city then by trolley, because they had no car, and besides it was fun to ride the trolley, especially at this time of the year when the conductor always wished you "Merry Christmas" when he took your fare. Daddy and his family had come in to do their Christmas shopping, which was mostly for warm coats and boots, and one toy for each child, and afterwards Grandpa brought them all here for a Christmas treat. Mommy, they said, was not so lucky. She had grown up so far from Driscoll's that she had never heard of it when she first met Daddy — imagine that! But the very first Christmas time after he met her he had brought her here, of course, and every Christmas time since; every single one.

"I was still at La Salle that first time."

"The next time, too. I thought you'd never finish at La Salle."

"Your father was born with no patience. What he has now is self-made."

"You had a Persian lamb coat and a red hat. A *very* red hat."

"You think I wore a red hat both times?"

"That's the one I remember. It came up to a high peak. Shiny things all over it."

"Sequins."

"Your mother was quite a catch. Not so pretty as she is now, either."

"Your father was quite a catch, too. He had what he called a mustache. An itty-bitty brush on his upper lip."

The children were getting sleepy, trying to suck up the last drops in the bottom of the glasses, lapping their spoons. Nobody reminded them of their manners. Their parents suddenly had eyes only for each other.

"I asked my mother this year," Margaret told Audrey, "if we had ever gone to Driscoll's except at

Christmas time and she said yes, of course. But I can't remember it. She said low that she hoped I still liked to go, because Daddy did so much, and she was sure none of the other children did, only the grandchildren. Said the others had lost interest in ice cream, wanted to go where they could get, if not cocktails, then at least coffee and weird-sounding sandwiches. I said I loved ice cream and I loved Driscoll's and it would hardly be Christmas for me if we didn't go there . . . Am I boring you, Audrey? I know it doesn't sound important yet."

"Oh, it does. I'm living it right with you. Go on."

"Well, then, if you really have been there with us when I was little, and sort of with Daddy when *he* was little and then when he first took Mommy there, and with them all the other times they went, and now you've heard Daddy say in a voice rich in relief and anticipation, 'Praise the Lord and pass the ice cream. We're going to Driscoll's,' and you're following fifty-year-old Mommy's only slightly thickening figure and kept-blonde head (because Daddy doesn't like to see the gray in her hair) topped by a saucy little red hat with a visor down that dim, narrow alley, hearing Daddy's step (not quite so buoyant as it used to be) behind you — if you're there with us when we turn the corner, maybe you'll feel something of what I felt when I couldn't see those old iron gates. Mommy couldn't see them either. She stopped, puzzled, and looked back past me at Daddy as if to ask, 'Where are we?' "

The reason they could not see the gates was that

they were not there. But the sign DRISCOLL'S ICE CREAM PARLOR in big brass letters was still over the heavy double doors and the chandeliers were lit, so they hurried inside, more eager than ever before for the reassurance of warmth, light, and the smell of chocolate, of a happy dream, of a Christmas welcome to a heavenly parlor.

But all was changed. The angels had flown away, the cupboards were empty and had no tufted scarlet linings. The chandeliers looked down bleakly upon a few widely scattered tables, one long counter with no high stools, and one elderly man in a stained white apron halfheartedly wiping up a pool of cream.

"Daddy asked, sort of stunned, 'What's happened here?'

"The counterman said, 'Oh, they're closing this place at the end of the year. Lease runs out then. Opened a new one over on Tewksbury Street two months or so ago. You didn't know?'

"Mommy said in a small voice, 'No. No, we didn't. How — how awful!'

"The counterman said, 'Well, some folks think so, and I'm one of 'em. Been on this counter for forty years. But there ain't enough of us, seems. The new place is going great guns. Twice as big as this. Two levels. They call it the Polynesia. Serve full lunches. Outlandish stuff young folks like. Have 'em waiting in line over there most of the time.'

"After a minute Daddy asked, 'They make the same ice cream?'

" 'They say so,' answered the counterman, noncommittally. He took a few more swipes at the pool and repeated, 'They say so.'

"Well, finally Daddy asked if we could still get the usual flavors here, and the counterman said, 'Most of 'em,' so Daddy waved us to the nearest table and ordered Mommy's favorite all-strawberry ice cream soda, and my coffee soda with chocolate chip, and his butterscotch sundae with whipped cream and nuts, and brought them to us all spilling and slopping over with deliciousness the way they always did. But, you know, not one of us could finish what we had! There was that sick feeling of being the only ones left in a beloved house that has been stripped of its furnishings and even part of its foundation because tomorrow the floodwaters are to rise and sweep it away, even bury forever the familiar little dips of its dooryard and the fitted stone of its garden wall."

Margaret's reaction to that sick feeling had at first been one of anger. She wanted to run out and find authorities to whom she could protest, then to picket the new Driscoll's on Tewksbury Street, and finally to stand with a gun where the gates had been when the workmen came to complete the destruction, almost the desecration, of the heavenly parlor. And she was puzzled by the patience in the sadness on her parents' faces, like that on the counterman's.

As they were leaving, her father asked, "Do you go into the new Driscoll's when this closes?"

The counterman answered, his hands busy moving a few dishes from one sink to another, "I guess I'll have to. I don't want to, but I guess I'll have to. I'm too old to start over with another company."

Her father nodded. He hesitated, trying to think of something more to say, and gave it up, gestured his wife and daughter toward the door. His wife looked back at the counterman, shaking her head a little in its red hat, and smiled a sad, sweet smile at him. Margaret thought of glancing to see if he returned it and decided against it.

During the quiet walk to the garage, the quiet wait for the check to bring their car down the ramp, the quiet ride home, Margaret had the first of her revelations.

It did not come in a blinding flash, but slowly and softly like daybreak. She saw that the patience in her parents and in the counterman was a quality, a reaction to loss, to bewilderment, painfully acquired by most of their generation in self-defense against an environment in which they were forced to spend their latter years, and where, at a time of life when earlier generations had begun to rest on their laurels, they were granted no laurels on which to rest but were under constant assault from change on every side — change in values, in communications, in transportation, in areas of human knowledge, in personal and professional relationships, in architecture, in all art forms, in all routes from where they were to where they might go, in everything which had once been solid, familiar, reliable and now, if it had not vanished completely, was so altered as to be almost or quite unrecognizable.

"And nobody thinks this matters, Audrey. The movers and the shakers of our time have actually assumed that they can make a good world while putting and keeping everyone past fifty figuratively in a concentration camp. Here are *millions* of human beings who have survived this cataclysm of change with rather more stability so far than younger ones, but the young don't want anything from them, won't take anything from them except their money and their jobs, just want to get them out of the way where they won't be seen or heard from. That they continue to live is resented, and they feel this. Every morning when they are waking up they must think, like the counterman, 'I guess I'll have to. I don't want to, but I guess I'll have to.' Like him, they are too old to start over with the new company on its terms, and the new company is offering no terms; it does not want them — their skills, their experience, their advice, their taste, their affection, or even their respect."

What had come to Margaret on the ride home that starry night was the realization that true progress would never be achieved but by the joint, combined effort of every earthly generation, of every segment of society straining together, each to its peak potential, toward that end. The human race could not afford concentration camps. If it was to survive it must honor and employ every possible resource. And it could not afford an attitude of patience toward all that was draining sweetness, dignity, and trust in the decency and worth of one's fellow man out of daily life and human relationships.

She waited in the hope that how this revelation might be shared and bear fruit would also be revealed. But it still had not when the three Sheaffers reached home.

"We had planned to decorate the tree then," Margaret told Audrey, "but Daddy said he'd like to lie down awhile first. He said his eyes were tired from the headlights. Mommy said that was a good idea. She would call Deb now about the velvet dresses and then address the last of her cards. We'd have a light supper later — it was already in the oven, she had only to turn it on — and do the tree. I had a feeling they both needed to be alone. So I went in where the bare tree stood, and looked at the waiting boxes of decorations — and idly turned on the television. Then, my dear, came the next revelation. Not really connected with the first one, yet in a way it was."

The television program, already under way, followed the course of the actual preparations for the opening of a great new metropolitan opera house; the largest, most luxuriously appointed, and most elaborately equipped structure of its kind in America and probably in the world. Margaret — and millions of other viewers — saw the Mighty Manager at his desk, being besieged by complaints by harried members of his staff, solving their insoluble problems while being interviewed by the press and answering one telephone after another on his several open lines. She heard that the first opera to be presented in this great new house had been composed for just that purpose and the leading role created for one Mighty Singer, an extraordinarily gifted young Negro woman from a little town in Mississippi, where her mother had been a midwife and her father a carpenter. They watched her rehearsing with a Mighty Director and heard the splendor of her voice, the beauty she produced apparently almost effortlessly. They were there when it was discovered that the stage, tremendous as it was, would not accommodate an army going into battle according to the composer's plan, and when it was announced to composer, stage designer, directors, and artists that whole scenes must therefore be rewritten, restaged, learned, and rehearsed in two weeks' time. They saw the way in which all concerned rose to this challenge, as the hard-pressed composer brought in his new music; heard orchestra and singers tiptoe through it; saw hundreds of workmen transforming the designer's visions into what was tangible, three-dimensional, and must work, while hundreds of dancers practiced routines in three rehearsal halls; saw the small, pleasant man who was the Mighty Designer trying to find words in which to express to interviewers his visions and how they came to him and how he felt about them. If any part of all this was more important than any other to the Designer it was the great pyramid which must lie open, all its four sides flat on the stage, until they rose and curled and slowly closed like the petals of a giant flower around the Mighty Singer at the conclusion of one of her numbers, after which the whole must move slowly from the center of the stage to the seclusion of a wing and there release her.

Margaret — and millions of others — reached the

dress rehearsal, knowing the racking uncertainty in the mind of every participant and the exhaustion of every muscle, the intoxication of every spirit. Here were the dreams of gods trapped in the bodies of men and women. Could these dreams find a way through these tired fingers, feet, and vocal cords and fill this mammoth temple?

The focal point of doubt was the mechanized pyramid . . . Its crucial moment came and the Mighty Singer took her place in its heart. Its petals slowly rose and curled and closed about her. It moved a foot or so — and stopped. It did not move again. The curtains had to be drawn and the Singer extracted from her metal prison. Man is but man.

But that was only the dress rehearsal.

Now it was the opening night.

It was the opening night and the boxes were filling with the great of the land, the orchestra seats with black ties, tuxedos, gowns by famous designers, and wraps of rare furs, the tiered balconies with the long-haired young in brief, glittering frocks and dark coats. Television cameras whirred, and everyone was bowing and smiling at acquaintances and at the cameras, clearly unaware of and unconcerned with all that was known to Margaret and millions of others who had been behind the scenes. The audience had come to see the house, to hear the music, and to applaud the performers. They did not know as Margaret did that even now the workmen were driving themselves to the point of collapse to complete the fireproofing of the Mighty Designer's vision because until it was complete the city fire department would not permit the performance to begin; that even now the Mighty Director was in receipt of an ultimatum from the musicians' union to the effect that the members of the orchestra would vote at the first intermission as to whether they would play for a second performance of this Mighty Opera.

They were not, as Margaret was — and millions of others were — with the Mighty Designer where he stood combing and recombing his hair, looking for encouragement into his own eyes as reflected from a mirror, saying in an undertone, "It'll do. It'll be all right. There's no reason why it shouldn't. We must have allowed for everything"; or when he came out to where a dancer was crying, half-hysterically, "I found my own way through! It's the very first time I haven't got lost!" and answered a reporter's question about what he would do after the performance with, "Oh, I shall run off. Before the final curtain goes down I shall have run off. Far, far away. Once it has left me — really left me — I cannot bear to think of it, or be reminded of it."

They were not, as Margaret was, in the dressing room of the Mighty Singer where her face was being rebuilt into that of an Egyptian, her head and shoulders weighted down with heavy crown and heavy robes, and she was saying when asked how she felt, "I am terrified out of my wits, and excited out of my skin —"

Thus what the theater audience saw was the first performance of a great American opera in a magnificent setting, while Margaret watched with wonder, anguish, reverence, and terror the struggle of human beings to give birth to a child conceived months ago in an overwhelming encounter with the god of Beauty, and carried to term, in a constantly threatening environment, by sheer faith, determination, and devotion.

"This is what I can't possibly describe," Margaret told Audrey, "or its effect on me. The *process*, I mean. It's easy to say there was a happy ending. The pyramid did move, not quite so far into the wings as it was supposed to, but far enough. The union was appeased and the musicians did not strike. The opera was a success — though puzzling to many — and the great new house was opened in a blaze of glory. But what those human beings felt obligated to undertake, and did undertake, and to a remarkable degree succeeded in doing, with only their fragile bodies, their stretching minds, their reaching hearts, their puny knowledge of the ultimate, their feeble instruments, their wires and wheels, their scraps of metal and cloth and paper and glass — that was what was really important, and truly astounded me. I've often castigated television, but how else could I have seen this whole? For the audience seated before her that night the Mighty Singer was the Queen of the Egyptians. But I saw her running back to her dressing room in tears, after the final curtain, pulling off her Egyptian patches and throwing her arms about her mother and her father, saying, 'Oh, isn't it wonderful the people at home are going to get to see this? That's the best part of it all. Daddy, you're up late. You know what the doctor said. Mom, you take him back to the apartment. The party's all ready. I'll come as soon as I can. There's champagne in the icebox and you just be sure there's a cup left for me!' . . . You see, Audrey, how it did tie in with what had come to me riding home from Driscoll's?"

"I think so. It seems quite clear. Gigantic as it was, it was an example in miniature, really, of what can happen when — when every segment does strain together, as you said; when every resource is drawn on. It must have been a terrific experience. How I wish I'd seen it! But I'm sure I wouldn't have seen all you saw in it. I guess I'd rather see it now."

"Maybe it will be on again. I wrote in and asked for it to be repeated. I hope many will. Why don't you?"

"I will."

"It *was* an example of what you say. And of a lot of other things, too. I'm still adding to my list of what that program signified to me. Among other things it was a kind of warning. It showed, for instance, just what Lisa Price told us that first day you came to St. Dom's — remember? Though the straining was combined to bring about the result, actually it was done separately; each artist was alone with his vision, in a frightening but wonderful aloneness, straining to meet the challenge to what he was, what he had. To do this they were often pitted against one another. The results of their individual effort had to be brought together, and this was a work of art in itself; the responsibility of the producer and the conductor. So it warned against exactly what Lisa warned against.

And something else I felt and couldn't analyze. But, with no reference to the opera, it was analyzed for me the next day."

The next day the Sheaffers went to a convocation and luncheon given in honor of a man who had contributed a million dollars toward a city college library being dedicated that day. Margaret's father was an alumnus of this college, and the dedication took place during the holidays because, as the alumni had raised the money to complete the cost of the structure named for its chief donor, it seemed fitting to have as many as possible of them present, and dormitory space was available to them only when the students were not in residence.

The convocation was held in the gymnasium, and the alumni filled every chair, spilled over onto the bleachers around three sides. But the two or three top benches of the bleachers, Margaret noticed, were occupied by the very young, probably local students and their friends on "a busman's holiday," drawn "back to the scene of the crime," who had taken a streetcar across town or come in sports cars or on motorcycles to see "what went on." Most of them wore slacks and turtleneck sweaters, wool shirts, desert boots or sneakers; the boys' hair was long and curly, the girls' long and straight, and this was how you distinguished between them; all were pale, looked tired, as if the night had been sleepless; their eyes shone, but not with health. They were in marked contrast with the alumni among whom Margaret sat, most of them younger than her parents, perhaps in their thirties

and forties, substantial, well dressed (in some cases
conspicuously so), well mannered, apparently self-
respecting and yet with an underlying tension revealed in the lines around their mouths, in their pos-
ture, even in their motionlessness as they waited for
the exercises to begin.

The college orchestra played.

The president of the college explained the Cere-
mony of the Library Key as it was passed from the
chief donor to the president of the alumni association
to the architect to the chairman of the board of trustees to the chief librarian, who then made a speech
expressing his appreciation and introducing the chief
donor.

The chief donor was a thickset, elderly, smooth-
shaven man of modest mien and benign countenance.
He had, he said, come to this country as a small boy
with immigrant parents from Armenia, and found it
indeed a great, a wonderful country which had been
infinitely good to him in that it offered opportunity
unlimited. (The very young in the high rows of the
bleachers exchanged glances as if on a barked order
from a superior officer —"Guide RIGHT!" or "Guide
LEFT!" — with raised eyebrows, a jerk of the knees,
and lips either grimly set or wryly twisted. Most of
them were Caucasians, perhaps one in twenty-five of
another race. Curiously, one tall, very thin, middle-
aged nun sat among them, like a lighthouse on one of
a throng of tiny islands, her hands serenely folded and
her calm eyes fixed on the speaker, who was clearly of
another race and religion than her own.) He felt, he

said, that the future of civilization depended on this country and its people, on its ability to hold to and promote the ideals of its founders and on their capacity and willingness to repay to its future favors of incalculable value granted to them in the past. He hoped that this new library would help to show students what the debt of each was to his country and in what coin he would be best able to pay it, enable each to prepare himself for loyal and productive citizenship in the most demanding period the world had yet faced; he hoped that students reading here would be influenced to develop constructive rather than destructive habits, ideas, theories, philosophies, and systems, would find positive approaches to clear and present problems, realizing that blind opposition to current practices, without a well-thought-through substitute program to recommend, did far more harm than good. (Glances were again exchanged along the high rows, and lips curved in cynical smiles. The chief donor must have felt this, though he could not have seen it, for he was looking genially, paternally, at the alumni.) "It may sound corny," he said gently. (The high rows shook with silent laughter. He continued in the same vein.) If this could be accomplished, he said, in a building to which, as an American citizen, he had been so fortunate as to be able to make some contribution, and which the trustees of this college had been so gracious as to name in honor of the parents who had brought him to this great country, he should then regard his share in this achievement as less part-payment on his personal debt than as still more to be grateful for and to seek to make return for, as he trusted the students who found their solutions here would also be making returns and insuring that the future of this Land of the Free would be even more glorious than its past.

"I went with the alumni to the luncheon," Margaret told Audrey, "my mind reeling from the impact of this man, these alumni, and those students on what had happened to me the night before. I was asking myself why this man differed so much from those of his generation I had been sorry for at Driscoll's; how the alumni differed from those who had opened the new opera house; whether the students in the bleachers had ever been like my seventh-graders at St. Dom's, and if so what had changed them . . . And, Audrey, if you can believe it, the luncheon speaker up and told me! At least, it seems to me now he did . . ."

The luncheon speaker, a recently retired professor who had been chairman of the college's department of psychology for many years, was introduced as the unanimous choice of the alumni library fund committee, the man from whom all its members most wanted to hear; and the committee believed that in this choice they would be joined by the great majority of contributing alumni.

The applause which greeted him substantiated their belief.

He was a short, slight man, with dark hair still untouched by gray, intense dark eyes, and a smile which came and went in a flash. He struck you at once as a man with a mission, a man in a hurry. He walked quickly to the microphone, lowered it quickly, and began to speak with a rapidity which increased as he continued. His voice was like a musical instrument and unconsciously he used it that way. With his first words the thousands in his audience leaned a little toward him, gave themselves up to him.

"He had what lately we call charisma," Margaret told Audrey, "though that was obviously no concern of his. His full attention was on his convictions and the techniques of expressing them effectively. He used no notes. I only wish you could have heard him. He is a hard man to resumé."

But the gist of what he said was that he had been much interested in the convocation, which seemed to him to confirm impressions gained wherever he had been during the past year of visiting campuses and meeting with faculties and alumni of various institutions. The college was most fortunate to have such a generous benefactor and so many loyal alumni. But it should be noted that the benefactor, like himself, was an elderly man, and that most of the alumni present had been out of college fifteen years or more.

"Something has gone amiss," he said, "since our benefactor and I were young. Something has gone amiss since your Commencement. Actually it was going amiss for many years before that, but few of us were aware of it, unfortunately, until quite recently. Now nearly everyone knows that something basic in our culture is deeply wrong. Most of us have little idea what it is, far less how to rectify it, but practically

all of us feel we know whom to blame — and that is
some other generation than our own. Well, I say we
are *all* to blame for just one serious, continuing short-
coming — and that is in not having begun to dig and
dig hard for reasons and solutions the minute we as
individuals, of whatever generation, woke up to the
existence of a grave problem, whenever that minute
came."

He took his own full share of blame, he said, for his
years of tolerance of those in his field and in his own
department who were more scientists than philoso-
phers, more sociologists than psychologists, studied
rats rather than people, and capitalized society while
decapitalizing God.

"There was an academic battleground on which we
did not choose to fight, and a battle not fought is lost.
There the fortunes of war turned against us. Since
then many who might have been aligned with us have
transferred their allegiance, or ceased to have any.
Thus our numbers now are pathetically small compared with what they might have been. Nevertheless,
late as the hour is, we must now take our stand and
never again call retreat. I call on all my former students to sign on with me in defense of the individual."

He went on to say that astounding technical ad-
vances, particularly in transportation and communications, had placed an almost intolerable burden on
the minds and hearts of human beings, but they could
have learned ways of adjusting to these new pressures
and demands if anyone had been prepared to teach

them, and perhaps by trial and error without teaching, if at the same time institutions in which potential leaders found themselves had not been indoctrinating them with the idea that all must adjust in the same way, that whatever society expected was right, that one who differed from the majority was sick, that personal ambition was ignoble, that only team spirit was a fine spirit, and that if you thought God told you anything else you had delusions. Thus individuals — especially the young — had been cut off from God and turned over to a voracious, insatiable computer society which was in the process of controlling their actions, their thinking, their present, and their future, consuming a little more of them each day.

"This we must stop," he said. "We must draw a line and stand on it, religiously, politically, and educationally; and then we must advance, winning more and more freedom, respect, and safety for the individual, and more and more opportunity for him to grow, to perform, to achieve at his own level, at his own rate, and in his own metier. It must cease to matter what his age is, or his generation. He must cease to feel that unless he can go to the moon it is useless for him to fly a plane, that unless his painting is acclaimed as a work of genius he should throw away his brush, that what he does in a company is far more important than anything he can do alone, that to be alone is to be friendless but that whatever he does in a company should and will create a brand-new world. The world was created long ago — and the human race considerably later. The part of each of us is to become worthy of that creation. Man must give God the honor He deserves, and must himself be deserving of honor. One of the best grounds, if not the best, on which to begin the battle to bring this about is the college campus, for once some success is won there, it will be carried into every walk of life, perhaps most effectively at first into our secondary and grade schools, where our children and grandchildren are more closely and constantly under adult guidance than anywhere else, except possibly at home. A child who does not see reason to trust and respect himself, and is not shown how to find and develop that reason, will sooner or later destroy himself, if only out of a sense of unworthiness. Only a few generations of such children, in sequence, would be enough to destroy this civilization. Our benefactor today spoke of his debt to his country. What is our debt, yours and mine, to it? And to him? And to ourselves? I want you to think about that."

"I'll wager everyone who was in that room has thought about it," Margaret said. "I know I have. And you know what I think, Audrey? I think I know of the right place for me to start doing something about it!"

"Where?

"I'm going to open a school of my own."

"Margaret! How can you? You — aren't coming back to St. Dom's? I was sure they'd keep you on even if Sister Mary Grace didn't stay on at the conservatory —"

Margaret laughed.

"Oh, I *am* going back to St. Dom's. They've de-cided that Sister Mary Grace is to finish her year. Of course I can't open my own school *now*. There's so much to be done first. It may be years before I'm ready. But the thing is to start getting ready right now. I'm getting ready by telling you that's what I'm doing and what I'm going to do. I *love* teaching, espe-cially the upper grades, and I don't want always to teach only Catholic children. I want to teach children of all religions, and no religion. I want to *live* with kids, and with other people who feel about them the way I do. And I want us all free to do what we can do best in the best way we can do it, and then to be judged by how well it turns out. Wouldn't that be glorious?"

"Oh, I'm sure it will be."

"Are you? Then you be thinking whether you'd like to do it with me."

"Me? You think you'd want me?"

"I don't know yet. But I know it depends on how much you decide you would like it, what you decide you want to learn that you don't know, what you choose to unlearn that you've been taught. On a lot of things. When I get to the point of choosing a faculty I'm going to be mighty fussy, I can tell you. But I will say that right now you're the only person I know that I'm sure could do it if you want to enough."

"What if — I'm married by then?"

"My dear! I've nothing against married teachers! Figure to be one myself someday, with a little bit o' luck! In fact, that's one reason for opening the right kind of school — so I'll be sure of one for my kids to go to."

At the end of Dockham's Road, that narrow, rutted, ungraded mile, Ellen had just cleaned the stanchions and spread pink sawdust under her two cows, fed them, and milked them. Now, as she crossed the yard with the milk pail and lantern, she paused and looked up at the stars. Dark came early now. Christmas was one of the shortest days of the year.

Something rubbed against her leg, just above the top of her boot. She swung the lantern and saw two yellow eyes down there, like amber beads.

"Well, pussy!" she said. "Where'd you come from? You looking for your Christmas dinner? Well, then, you come along. You follow me, and soon's I strain this milk — "

She closed the kitchen door behind them, and dropped the bar across it. No need of the bar, except against a wind, but it seemed more cosy. She set the pail on the counter by the sink, blew out the lantern and hung it up, dropped her coat and shawl on the couch, and took a piece of cheesecloth from a drawer.

The kitten jumped lightly to the couch and made itself a nest in the folds of the shawl. It sat there watching Ellen and washing its paws, by turns.

"Warming your little backside, ain't ye?" Ellen said. "You pretty thing, you. Striped just as even ye be, gray and white, 's if somebody had knit ye on needles or crocheted ye with a hook." She spoke as her grandfather might have.

Filling a saucer with the warm milk left in the pail from the straining, she set it on the floor behind the stove and the kitten came to it. Now Ellen watched the kitten, hands on her hips, as the kitten had watched her.

"When you're through," she said, "I'll put you up attic for a while so you can catch your Christmas meat. I heard mice after my corn there just last night. Hadn't been for you happening along, I'd 'a' had to set a trap. So I'm real glad you've come."

She smiled to hear the scampering overhead as she sat at the table sturdily chewing between her hard gums a piece of the fowl she had stewed and fricasseed for her Christmas dinner. Later, she called the kitten downstairs and let it outside while she brought the plants in from the windowsills and warmed in the oven an old piece of flannel which she laid over the cover of the woodbox.

"Come, pussy! Come, pussy! . . . There now, here's your bed. You've had your Christmas and I've had mine. Now we'll both of us go to bed. Tomorrow is another day, and we'll see what happens then."

She blew out the lamp, for the moon had risen. Through the gable window it picked out the treads of the stairs, and her chamber was as light as day. She tucked a hot beach rock between her cotton blankets, and said over in a cracked singsong, as she undid her strings and buttons, the words of "Silent Night."

6

WALT *Ross to Audrey Mason:*
"... You might be surprised if you knew
what guys in a place like this find to talk about. One
unlucky joe — no girl to write to him — watched
while I was reading my letters, until finally I told him
that most of what I was reading was about a girl you
had met and liked. Even mentioned her name and
right away he was excited, wondering if she was the
Peg Sheaffer he went to school with. Where did she go
to high school anyway? His name is Padraic Breck.
Calls himself Paddy . . ."

Audrey to Walt:
"Small world! Margaret remembers Padraic Breck;
says he was a freshman 'and awfully cute' when she
was a senior. She remembers his older brother even

better; he directed traffic at the crossing near her school when she was in third grade, and she adored him — used to pretend she was afraid to go across so he would take her hand and lead her over; actually I don't believe she was ever afraid of anything in her life! You must have by now my letter telling you about her determination to start a school of her own, and maybe she will want me to teach in it. Can you imagine that might be possible? I mean, do you have any idea yet where we might be two or three years from now, and what you would like to be doing? . . . Margaret is staying on campus with me tonight, and encloses a letter for you to give to Padraic. If he isn't able to write, let me know and tell me more about him to tell her. She can't address an envelope to him because she doesn't know his rank, but says to tell you she is paying her fair share of the postage, which she is sure will NOT be half . . ."

Margaret Sheaffer to Padraic Breck:

"Just heard you are a hospital neighbor of one Walt Ross, boyfriend of my girl friend, but have no more news of you than that. What's up? Did you get sick, or were you wounded, or are you on the hospital staff? There is no way of telling from what Walt wrote Audrey. He just said he mentioned my name to you and you wondered if I was Peg Sheaffer of Rushford High. Well, I surely am. Or maybe I should say I was, for nobody has ever called me Peg anywhere I've been but there. Good old Rushford High! The building was the best part of it; didn't you think so? How I loved that pile of granite with the ivy growing over it! They must have closed it before you graduated, didn't they? Now the kids in that part of town have a new school with a different name; all on one level, all windows, and bare as your hand, of course. I wouldn't like it. Wonder what they did with all that lovely granite. Do your folks still live around there? My parents moved out to South Fawcett several years ago. Did I ever tell you — come to think of it, did we ever talk together? I can't be sure of that, though I remember exactly how you looked. I can see you now, standing in the middle of the front row when the boys' glee club sang at assemblies; Irish as a four-leaf clover; real cute. I used to wonder if you would grow to be as big as your brother. Have you? He used to be at the crossing in front of West Intermediary when I went there and he was the greatest; I'll never forget him. That was what I was going to ask — if I had ever told you how much I admired him. He made such an impression on me that the first time I heard your name at High I asked around whether you were related to Officer Breck, and found out you were his brother. I think somebody told me you lived with him. Lucky boy! He must have taught you a lot. He taught me a lot just taking me across the street now and then . . . I hope you are able to write, Padraic, and will write to me. I'd be much interested in anything you can and want to tell me about what you have been and are doing in Vietnam and how you feel about it. All of us here at home are greatly in your debt. I am proud that I know you. What can we send you that you could use? . . ."

Padraic to Margaret:

"Maybe you thought I was never going to answer your welcome letter. It took quite a while to get where I am and do not get much chance to write over here. Was only in the hospital a week. A bullet grazed my head but my head is hard. No. I am not as big as Mike but I am tough. They say a little guy is the toughest. Can not say much about what is going on over here. You have to see it to believe it. It would be great if you could send to the above address any of the following — raisins, dates, figs, nuts (kind of soft ones as many here even kids do not have much to chew with) , chocolate bars, cocoa you can mix with water, gum drops, Necco wafers, small blankits or pieces of big ones to wrap kids in or like a woman could put over her shoulders. Better write on the corner of the package something like if I am not there hand to any soldier guarding the village of Lolu. Soon as he sees it he will know what to do with it. Far as I know I will be here some time but no telling when things will change. Your letter kind of set me thinking about home but I don't think about home much, only how Mike's wife and kids are making out. It is a different world over here but after a while you get to feel like you belong to a village like this. The people here are kind of like the kids at West Itermediary. They need

somebody to man their crossing right now and maybe
for quite a while. Long as they do it suits me to be the
man. Seems a long way back to Rushford High. I left
before they closed it down. I did not graduate. So
long, Peg. Thanks for writing . . ."

Eric Tucker to his wife Kimberly:
    " . . . Hey, what's up politically at home? You
didn't mention the November elections, and our unit
was so tied down then I didn't even remember they
were going on. But lately I've been coming to that
things are happening over there as well as here. How
do you figure it, baby? Sounds like all of a sudden
people have come into office who talk sense. At least,
what I can pick up of it sounds like sense to me, and
that's new. Naturally a lot of people don't like it, but
must be more do, for a change. *Time* sounds as if it is
trying, more or less, to stay on the fence. Ma sends me
the home paper, and seems after having a Rep. governor and Dem. legislature, we've now got a Dem. governor and Rep. legislature. How's that for a shift, and
what in heck does it mean? Maybe you can't account
for that from where you are, but what do you think of
this new U.S. Senator from Massachusetts? They say
he stays in the Senate chamber and listens when another senator is talking, whether anybody else does or
not. How about that? And what about this new governor out in California? I heard him give a speech on radio in the last presidential campaign — in fact, I heard
it three times and it got me out to cast my first vote.

Last night I read most of his inaugural address in a little publication called *Freedom's Way* that a buddy of mine subscribes to, and I thought it was purely great. Then the editor went on to tell what a fuss the California colleges are kicking up about a reduction in their budgets. There's something about that in *Time,* too. And you know what, honey? They've managed to get you off the hook about why you didn't learn more while you were in college — more that I thought everybody learned there. Maybe there aren't as many brains on campuses as I thought, or else they're being used in a funny way. Look, what kind of a brain tells you you can keep on spending more money than there *is*? Didn't they ever read that story about killing the goose that laid the gold eggs? Now they say if they can't have all the money they want, they can't take in any more students. Great idea! I can just remember when my dad came home and told us he'd been laid off from his part-time job in a pulp mill; we'd have to get through the winter, anyway, on what he could get for his lobsters. Now I suppose if he had been a big brain he might have told ma, 'Of course that means we'll have to get rid of some kids. I don't know how many, but Ricky's the youngest so set him outside right now. It's going to 30 below before morning.' If he'd been that smart, he might have had the makings of quite a Tucker graveyard by spring. But pa's brain was only average size, and he never went beyond district school, so he just kept his old dory riding the waves, and his twelve-year-old truck running to haul the lobsters into town; he told Tim, who was in high school, if he wanted to stay there he would have to see to it himself, so Tim went in town and got a job for afternoons and Saturdays to pay for his room and his groceries and whatever else he needed. Argie and Ben, I guess they were maybe twelve and fourteen, fished off the rocks and went clamming and hauled potatoes and dry wood to the neighbors on their sleds. Reason we had wood to sell was that we stopped having a fire anywhere but in the kitchen stove, and reason we had potatoes to sell was that we pretty much stopped eating them. We sold most of the eggs ma's hens laid, too; and lived on chowders, parsnip stew, and oatmeal. But nobody starved — not even the cow — and nobody froze to death. We lived 'til spring, and the first warm Saturday ma and Judy (she was nine) began cleaning summer cottages. They started at one end of the beach and worked right up through to the other end by June. That was the year Tim graduated and went to work in the bank. He got the chance because he had been bank janitor all his senior year, besides getting a medal for best in the class in the commercial course. There's always plenty of work around a beach in summer, and the pulp mill started up again in the fall . . . I'm still set on getting an education, baby, but you can bet I'm going to hang onto what brains I've got while I'm doing it. It's lucky, I guess, I can't go to any college full-time, even if I wanted to, being as how I'll have a wife to support. It's probably best and safest to mix a lot of other things in with education.

Looks like taking it straight may be as risky as playing around with LSD . . ."

Eileen Breck to Padraic:

". . . It was funny you should ask about that Andy Pollister. I aint heard from him more than a few times since he went off but right the day before Christmas this year I got a letter from him with a check for $25 in it to buy us all presents from him he said. That long with what you sent made us a real nice Christmas I can tell you. I knit em all sweaters and caps and mittens same as usual and we all got shoes and a turkey for dinner and besides that there was oranges all around and skates for them as had outgrowed theirs and some pretty books and a doll for Evie that draws her mouth down like she was crying when you move her arm one way and grins when you move it the other way. What they won't think of next for kids. I was going to tell you what that Andy said but I might as well put his letter in with this then you will know all I know better than I could write it out. I have wrote him I was pleased to hear and how we used the money . . ."

Andy to Eileen:

" . . . If I wrote to you every time I think of Mike and his family, you would be swamped with mail. The Brecks are very big in my life. You were all always swell to me, and Mike was the best friend I ever had, not counting my dad; the only friend I had when I needed one the most I ever did. He shouldered a lot of my troubles with me when I didn't have much else to share. Now something mighty good has happened to me and I keep wishing I could tell him about it; the nearest I can come to that is telling you. You may remember I've been working on my father's weekly newspaper since I left the *Sun,* and this fall our *Clarion* landed with all four feet in the middle of the hottest political battle this state has seen in a good many years, if not ever. If you can believe it, ours was the only paper in the state supporting the candidate for Congress who had already been sent to the House three times with big majorities but the fourth time by the skin of his teeth. This fifth time the other papers took out after him and seemed to think they really had him down, but he kept talking and we kept printing everything he said and praising his record editorially — and not only did subscriptions to the *Clarion* triple and we keep selling out on newsstands that had never carried us before, but our man got reelected by a very safe if not huge majority. So the Pollisters got Christmas in November this year, and it has lasted right through, but Mac (the Congressman; his name is Rorer Maxam but only his opponents call him Rorer) recommended me to Senator Readfield, of a neighboring state, who has offered me a job on his staff in Washington, starting next fall when one of his present assistants is leaving to run for office himself. Meantime I'm in charge of Mac's office in Capital City and handling his press releases. What a break! For quite a while I've wondered uneasily if Mike would think I was a turntail to come back here, but it was the best I knew of to do, and now I feel sure he would have seen and said that the best I knew of to do was the right thing, whatever it was. I can still hear him say, 'Never give up, kid. That's the thing. Never give up.' Well, I didn't give up. I was pretty close to it sometimes but, mostly because of Mike, I never did. Now I'm registering for courses at State U. for next semester. When I get to Washington I'll transfer all my credits to some college down there and get my degree. Soon as I have, if I still feel as I do now, I'll go for a law degree. When I've been admitted to the bar, Mrs. Michael Breck, if you ever want any legal advice, you'll know who to call on and it won't cost you a cent. Remember me to the kids. What's Padraic doing now? . . ."

Padraic to Andy:

"Eileen sent me the letter you wrote to her around Xmas. I see you asked what I am doing. This is to tell you I am over here trying to look after a Viet village near as I can way Mike would if he was here. I take it you are doing what you can for things back home. Hard to tell how much is getting done. Things are tough all over. But like Mike said just dont quit kid. It always bucks me up to hear from somebody that remembers Mike. I know an awful lot of people must but over here I do not meet up with them. Or maybe I do and we just pass by, they not even knowing my name is Breck. Only a few weeks ago I got the letter I am putting in with this. Eileen sending me yours give me the idea. You see she says she heard I was in a hospital. Scalp wound from a V C sniper. All healed up now but hair dont grow there yet. I look kind of as if somebody had started on me with a tommyhawk. Ha Ha. Like she says she and I was in school together and she remembers Mike. I was real glad to get the letter and I have wrote an answer to it but if she writes again I may not. You can see by reading her letter I cannot make much of an answer to things a girl like that says. I never was much for writing and this is a real smart girl. She went to college and the girl friend of this guy I talked with in the hospital wrote him that Peg is a teacher now. Teachers always scared me to death. So if you should ever run across this girl that cannot be living very far from you I should not think by the address tell her you know me and knew Mike. Then if she says she wrote to me and I did not answer tell her the best way you can what I have wrote here. It would take me a week of nights to try to explain it out and I should be wore to a frazzle. Then I do not dout she would write back and I would be as bad off as I was before. She is a real nice girl and a sharp one too and if I was as near where she is as you are I would look her up. Best of luck, Andy. Make some good laws and get red of the bad ones. Hope to be back there in time to vote for you for president. So long for now."

Andy to Margaret:

"I had a letter last week from Padraic Breck in Vietnam. He seems to think that you and I are neighbors and that since we were both admirers of his brother Mike we should meet, and so he has sent a message for me to deliver to you in person. I'd like very much to do that. Actually, on checking the map, I find that we are about a hundred miles apart and I can't say just when I may be in that area. Right now I have a full schedule writing the editorials for this newspaper (may I send you a subscription?) while bulling around the china shop of state politics and starting up a college course I blew a gasket on three years ago. However, I do have to drive north through your state in six weeks or so, and would like to call you from Route 95, either going or coming, if you will give me a number at which I might reach you. Take you to lunch? Or would supper be better? Or is supper dinner over there?"

Margaret to Andy:

"Dinner is supper. Supper is better. Lunch is possible. My landlady's number is 324-9015, and she is practically always in. If I am out, she will take a message. I could be there almost any evening if you can let her know or drop me a line to say when you will phone. Do send the *Clarion*. If I don't read anything else in it, I shall certainly read the editorials."

Andy to Margaret:

"I have had briefer and less enthusiastic responses when I asked for a date, but not much. Are you receiving the *Clarion*?"

Margaret to Andy:

"Supper in Dewey is not a date. It is a nightly necessity, available to the homeless only at counters where one sits on a stool. Uncomfortable and maybe greasy, but cheap. Even I can afford it. I am meeting you — if I ever do — to relieve you of a message with which you are burdened. What have I to be enthusiastic about in this connection? Will the message, when I get it, make me ecstatic? Yes, I am receiving the *Clarion*."

Andy to Margaret, on a postcard:

"It is not the message, actually, but its anticipated delivery which should make you enthusiastic, if not ecstatic, and would if you had any imagination. What do you think of the *Clarion?*"

Margaret to Andy, on a postcard:

"Good heavens! I have enough imagination so that when it started to work on your latest communiqué, I turned off the switch. Padraic better not have sent me what you could be implying that he did. And I never anticipate. Life is too full of surprises, bad as well as good. I cannot tell you on a postcard what I think of the *Clarion* and I shall not invest a penny more than you do in this minor but mysterious operation."

"Year's subscription to the *Clarion*, $5.00. *A.*"

"Cancel subscription. Never ordered it. *M.*"

"Have it here in your own hand: 'Do send the *Clarion* . . . Shall certainly read the editorials.' Have you? *A.*"

"I was robbed. That is to say, tricked. *Don't* send the *Clarion*. The answer to your question is yes. *M."*

"And they're not worth $5.00? *A."*

"I don't have $5.00. *M."*

"You have already been mailed five issues of the *Clarion. A."*

"So I have read between ten and fifteen editorials. Isn't that a fair exchange of favors? No use to ask for the papers to be returned. I threw them away. *M."*

"Even the editorials? *A."*

"I admit to having kept three editorials to confront their author with, if I should ever encounter him, which with each day (and postcard) seems less likely. What will you give to get them out of my files and back in your hands? *M."*

"Blackmailer. *A."*

"No wonder Padraic thought we had something in common. *M."*

It was April before Andy crossed the state line. That was the spring the district attorney of a Southern city was at work to discredit the Warren Commission Report on the Kennedy assassination; the first Love-In was held on Boston Common; churches dis-

covered in way-out music and dancing a modern form
of religious worship; the First Lady rode up a Green
Mountain in a chairlift with a watchful Secret Service
man swinging beside her; the Democratic Postmaster
General called Republicanism a disease; the death
toll in defense of the independence of South Vietnam
mounted to twenty-five hundred weekly; the world
champion heavyweight fighter refused to answer his
country's draft call; the Arabs closed the Gulf of
Aqaba to Jewish shipping; on order of President
Gamal Abdel Nasser of the United Arab Republic,
the United Nations hastily withdrew its peacekeeping
force from the Gaza Strip and went into a long series
of extraordinary sessions concerned with how best to
keep the peace; meanwhile the Israelis overran not
only the Gaza Strip but the United Arab Republic,
and not only these but Jordan and Syria too, in three
days; the Supreme Court made many five-to-four deci-
sions; above low moans and loud outcries for world
unity and universal love the thunder of disunion
rolled, the lightning of anger flashed, and the steel
boots of hatred tramped. The most moving and constructive broadcast over the airwaves encircling every
American home was provided by small children explaining to their elders how to prevent forest fires and
artlessly expressing their affection for Smokey the
Bear.

Audrey Mason was completing her junior year at
the State Teachers College and transferring her
credits to a small private college downstate where she

planned to major in history. It would probably require a fifth year to accumulate the credits required
there for a degree, but she was not greatly concerned
about time. Besides, Walt should be out of the service
in another year, they would be married, she did not
yet know where they would be living, and she might
never get a degree from anywhere. What she wanted
was to study in the field of history. Costs of education
at the private college were considerably higher than at
the State Teachers College, but the cost of hers to her
parents would be no greater, as she would earn her
room and board in a private home. The college had
assured her there were more such openings for women
students than could be filled. She had had enough —
more than enough — of campus life.

Maisie Frome had disappeared. Her family thought
she had gone north with her school skiing team, but
wherever she was, she was not with them. The coach
and the team, of which she was not a member but one
of several substitutes, supposed she had preferred at
the last minute not to come and was at home. She was
not at home. Her mother quickly decided not to notify the police, after a check revealed that Maisie not
only had taken with her everything she ordinarily
used or wore — guitar, shirts, skirts, sweaters, tights,
both pairs of high boots, and leopard coat — but had
also taken from the family safe (where nothing else
was disturbed) a ring and a brooch left to her by her
grandmother and together evaluated for inheritance
tax purposes at nineteen hundred dollars. She had her

checkbook, too, almost certainly, and the last monthly report from the bank showed her balance to be seventeen hundred dollars, though Maisie probably thought it was seven hundred, as she never opened those big brown envelopes from the bank; her father, a bank director, was conscientious about seeing that no Frome checking account ever fell below a thousand dollars. And her car was gone.

"No," said Maida. "I'm sure it is best to handle this matter privately, confiding perhaps in a few close friends and, of course, the bank. The child is impulsive. She has simply dashed off somewhere. She will dash back any day. Or call up from Sun Valley."

"Or maybe Acapulco," said Sue. "With all that loot to travel on. It's really disgusting for an eighteen-year-old to have so much money to throw around, and even know the combination of the safe. What you were thinking of —"

"You all know the combination," Maida told her. "When I cannot trust my family with knowledge of how to open the family safe —"

"Well, could you?" asked Nat, almost with relish.

"The ring and the brooch were willed to her. She took nothing which was not hers."

If Nat had been a member of W.C.C. or F.F.L. she would have caught her cue from Maida's tone and might not have pressed on, but she had never seen Sue's mother in her official capacity, only as a faintly bewildered, patiently hospitable, hopeful-to-the-last-gasp female parent.

"Of course I wasn't invited to hear the will read,"

said Nat, "and I have never seen it, but I understood it said that jewelry was to be held for Maisie until she was twenty-one."

Maida rose, gathering up some papers, and crossed the room. In the doorway she turned.

"You were not invited to hear my mother's will read because you are not a member of the family. If you think you are, you are mistaken and I may have contributed to your misunderstanding. If so, I regret it. Let me say distinctly that if you have a family, it is not this one, this is not your home, as a guest you have worn out your welcome, and you will please make other living arrangements at once. It is now four-thirty. I am going into the library to do some telephoning. When I come out for dinner, I do not expect to find you or any of your belongings here."

She closed the library door behind her, and bolted it.

Sue turned in blank astonishment to her father.

"She doesn't mean that, does she, Daddy?"

"Don't ask me," said Max Frome. "I'm going downtown."

He went into the hall and a minute later Sue and Nat heard the outside door close and the Cadillac start up.

"She's more wrought up than we realized," Sue said. "She can't mean that."

"I think she probably does," Nat said, shrugging. "Just goes to show —" She uncurled from the sofa. "I'll take off. A little rough I can't even call anywhere

for a cab and a reservation, but looks like she's keeping the telephone tied up. Oh, well. C'est la vie,
l'amour, and all that."

Sue paced the living room for a few minutes, then
knocked on the library door.

Maida completed a brief conversation and asked
briskly, "Yes?"

Sue said, low, "Nat is packing, Mom. If she goes, I
go. You know that, don't you?"

Maida did not reply at once. When she did there
was pain in her voice but it was steady.

"Suit yourself, Sue. You must know by now what
you want if you are ever going to."

" . . . Will you come out, Mom? Or let me in?"

" . . . No . . . No, my mother is dead. Kim is
married. You are twenty-eight years old. If I have responsibility for anyone today it is for Maisie. I must
not delay these telephone calls. I shall not be out until
dinner time."

Thus when Kim Tucker came home for dinner she
learned that Maisie's whereabouts was unknown, that
her father had engaged the services of a private detec-
tive agency which within an hour had discovered her
car, stripped of number plates, in a used-car lot, and
that if she had taken any flight from the airport in the
past three days she had not given her own name; also
that Sue and Nat had moved out, bag and baggage.

"Do you think," Kim asked, "there is — any connection? I mean — you don't think they all went together?"

"Certainly not," her mother answered. "Maisie has

been gone four days since we thought she went north with the skiing team. The others were here at four-thirty when I went into the library to — do some telephoning. When I came out a few minutes ago they had left. I went up to change and glanced into their room and all their things are gone."

Kim heard her own caught breath of relief and her voice saying, "Oh. That's good."

"Good?"

Kim looked at her mother standing straight, almost regal, in a black dinner gown with soft black feathers brushing her upper arms, wearing antique garnet earrings and pendant and bracelets, and with her face both the hardest and the saddest Kim had ever seen it.

"Oh, don't mind me, Mom. I shouldn't have said that. You must be so —"

"Of course you should have said what you think. This is no time for pretense. What is good about it?"

"Well — I just think it is good they aren't together. I mean, better for Maisie, wherever she is . . . Mom, Maise is a crazy kid, but she *is* a kid. She'll find her way if somebody older — that she trusts — doesn't mix her up. If she left on her own, she had her reasons, and I think she'll come back . . . I'm sure she'll come back, Mom."

Maida nodded, her eyes fixed on Kim's. Her hand groped for a chairback.

"Don't — look like that, Mom. Maise will come back. Maybe she just needed to be alone. Sometimes a person has to —"

"It isn't Maisie — so much — now. It's Sue. What have I done to Sue?"

"I don't know, Mom. Sit down. You have to sit down. Look, we'll both sit down. Now — what do you think you have done to Sue?"

"I — drove her out."

"You *drove* her out?"

"I told Nat to go. I've — endured her and endured her, for Sue's sake. But when she said something about Maisie that I — I couldn't stand, I couldn't endure her any longer. I gave her just two hours to be out of this house, and I went into the library and locked the door . . . Sue came to the door and told me if Nat left she would leave, too . . ."

"What did you say?"

"I said — she must use her own judgment . . . She wanted to come in or me to come out — and I refused . . . I — I couldn't talk about it. There just — didn't seem to be anything to say . . . Oh, *Kim* —"

Maida turned away her head. She had seen her mother cry, and resolved before their birth that her children would never see their mother cry.

Kim knew that her mother was crying. You do not cry only with your eyes, your face, but with your voice, and the more you try not to the more you cry with your whole body.

After a minute Kim got to her knees on the rose damask upholstery, put her arms around her mother's shoulders, pressed her cheek against the shining upsweep of her mother's perfectly arranged hair. She did not recall ever having done this before, but perhaps she had when she was very small.

She said, "Mom, listen to me. I think you did exactly right . . . Are you listening to me, Mom? . . . Do you care what I think?"

" . . . Of — course I do. Yes. I'm listening."

"Then I'm going to tell you. Straight. Because I've been thinking about it a lot ever since I came home after I was married. I'm sure what you did to Sue tonight was right. Probably what you had been doing to her all the years before that, ever since she was born, was right, too. It was the same thing you did to me, and have been doing to Maisie. The same things most parents have done to people of our age. Everything you did added up to a terrific problem for us — you made it *so* hard to leave you! Now keep in mind I don't think that was a bad thing. I think it was really a very good thing —"

Maida turned to look at her middle daughter. Kim had to free her a little.

"What are you saying? Hard to leave me? It is years since I've thought any of you felt any real attachment to your parents —"

"Mom, keep on listening. I'm being absolutely honest. There is a drive in people toward growth, toward independence, toward self-realization, toward being responsible for one's self and others and solving one's own problems. You and Daddy did so much for us — with the best will in the world, with the best intentions in the world — that you left us with just one problem only we could solve. That was how to find the courage and the stamina and the determination to pull away from this sunny dock and lay to the oars and set our own lobster traps and tend them no matter how cold it was out there, no matter how stormy, and whether we felt like it or not. Gram had plenty of problems — she used to tell me about them — leaving a farm for a village school, going on to a finishing school and a conservatory of music, marrying a village boy who was becoming a city doctor. But she was trail-blazing and she knew it, and she was getting more physically comfortable all the time. *You* had plenty of problems — Gram told me about them, too — how she and your father pushed you into social situations they couldn't have coped with but thought were to your advantage. She said she worried about it, but it seemed the only way. And after you managed that, you fell in love with Daddy, who had a lot of money (which was one of the things Gram and your father wanted for you) but lived in a different part of the country, so when you came out here you had to unlearn a lot and learn a lot of new things to be the kind of wife you felt he needed. And *you did it*. Gram made her way, and you made yours. That's what Sue wanted to do, and I wanted to do, and Maise wants to do. But because of all you'd done, you had so much to give us, and you were willing, and so capable, and so patient, you made it so easy to stay here and take it, so terribly hard to get up and go. That's why I say it was a good thing — you gave us the one big challenge we had. The question we had to answer — and we all knew it by the time we were fifteen — was *did we have the guts?*

"I found I did, and it was glorious. You didn't want me to go east alone, and you didn't like it that I married Rick. But that was when I stopped being scared. That's when I really started to grow. And that's why I've kept so separate since I came back. I was afraid it hurt you, and I was sorry about that, but I just wasn't going to get tied to this sunny dock again, and I never will. I'm a woman and, if you want to, you and I can be friends."

They were apart now, sitting side by side.

"Kim," Maida said softly, "what a lovely word!"

Kim laughed, with a note of nervousness, slipped a hand over Maida's, and sobered.

"We can't tell yet about Sue and Maise. I honestly think it is a very good sign that Maise has gone. You must be awfully afraid of what may happen to her. I am, too. Because it is too soon, and I don't like the way she did it. But we'll just have to 'hang to the rigging,' as Gram used to say, and see how it turns out. If she does something with this freedom, something that really makes sense to her, she'll be older and more responsible when she comes back, and I hope you'll treat her that way. You made a web, she was born into it, she's broken out of it. Now let her make her own . . . Sue — well, it's different with Sue. I mean, we have to face it, there may still be hope for Sue and there may not. She's never done anything yet — anything positive, that is. We all started by being against people and things. Maybe everybody does and always has, though other generations haven't been as frank about it as ours. Somewhere along the way we got converted to brutal frankness as if it were a religious creed. But Sue's never gone beyond negativism, and she's far from a kid. She went through college hating all but a few of her courses, fighting the rules, despising the traditions; but she didn't drop out or even transfer. All that time she was hating the family, despising the city where she grew up, embarrassed to death by everything you and Daddy did and by your way of life. But she snapped up your offer of a European tour when she graduated, and went on it, kicking and screaming all the way. *Then* she came back, grabbed onto Nat, and moved right in here to *use* you and everything you had as a base from which they could trail all over the country like a couple of lost souls, protesting everything, and where they could always fall in for good food, warm baths, and a chance to insult and abuse everybody here. Frankly, I didn't think she would ever really leave. I don't believe she would have, either, if she hadn't been pushed. That's why I say what you did was right. It's making Sue get her answer to that big question. She may not like the answer she gets, and if she doesn't like it, we won't. But anything is better than no answer. Here she was no good to herself or anybody else."

"If she wants to come back — shouldn't we let her?"

"Discourage her. Set your own terms for any coming back. This is your house. She's very unlikely to accept them. And she shouldn't, for more than a brief visit."

"Do you — think she will break with Nat?"

Kim drew a long breath.

"I hope so. How I hope so! But if she doesn't, there is our final hope. Nat may break with Sue when she can't provide oases of lazy and luxurious living between their safaris over the desert of man's inhumanity to man. I see Nat as a gal who thinks the world owes everybody a bed of roses and a jug of ambrosia, and makes sure of hers to start with. If I never see that one again it will be too soon . . . Mom, it's way past dinner time. Aren't you hungry?"

" . . . Why — yes! Yes, Kim, I think I am. Or something like that."

"Where's Daddy?"

"I don't know. I haven't seen him, either, since I went into the library. But he did call from the office, around six, to tell me about Maisie's car."

Kim laughed.

"Good old Daddy. Wherever he is, we know he'll be back. Nice there's *somebody* to be sure of. I'll be down in a minute. Then let's eat. I'm starved."

As Kim ran upstairs, Maida went to the kitchen to tell Kirsti they would not wait any longer for Mr. Frome, so please fill the tureen and warm the soup plates.

Kirsti's round blue eyes were darkened by compassion. She stood with her hands tight clasped under her little white apron. Her mother Bertha had been with Maida when both were brides, and had stayed until

Kirsti was old enough to be trained to take her place. Bertha and Maida had been and remained close friends. In a way, Kirsti had two mothers as many English children have both a mummy and a nanny, loving and respecting them both.

She said, "I — set three places, ma'am. Was that right?"

"Three places. Yes, dear. That's right. But keep back some of your good soup for Mr. Frome. And don't put on his plate until he comes."

"Yes, ma'am . . . Oh, and I made these little cheese biscuits that you got the recipe for from somebody at your club." She turned back a cloth on the counter. "I just happened to think you might like them with the soup better than crackers. They're almost all crust."

Maida looked down at the panful of small, golden-brown circles, and from them to Kirsti's anxious face below shining, piled-up blonde hair.

"Kirsti, they look delicious. Bless your thoughtful heart. Whatever would I do without you?"

"You won't have to, ma'am. No matter where I am, even if I should get married or something, if you ever really need me, you say so, and I'll come." She added quickly, "I just wanted to tell you that. I'd rather you wouldn't say anything. We don't want to cry into the soup. I'll pop these plates into the oven. That was an awful nice roast of beef you picked out this morning, ma'am. I'll bet it'll just about melt in your mouth."

Maida and Kim were still on the soup course when they heard the car driven in, the garage door lowered, and Max coming heavily up the stairs to the back hall. Kirsti opened the kitchen door and asked:

"You want to wash up in the lavatory and eat as you are, sir? Or would you rather change first? Mrs. Frome and Kim just sat down. They didn't know when you'd be coming."

"You mean — they're *eating*, Kirsti?"

"Yes, sir."

"As if nothing had happened?"

He must have raised one eyebrow — Maida remembered how he used to raise an eyebrow in imitation of General Eisenhower hearing the news that President Truman had relieved General MacArthur of his command — for Kirsti giggled.

"Just about, sir."

"Well! You don't tell me, for crying out loud, who'd a thunk it, and all those other obsolete slang expressions I picked up in childhood and have been trying to forget ever since! Also, what's cooking?"

"Onion soup, sir. Your favorite. And a prime cut of beef barbecuing. Carrots steaming in cabbage leaves in the well. Baked potatoes with sour cream. I'm tossing a watercress salad —"

"Hold! Enough! I'm washing up right here."

Maida was remembering what Kim had said. *Nice there's somebody to be sure of.* Suddenly, as he came into the dining room, she wanted to jump up and throw herself into his arms; but if she had, she would have burst into tears, and she did not want that, he did not need that. She kept to her chair and smiled at him.

"You're just in time, dear. Would you like some sherry? It's on the sideboard."

"You girls have some?"

"Not yet."

He poured three glasses, set them on a small silver tray, and brought them around the table. As he put Maida's beside her goblet, he stooped and kissed her cheek. From behind Kim's chair he kissed the top of her head. Dropping into his own chair, he sat sipping the sherry, looking across it from one to the other, and sighed luxuriously.

"Goes to the spot."

"You're tired," Maida said.

Kirsti brought his soup.

"Been quite a day," he agreed mildly.

"But everything's done now," Kim said, "that can be done. So let's all relax. Celery, Daddy? Olives?"

He shook his head. "Spoil the flavor of Kirsti's special." He raised his voice. "This is the best soup she *ever* made."

He seemed to concentrate on the soup, Maida and Kim on the sherry and bits of cheese biscuits.

She's taking it better than I thought she would. Five times I rushed her to the hospital and only every other time she got a baby to bring back. What she wanted more than anything else was a big family. A big, happy family. Because she'd been an only child and knew what it was to be all her parents had. That was so lonely, she used to tell me. But she couldn't have a big family, and she didn't get a happy one. Poor girl. She's tried all kinds of substitutes, but they never worked. She's never told me that. I just know it. Maybe there isn't any substitute for a family for a woman like Maida, but if only . . .

. . . I have such a strange feeling. I don't understand it. It's a kind of relief. A sudden sense of peace. I shouldn't feel this way. I'm scared. It's so quiet, all of a sudden. The candlesticks are so tall. The candle-flames seem to be opening slowly, softly, like night-blooming flowers. Kirsti's step is light and firm. Kim said we could be friends now. And Max — Max has come home. He looks at me as if — as if he has something to say to me, something to tell me, something to ask me. Not now, but later. I didn't think he would ever look at me like that again. It's been so long. Why am I frightened? Is it because this is happiness, and I know I can't really be happy tonight? It can't be true. That's why I'm frightened. Because it's a dream I can't bear to wake up from . . .

. . . I wonder if Mom is jealous when Daddy praises Kirsti's soup. I never thought of that until just now. Before Kirsti it was Bertha's banana fritters and her broiled mushrooms and her sponge cake he used to raise his voice about at the dinner table. He knew just how to please Bertha, and now Kirsti. He must like to please people. Doesn't everyone, really? But he must have despaired of his own family years ago. Sue, and Maise, and me — and Mom, too. He must think there's no joy in any of us. There was in me, and Rick found it, and brought it out. But I haven't shown much of it here, because I didn't want to be here. Why didn't I want to be here? Mostly because I

wanted to be with Rick, but partly because of Sue and Nat. It didn't really have anything to do with him — or Mom. I wish they knew that . . .

Kirsti had taken away the soup plates, brought in the roast, the hot vegetables, the salad.

"Hey," Kim said suddenly, "let's play something after dinner. There was a time after Sue went away to school and when Maise was put to bed very early that the three of us always played games for an hour or so after dinner unless some of us were going out. I loved that. Daddy claimed to be crazy about dominoes and usually won. Mom was the card shark. But Scrabble was my dish. If nobody has a date tonight, Scrabble anyone?"

She watched the startled response on both her parents' faces change to vague incredulity and finally, as their glances met over the length of the table and between the candles, give way to something childlike and touching, like mischievousness.

"What do you say, May?"

Kim could not recall that she had ever heard her father call her mother May before, as sometimes her grandmother had.

"Why not? Though we're sure to lose. If she can find the Scrabble set, which I doubt. It's years since I saw it."

"I can find it," Kim said positively. "I know exactly where it is."

It was in the drawer of the desk in her room. Many nights when she could not sleep for thinking of Rick she had played it as solitaire.

An hour later the kitchen was quiet. Kirsti's little car had putt-putted away into the spring evening. The three Fromes sat by a card table in the family room, between a low fire and a window open to the scent of budding lilacs. Kim's count of words completed on the board was so much higher than either Max's or Maida's that they had ceased to compete with her — if indeed they had ever undertaken to do so — and she was laughing at the concentration each was devoting to possible combinations as they kept reversing order behind her. The only race was between them.

"Oh, stop it, Kim," Maida cried. "You didn't need that word, and I did. I could have made it, too!"

"Good for you, Kim," Max said. "Just the break I wanted. Now I've —"

The telephone rang. Maida blinked. Max stiffened. They looked quickly at each other.

"Do you want to take it, May?"

"Oh — I wish you would, Max. Please?"

He pushed back his chair, jostling the table. The lettered squares slid into heaps and windrows. He went into the library, leaving the door open behind him. The women heard the click as he picked up the receiver.

"Max Frome speaking . . . Well, hullo, Maisie! Where on earth are you? . . .

Maida's hand went out, and Kim's covered it.

" . . . Well, we knew *that*. The rest of them came home this morning. So where have you been, and where are you? . . . Well, I must say you might have told us. When are you coming home? . . . Well, none of this makes much sense to me. You'd better explain it to your mother . . . Why not? . . . No, she isn't either. She'll be all right now she knows you're all right. This finding that a kid hasn't been where she left for four days ago, and her car turning up in a used-car lot, would shake up anybody . . . Yes, that, too . . . Well, I hope so . . . No, they're — out . . . Yes, she's here. We're playing Scrabble . . . playing SCRABBLE . . . Okay, you play your games and we'll play ours . . . I'll see. Kim! Can you come to the telephone? . . . Here she is —"

Max Frome returned to the family room, sank into a deep chair and raised an eyebrow at his wife, as he fumbled in a table drawer for his pipe.

"So that's that," he said. "She's all right. She's in New York. She's got some kind of a crazy job."

"Max! A job? What kind of a job?"

"Playing that damned tambourine. Or oboe. Or whatever it is. Part of an act in some floor show. Or coffee house. Or something. Seems she's been writing to a group of kids that make records she likes, and the day before she was going on that skiing trip she got a letter from one of them saying somebody was dropping out of the act and did she want to audition. So off she went like a shot out of a gun."

"But — why didn't she tell us?"

"Because she thought we'd stop her. Or at least delay her. And wouldn't we have tried? Of all the crazy ideas — that a kid could get a *job* by writing a letter to a bunch of other kids and getting one back — that

anybody would ever *pay* to hear her strum that
thing —"

"But somebody *is* paying her?"

"Says she's getting seventy-five dollars a week and
living on it — in an apartment with two of the girl
singers. Says she sold her car for five hundred dollars
— I call that practically giving it away, but it was her
car — and went to New York by bus. She's put four
hundred dollars in a bank there, to tide her over between engagements; she hasn't written any checks on
her account here and is going to try not to; and she
hopes the pin and the ring she took from the safe will
get here by tomorrow. She has sent them to you by
registered mail —"

"Max — she didn't want to speak to me, did she?"

He stopped trying to light his pipe, and dropped it
back into the drawer.

"No, dear. She — didn't seem to. Seemed to think
you must be all upset . . ."

"How did *she* sound?"

"Hard to say. Pretty excited. Talking very fast.
Happy, I think, but nervous. Ridiculously young and
— proud, maybe. Yes, maybe *proud* is the word. And
don't ask me what she thinks she has to be proud of,
going off half-cocked, scaring everybody to death —"

He had risen now. He was beginning to get angry.
Maida rose, too, and stood close to him, touched him.
They were the same height. Then he saw that, though
there were tears in her eyes, she was smiling.

She said, "I think I know. From things Kim told me
this afternoon. I heard you tell Maisie it didn't make

much sense to you, and it *doesn't* make much sense to us — what they say and do and even — what makes them proud. Apparently what we say and do — and what makes us proud — doesn't make sense to them, either. The difference is that we will listen, and try to make sense of it, if only they will explain —"

Kim came back and when her father looked at her he saw in her face what he had heard in Maisie's voice.

Baffled, he said gruffly, "If you're off the phone, I'd better call the agency," and strode past her into the library.

Kim caught her mother by the shoulders and spun her round.

"Glory hallelujah, Mom, Maise did it! She really did it! She wants to talk to you, but not until after I've told you what I can. She can't *believe* you aren't practically out of your mind. I don't know where she got that idea about you. I never had it. I never thought you were really trying to hang onto me. I didn't think you'd like it when you got my wire saying I was married, because I thought you counted on one, two, three huge weddings splashed all over the society pages. I thought you'd be mad, but I certainly didn't think you'd go into a tailspin —"

"Maybe," Maida said ruefully, "she got that idea from being here when we got your wire! But never mind that now. *When* does she want to talk to me?"

"Tomorrow. She wants you to call her between four o'clock and eight. She works from ten to two at night, goes home and has supper and sleeps until noon, has breakfast and rehearses until three-thirty or so, and then is free until time to go to work again. But usually she goes out for dinner about eight. She gave us her address and telephone number. I wrote it all down. It's there by the telephone. Mom, she really is working — *hard* — and she's never worked at anything before. You know she's always loathed school, but she loves this job. She really loves it —"

"But how did she get it, Kim? *Writing letters!*"

"She got it because she wanted it so much, and she wanted it so much because she knew she could do it. That combination's bound to win, sooner or later, if a person has the drive and the courage to go after what he wants as soon as he sees it. I didn't used to be sure of that, but I am now. And Maise is certainly proving it. From her point of view, she's done the best she possibly could. She didn't tell you what she was going to do, she says, because she couldn't risk being talked out of it — or your insisting on going with her and *then* talking her out of it. She took her pin and ring before she was supposed to, but only to sell in some future extreme emergency. If she hadn't got this job, she wouldn't have come home, she says. She'd have stayed until she did get one. But she got the job, and the jewelry is on the way back to the safe. She sold her car cheap, but she had to sell it quick, and secretly. Now she has that money for reserve. She doesn't intend to draw on her checking account, says that is really Daddy's money. She is determined to be independent and make her own way, doing what she loves to do and can do best. It may not seem like much to you — it may not be much — what she is doing now, but it's a start. She may get to be great. Anyway, she's on her own and that *had* to be her first step."

Max had come back and was listening.

"Oh, I'm *proud* of her," Kim said, "and I hope you both are. Now I'm going upstairs and write Rick about it. Good night, Mom. Good night, Daddy."

She kissed them both. It had been many years since she had done that when she said good-night. Often she had not even said good-night.

". . . Honey, you'll never know how wrong I thought you were when you insisted on my staying here while you're away, how much I thought we were both risking by it. But nothing I foresaw has happened, and some pretty wonderful things I never expected have happened. Especially today! Sue and Nat have MOVED OUT, and may joy be with them, wherever they are. And Babydoll Maisie is a baby no longer; she has run off to New York and got a job. Somebody is actually paying her seventy-five dollars a week to strum that guitar! (You know, she may be really good? One thing I'm sure of, she can't *compose* — but maybe she can play other people's music and sing it, too, if she settles down to it. After all, Gram had a beautiful voice and — I've heard — might have become a concert singer if she hadn't preferred to be a good wife to her doctor; and Mom's no slouch at the piano.) At first Mom took it hard and Daddy was great. Then Mom and I had a real straight-from-the-shoulder talk and she saw the light. Like you said, she is a darned good egg. Soon as she felt better and Maisie called up, so they knew she was all right,

Daddy started getting mad. I suppose that's about all a man can do sometimes with a family of crazy women. I do hope for your sake *we* don't have all girls! I did what I could. I don't mind saying I think I did fine. Reckon I'm *mature,* at last. At school that was what everybody wanted and thought everybody ought to get to be overnight. Now I'd say I've finally made it . . . They just went past my door, talking low, as if they were strolling in the park. What I overheard I won't repeat. I'm sure they don't even remember I'm here. And that's great. Because I'm really not here. I'm there. With you . . ."

A week later word came to Kim that Rick was being returned to the States and would be based in Rhode Island for the rest of his period of service. She gave her paper two weeks' notice and went to Providence to look for an apartment and to be there when he arrived.

In early June Mr. and Mrs. Max Frome flew to Scotland for the summer. Unless unexpectedly called home, they would probably go on to Switzerland in September and might stay to take a Mediterranean cruise at Christmas time.

7

ONE hazy August morning about nine o'clock Vi
Morrison had cleared up after breakfast, done
the chamber work, drawn the parlor shades and put
the curtains to soak, and was testing the heat of the
wood-stove oven in the shedroom when she heard a
car in the dooryard. She had an electric stove in the
pantry now and an oil range in the kitchen, but in
summer she never baked in either. Using the shed-
room stove kept the heat out of the house, and she still
liked a wood oven the best of any.

When she heard the car she made an impatient
sound, for she did not like to be interrupted in her
morning work. She was about out of pie, Chet depended on his pie, she had already taken from the icebox the pastry which had been chilling through the
night and it would not take long for it to warm up,
and she had counted on having the first two plates in

the oven before the telephone rang. Her daughter Dorrie, who lived in the village, usually called up as soon as she could get the line after twenty minutes past nine, when she put the baby to bed for his morning nap. But Vi banged the oven door shut, picked up her crutch, swung the stump of her left leg off the cane-seated chair, and went to the door to look out.

The car appeared to be full of young people and had out-of-state license plates. Vi sniffed. They would inquire the way, no doubt. Every so often in summer strangers drove along this road looking for some place they would have found a good deal sooner if they had not turned onto this road in the first place. Not that you could not get by this road anywhere you wanted to go, but it took longer, and strangers were generally in a hurry and couldn't understand anything you told them. She would never forget a Sunday afternoon years ago — it must have been as long ago as before she lost her leg from that blood poisoning, because she remembered that she and Chet and Dorrie were on their way to Willett's Pond to go out in the Percys' boat after pond lilies — when the nose of a great hulking car with New Jersey plates swung into the narrow stretch between Lafe's Ledge and the Witches' Kettle, coming slowly right at them. There was only one track then, not only between the Ledge and the Kettle but for quite a ways this side. That was before they put in the fill along the edge of Old Billy's Swamp, to widen the road. Well, finally the New Jersey car stopped, big nose almost up against the front of Chet's pickup. The top of it was down, and it would have held a dozen, but there was just one man in it. First he glared, but Chet just sat and looked at him, kind of interested. Then the man shouted around his windshield, "Do you know where I am?" Chet snickered. The women had to laugh, too. *Do you know where I am?* He was between Lafe's Ledge and Old Billy's Swamp, just this side of the Witches' Kettle, was where he was. Finally Chet said, "Yes, I know, but I can't tell you. So's to mean anything to you, that is." And there they sat. "Then how do I get out of here?" the New Jersey man asked, sounding kind of aggravated. Chet thought this over. "Well," Chet said, depends some on where you want to get *to,* don't it?" Vi and Dorrie were laughing so hard by then they had to cover their mouths. Of course in time Chet got him straightened out and backed up to where he could pass, and they were rid of *him.* But Vi smiled now, remembering it.

The driver of the car, coming up the path, thought she was smiling at him, and he smiled back. He would have smiled anyway. Whenever he was not wearing a grin lately, one was coming on.

Vi spoke as soon as he was near enough so that she did not need to raise her voice. That mess of piecrust was getting warmer with every tick of the clock.

She said, with grudging indulgence, "You're lost, I s'pose."

"I don't think so. You Mrs. Morrison?"

"I think's likely."

"Mr. Morrison home?"

"Not exactly."

"Did the real estate man call you from town?"

"You mean Spike Bellamy?"

"I didn't get his name. I wasn't the one who talked to him. Sign said the Edwards Agency."

"Harry Edwards sold out last fall and went to Colorado. He's got asthma bad. It's Spike Bellamy now."

"He said when we left half an hour ago that he would call up here and tell you we were on the way."

"Well, didn't. Likely couldn't get the line. Or forgot."

"That's too bad. He said Mr. Morrison had the key to the Foye place that's for sale and would show it to us. Know when he'll be back?"

"Dinner time, prob'ly. Wait a minute."

She went into the pantry, slammed the bowl of pastry back into the icebox, and returned to the shed-room door.

"I'll bet you're right in the middle of cooking."

"Was."

"Darned shame to bother you this way."

"No matter."

"I don't suppose you could let us have the key?"

"Key to Foye's?"

He nodded, hopeful but doubtful.

She shook her head. "Don't have it."

"And you don't know where we could find Mr. Morrison?"

"No. Anyway, he don't have it, neither."

"Don't? You know who does?"

Vi took a long look at the occupants of the car. Two girls' heads were hanging out of it by now as if they were watching a puppet show. Another head, close to the open window, was a man's and not young. Middle-aged, anyway; maybe more. Her scrutiny returned to the young man before her. He talked right, and his number plates were from the adjoining state, so he was not altogether a stranger.

She asked suddenly, "Any of your folks come from around here?"

He shook his head, knowing it would count against him.

"Can't say they did, and guess I'd know if they had. Nice as it is round here, we'd have been riding this way every summer if we'd had any call. We used to come to Glenville a lot. That's where my mother grew up and she had a sister living there."

"Glenville ain't far. What's your aunt's name?"

"She's dead now. Was Lettie Trumbull. Her husband was Almon Trumbull. He was postmaster in Glenville for quite a while."

"Don't believe I ever heard of Trumbulls."

"Their daughter married a Hurd. They still live in Glenville."

"Not Paul Hurd, that has that big chicken farm on the side of Mount Zed?"

They stared at each other in incredulous delight.

"*Yes*. Yes, it *is* Paul Hurd, and they do have a chicken farm —"

"Why, what do you know? Chet's bought day-old chicks of Paul Hurd three years running! Quite a ride for 'em, Chet thinks, but they stand it fine. Awful good stock, Chet says. He took a hundred last spring and never lost a one. Not a one . . . You ain't thinking of going into the chicken business, I don't s'pose, that you want to buy a place?"

"Well, I might. Not right off, though. We're just looking for a place that's livable. Maybe only for summers at first."

"Well, the Foye place must be livable. Ellen lived there year round for ninety-seven years, lacking a few months, and all sole alone the last forty or more. You married?"

He cast a quick glance sidewise at the car, and then ducked his head a little, looking up at Vi under his eyebrows.

"Am I married?" he repeated. "Well — not yet."

She had to laugh at that, he sounded so roguish.

"I wouldn't blame you 'f you told me to mind my own business," she said. "Now 'bout Spike Bellamy 'n' the old Foye place 'n' us 'n' the key. It's all a tangled-up mess but I'll explain it as well as I can as quick as I can. See, Ellen Dockham — she was a Foye but she married a Dockham — never got off her place much. She was that kind, same's I am. And after she was left alone she never did. Seemed to affect her that way. Chet took to doing for her whatever had to be done outside. Well, there, somebody had to, and she was a good old soul. So he went in with her mail once a week to find out what she wanted, and like that. See, there's her mailbox right beside of ours. It used to be at the end of her road that turns right off this one just around the bend there, but Chet brought it down here. Handier for him and the mailman, too. After all, they was the only ones that used it. So Chet was the one that found her gone. Course they both knew it would be. He kind of dreaded it, I guess. But she didn't. She had it all planned out for him. She said when he come over the road in the winter and there wasn't any smoke coming out of the chimney he could be forewarned by that. Or if in warmer weather he didn't hear her sing out by the time he got into the clearing, or see the barn door open or signs she'd been stirring around outside. But it was winter. And she'd give him an address for me to write to, and told him she'd leave directions in the Larkin desk as to where he'd find her money. There wasn't much money, I can tell you. We never s'posed there would be. The address was her niece Betty's, born and brought up out in California. This Betty never was here. Ellen never laid eyes on her. Well, I wrote to her and said fur as we knew there was no will, so she and her brother must be the heirs. We had the funeral here. I felt bad it couldn't be over there, but the traveling was bad and the ground was froze too deep to dig a grave, so the casket had to be put down in the tomb till spring. Then Chet had it brought home and buried with the rest of 'em. Nobody come to the funeral but our folks and the undertaker and the minister. Kind of sad in a way, but then again, all Ellen's folks was where she'd gone. Afterwards Chet asked the undertaker and the minister what to do about her cows and the key he had and what was to happen to the place. They told him he'd better see a lawyer and he did as soon as he could, but there's no lawyer this side of Renniford. When he did, the lawyer told him he'd better bring the cows over here. Well, that had been the *first* thing he done, weeks before. The cows and a few hens and a little kitten that come to her Christmas. He wasn't likely to leave them over there alone. He's got *some* sense *without* studying into law. He'd took what grain and vegetables and fruit and food there was, too, and what hadn't froze or otherwise spoiled we'd eat or put in our cellar, and he told the lawyer so. The lawyer said the only thing was to keep everything as 'twas till we heard from the heirs. He took Betty's address and he wrote to her. 'Long in April I got a letter back. Reason it took so long, seems she'd moved to Alaska, where her husband and her brother had staked out a claim and was homesteading. She didn't say much, only if there was anything coming to 'em, they'd sure be glad to get it. Chet told me to send that letter down to the lawyer and I did, and along about June he drove up here, and Chet went with him over to Foye's. He told Chet he was going to list the place for sale, and he wished we could get the house aired out and cleaned up. Said he thought it would be all right for us to keep the cows and hens for our trouble. So Chet got Dorrie up and she went over it, and we've never heard anything about it since. Till this young couple come that's staying over there."

"Somebody's living there?"

"Well, I don't know as you'd call it living. They're staying there for a spell. It's Suse Wentworth's granddaughter and her husband. She didn't know Ellen had died, and her husband was just out of the service, so they thought they'd come and see Ellen and tell her about Suse dying. Suse was nowheres near as old as Ellen but they went to district school here at the same time and after Suse went off they wrote back and forth some and once anyway Suse made Ellen quite a visit. 'Bout the only one that ever did. Chet told of it at the

time. The old Wentworth cellar hole's just down the
road apiece. You come by it. So when they called here,
noticing Ellen's name on the mailbox, I told her how
things was, and she said would it be all right if they
drove over to see where she lived. I said I didn't know
why not. She's a real nice-looking girl, looks like the
Wentworths, I know from pictures of 'em in Chet's
mother's parlor album. Got red hair, and I've heard a
lot of 'em did. Only thing, she rolls her r's awfully
when she talks. Well, they had New York plates. After
an hour or so they come back and that time her husband come to the door and wanted to know who they
could see about renting the Foye place for two or
three weeks. Said they was on vacation and visiting his
mother over in Ferrisport, only she didn't really have
room for 'em without putting out his sister and her
family who was househunting and had all their stuff in
storage, and anyway they kind of wanted to be by
themselves part of the time. Well, I'd known as soon
as he opened his mouth that he come from right
around here somewhere, and when I found out his
mother was a Ferrisport Stanley — Stanleys kept the
Duck Point Light for years — I told him I didn't believe but Ellen would want them to make a visit there,
if they wanted to, same as she would if she'd been
there, without paying any rent. Nobody else was using
it, I told him. Do it good to have somebody in there.
So I asked him when they wanted to go in, and he said
as soon as they could. Seems his wife had taken a great
fancy to it just from looking around and peeking in
the windows. Right then, he said, only he didn't
s'pose they could. I said well, *I* s'posed they could, to

go ahead and I'd take the blame if there was any. But when Chet come he said he guessed it was all right. They've been there 'most two weeks now, and Chet's been meaning to speak of it to Spike, but I guess he hasn't got around to it. So they've got the key."

"You think they're there now?"

"I know well enough. Always see 'em come and go. That's why I wouldn't let on about 'em to a stranger if I could help it, because I figured Suse's granddaughter — Suse that was about the only friend Ellen had — and her husband that's been in Vietnam has got about as much right there as anybody and deserve a little peace now they're back together again. But there's another side to it. Long as you're relation to Paul Hurd and looking for a place to buy, and after all that Betty and her brother, Ellen's own grandchildren, are sitting somewhere on a glacier and needing any help they can get, you might's well go along over and see if it's what you want. Next road to the right."

"Fine. Thanks, Mrs. Morrison."

But she was already turning back into the house, swinging along on her crutch toward the telephone, intent on finding out why it had not rung.

"I guess you couldn't get the line, could you? It's half-past nine . . . Well, that's what I thought, but it was free when I took down the receiver. Everything's all right with you, then? . . . Good. Well, I can't stop any longer now. Fire's down and I've got pies to bake and everything else. Been at the door a solid half-hour while a young fellow that may buy the Foye place talked me blue in the face. So much going on here all the time I can't keep up with it. Call back after dinner if you want to. Going to be hot, I guess. I'll be ready to set down and cool off by then. Goodbye."

Andy Pollister was backing his car out of the Morrison yard. He drove on around a curve, turned off to the right, and stopped.

"Did you get all that, everybody?" he asked. "If so, do we follow up this lead or proceed to the next place on the Edwards list, which is in North Farwell?"

Margaret Sheaffer, turning to crook her bare arm over the back of her seat and rest her chin on it, said, "Oh — what do *you* say, Dr. Gilbert?"

"I say I cannot bear to live out my days without having seen where Ellen lived and died, and which when sold will bring money to Betty sitting somewhere on a glacier, and where some relative of Suse's is staying in order not to put out her husband's sister. Time is *not* of the essence. We must see this place."

"Oh-h-h, Andy," Margaret sighed rapturously, her eyes coming back to him, "if I hadn't known he would say something like that, I wouldn't have asked him! I'm absolutely fascinated!"

"By what now, exactly?" Andy asked in his most elaborately indulgent tone, moving on.

The day before, the four of them had looked at three country places which were on the market, and Margaret had been fascinated by something about every one of them. In the house with no sills and the floors dropping into the cellar, it had been the flying staircase she could see through the glass panels beside the sagging front door. At the one on the riverbank, where the water obviously rose to cover at least the first floor in floodtime, it had been the river. At the new ranchtype, built over the cellar of an old farmhouse which had been picked out to be struck by lightning in the shadow of three — yes, three — huge, collapsing barns, it had been the barns. But Andy's tone was only a face-saving cover for his constant delight in this girl's capacity for enjoyment, and they all knew it. Audrey, who felt much as he did, laughed with a familiar note of anticipation in her voice. Dr. Gilbert, whose reactions after many years and long experience with the rotted sills, flooded floors, and broken beams of life were amazingly like Margaret's, waited silently and confidently for her answer.

"You *know*, Andy. By the same things he is. By everything that woman said. She was *marvelous*. And *you* were marvelous! What did you *do* to get her to say all that, when she obviously didn't want to talk to you at all?"

"Oh, it's a very special technique. It's country hocus-pocus. But I will tell you this much — you have to start by having a cousin who married Paul Hurd. No, as a matter of fact, it starts back of that. The day-old chickens your Paul Hurd sells to people have to live and thrive. If Paul Hurd's chickens died by the dozen we'd have been pulling into North Farwell by now, without ever having heard anything more about the Foye place than they told you at the real estate office in town and nothing whatever of Betty or Suse or Suse's granddaughter or the Ferrisport Stanleys . . ."

Audrey laughed again, but Margaret was not amused. She nodded solemnly, her eyes shining.

"Of course that's true. That's *it* exactly. That woman has her own ways of coming to a judgment as to the value and trustworthiness of a person. If a stranger has a cousin who married a man whose chickens are 'awful good stock,' that *is* something. It's a place to start. She's justified in talking to him, and if she likes the way he listens she'll keep on talking . . . Did you notice how she had her own ideas about what all those people had a right to, and how responsible she felt for protecting all their different rights? Oh, I — Sh-h!" She touched Andy's arm. "Don't say anything. Look, everybody! Just — look!"

Andy had been driving slowly through deep ruts which must be impassable for most cars in mudtime, on their left a jungle of interlocking bushes the height, perhaps, of a tall man's shoulders and on their right a swamp where nothing grew but long, sword-shaped, sword-sharp blades of swamp grass which, rooted in stagnant water, had cut their way up through hummocks like old beehives and then, drying at the edges, had bent to thrust their points back into the dark depths from which they had come.

Ahead of the car had been the steeply rising tree-line, and now they were in it, climbing, the road no wider but becoming rocky between bare ledges with evergreen trees — pine, spruce, and hemlock — growing out of their crevices, crowding their tops, like watchful but silent guards with folded arms. There was no motion anywhere, save that of the car, and the still air was heavy with August heat, the smell of pitch, and some intangible, nameless element — perhaps a threat, perhaps a promise.

Andy shifted to a lower gear.

"Do you feel," Margaret whispered, "as if — maybe — we should apologize?"

"Some people, perhaps," said Dr. Gilbert, quietly. "Not us."

After a minute she agreed. "No. Not us."

The road was zigzagging now, so far to the left, so far to the right, and the incline somewhat more gentle. It had been little used. Its stones were covered with a leaflike moss. Gradually the chasm walls lowered. The trees grew closer, and larger. The tips of their spiny branches met to make a roof between the car and the sky. Here it was dim, like a cathedral, the stones were covered with brown needles, a deep carpet on which the wheels made no sound, and the road leveled out. Andy could shift into high, and they rode almost silently in and out among the trees, following not so much a road as the spaces wide enough to admit the car.

No one had spoken again.

Then they came quite suddenly into the sunlight of an open field. The grass had been cut so recently that it had not yet been raked. The moisture still in it gave off the luscious scent of split watermelons. The road was two tracks and the ribbon of grass between them was uncut, silvery, soft as feathers. There was a light breeze here, very fresh, as if it came from where no man had ever been.

They were climbing again, and at the top of the hill, stark against the sky, stood three huge, sprawling maple trees and an ash in a row beside a red wooden pump, a small red barn with a fenced-in cattle yard and watering trough, a long, narrow, weatherbeaten shed, and the white story-and-a-half house in which Ellen Foye had been born and where she had lived — child, girl, and woman — for close on to a hundred years.

The car stopped under the maples.

The girl sitting on the doorstep stopped shelling peas to look at it. The man beside her put down something he had been working on, closed his jackknife, and strolled toward it.

Dr. Gilbert stepped down from the back seat and held out his hand.

"I'm afraid this is an intrusion. I'm Myron Gilbert, looking for a country home, and they told us at the agency in town that this place is for sale."

Margaret knew — and knew he knew — that these were totally inadequate and meaningless words to use here, yet — strangely — the only acceptable ones to explain their presence.

The young man, shaking hands, nodded and smiled.

"I'm Rick Tucker. My wife and I are here, you might say, as temporary caretakers. Actually, it's a sort of visit to — the place. Kim's grandmother was a lifelong friend of the lady who used to live here. We came to look her up. Didn't know she had died last winter. Mrs. Morrison said it was all right if we stayed on a few weeks. Like to come in, or rather look around outside first?"

The others came spilling out of the car. Margaret had a feeling of exhilaration as her foot touched the ground. She had an urge to step very lightly.

"These are the young friends who are helping me in my search. Margaret Sheaffer — Rick Tucker . . . Audrey Mason, Andy Pollister — Rick Tucker —"

The girl had left her pan of peas on the step and was coming down the path.

"Kim, this is Mr. Gilbert —"

"Good morning. This is Audrey Mason, Mrs. Tucker. Margaret Sheaffer, Andy Pollister . . . Let's all walk along the hill a little way first, shall we?"

"I'm afraid we don't know the boundary lines —"

"That's not important yet."

Margaret said, "I don't feel as if — it *has* any boundaries."

There was no haze now. The sun was hot on their left arms and shoulders and ears as they walked south on the rim of Foye's Hill. Dr. Gilbert had set off first, at an eager, rapid pace. Margaret followed a little more slowly, still with that feeling she should step lightly. Audrey was behind her, nearer to Andy than to her. Both sensed that Margaret felt alone, wanted space. Kim and Rick were together, almost with Andy but not quite. As they walked they looked off from time to time across the meadows where Foyes and Dockhams had found their wild strawberries in late June and cranberries in the fall. They passed through a small orchard of old apple trees which had long needed feeding, pruning, and spraying, but where the fruit clinging to the branches was beginning to turn red.

"See!" said Margaret softly, as if to herself. "Oh, see!"

From the hollow trunk of a tree with only one living branch a bird had flown out, and just inside four baby beaks were wide open.

Seeing the others stopped, Dr. Gilbert came back. The six stood around the four, all smiling as people do when looking into a bassinet.

"We found it last week," said Kim. "We'd have told you if you had walked by. But we liked finding it."

"We mustn't stay," said Margaret. "She won't come back until we've gone, will she? They're waiting for what she will bring back. I wonder what she'll find for them."

"Blackberries are ripe," said Rick. "We had some for breakfast."

They went on to where the hill dropped off and the evergreens began again, tall and dark. At the foot of the slope, through the trees, they could see blue water. Between field and woods there had been a barbed-wire fence, but now only a few rusty strands of it remained, entangled in low bushes and easily stepped across.

"I think this was the pasture," said Rick. "We went down to the water the other day, and it's more than a frog pond. Really a small lake. A few lilies are growing in it. We asked the Morrisons if it belonged to Mrs. Dockham and they said yes. It's fed by a little brook that used to be bigger and the first Foyes had a sawmill there. Do you want to go down? Pretty rough under foot."

"Not I," said Dr. Gilbert. He pulled out his hand-kerchief, took off his hat, and wiped away sweat. "I'm going to sit down and listen for the brook."

The bareheaded girls sat with him. The bare-headed young men stretched flat on the cool pine nee-dles. They all listened for the brook. They heard it. The girls thought of music. The men were reminded of their thirst, but found it lessened, as if the shade and the sound of running water had combined to slake it. They heard bird calls, too, and wished they could reply, the singing of the wind in the tops of the pines and wondered in what direction it was moving . . .

All of that which had been so familiar to Ellen Foye it seemed a part of her, like breathing out and breath-ing in — though she had never for a moment taken it for granted, knowing that no day, no hour even, was ever exactly like another, that Nature was a store-house in which God kept an inexhaustible supply of air currents from which an endless chain of surprises were created — was new to them, as new almost as a strange planet speaking in a language they strained to understand but did not. They were resolved to under-stand it and to find a way to make reply, yet felt under no pressure. It was as if they had received one message in their own tongue; just one.

Wait. Listen. See . . . Wait . . .

At last Andy sat up and looked at his watch.

Margaret turned to him, startled.

He said, "It's eleven-thirty. We might have brought along that lunch you girls put up."

"Are you *hungry?*" Audrey asked, with a note of shock which made Kim laugh aloud, remembering that her first adjustment problem in marriage had been to accept the fact of Rick's hunger at the most unlikely times.

Dr. Gilbert said, "It is a male weakness, my dear. Unless a man has just been fed, if he is happy, he is hungry. We must return at once to the vicinity of lunch. It will then be possible for Andy, Rick, and me to endure our pangs cheerfully while we make a quick tour of the buildings, whereupon we shall eat. Immediately thereafter our combined male judgment will be at its peak of reliability and at the same time, whether oddly or naturally, most susceptible to female influence."

He rose, put on his hat, and strode briskly back along the rim of the hill toward the barn. Andy was behind him, with a girl on each side. Rick and Kim followed, hand in hand, but at considerable distance.

Rick asked, "Do you think they're going to try to buy it?"

Kim nodded slowly, not looking at him.

"What ever gave us the idea nobody but us would want it?"

After a minute she said, "Lots of reasons. As far as we knew, nobody but Ellen had wanted it for so long. There's so much against it for most people. But these aren't — most people."

"What do you make of them?"

"I don't know. I feel as if they're — getting signals. And they give off signals, too. Especially the one they call Margaret."

"Sounds weird."

"I don't mean that. It's just — they're so alive. Who else have we ever known who was as alive as they are — except us when we're alone? It doesn't matter to them that they're not alone. They go right along being themselves, no matter where they are, because being themselves is more exciting than anything. Being with them is different from being with anyone else in the way pounding on a door and not getting any response is different from having someone open the door as you go up the walk. I think that's it. Being that alive opens all your doors and windows."

"Even the old man."

"You think he's old? I'd call him ageless. Really I think he and Margaret are equally alive, take in and give out to the same extraordinary degree, only to her everything is completely new and to him it is more a new combination of familiar things. She is more acutely sensitive and responsive. His is the joy of wisdom. Andy and the quiet girl don't give out as much. They're more like us in that. They must have had to take down barriers, somewhere along the way, that the others never knew. Now those barriers are down, everything comes to them that comes to the others, but — well, their sending signals aren't as strong yet."

"What do you figure the connection among them is?"

"Well, they wouldn't need anything else to bring them together, once they met, would they? Mr. —

Gilbert, is it? — said he was looking for a country home and they were helping him look. The girls may have been roommates at school. Schoolmates, anyway. And obviously Andy and Margaret are in love."

"So what do *we* do?"

They had reached the wellcurb and so had the maple shade. Kim sat down there, asking, "What do you mean, what do we do?" Rick pumped water, splashed it over his head and arms, filled the long-handled agate dipper and passed it to her. She drank deep, looking at him over the rim, and passed it back still half full. Drinking from it, he sat down beside her. Through the open barn door they could hear the others walking about . . .

These must have been the cow stalls. There are eleven. She couldn't have had that many horses . . . Horses have stalls. Cows have stanchions . . . Oh, look! This is a harness closet. Harnesses still hanging here . . . See the haycart hung to the ridgepole! To keep it out of the way, I suppose, when it wasn't being used . . . Oh, Andy! A sleigh! . . . Here are stairs going down. A barn cellar! . . .

"If it keeps on looking as if they are going to want to buy it," said Rick. "Or anyway. We've just been letting one day slide into another —"

"Hasn't it been heavenly?"

"Only, if we don't decide now, it may be too late. Do we want to buy it?"

"Do you?"

"Do *you,* Kim?"

". . . Oh, Rick, why haven't we talked about it before, when we had hours and hours? We don't even know what they're asking for it — you haven't made up your mind where we have to go this fall, whether you'll start college if you're admitted at the last minute, or if it would be better to wait a year and get a job — we haven't decided *anything!* We've just been dreaming here, as if we never had to wake up. I know I don't want to leave, but —"

"I don't believe the Morrisons would let it be sold to anyone else, if we tell them we want it."

"I don't either. Because of Gram. If they could help it. I don't know how much influence they have with the agency —"

"Well, I'm going to find out some of these things. Right now. I'm going down to talk with Mrs. Morrison."

He jumped up.

"Oh, Rick, I —"

"No time to lose. Depending on what she says, I may go on into town, to the agency —"

He disappeared inside the shed. As he backed the car out, she went toward it.

"Ricky —"

"Don't worry. Back in an hour or so."

He grinned, waved, and was gone. She returned to sit on the wellcurb, her chin in her hands. The yard grass around the soles of her sandals did not grow separately, each spear distant by the minutest fraction from its companions yet all smoothly matted together as that on city lawns does, or seems to, but rooted in small tufts so that when she looked closely at it, passed the palm of her hand over it, it neither looked nor felt like velvet but more like a candlewick spread.

Andy was the first to appear in the barn door, look speculatively around, and stroll toward the pump.

"Like a drink?" Kim asked. "I'll bring out some paper cups."

"You know better. The only way to drink well water is from a long-handled dipper."

He pumped and drank, watching the water he had not taken run down a trough to a tub in the barn-yard.

"We all had some on the way by. Never tasted better. Reminds me of the spring we used to dip water out of at my grandfather's."

"There's a spring back of the house. That's even colder than this. Ellen used to keep her milk and butter in it in hot weather. We've been doing that, too. In her containers. The Morrisons showed us where they were."

"Did you know her?"

"Ellen? No. I call her Ellen because my grand-mother always did. They went to school together when they were children. At least, Gram was a child. She said Ellen was one of the 'big girls.' It was a district school, you know, with pupils of all ages up to sometimes as much as eighteen, Gram said. The smallest sat in the front, nearest the teacher, and the oldest along the back. Gram tried to describe Ellen to me as she looked to her then, and that's the way I see her: sort of a fifteen-year-old Mona Lisa in a calico dress. But she was in her late nineties when she died."

"So Mrs. Morrison told us. And had lived here alone for around forty years. No children?"

"Several. But they all died long before she did."

"Quite a human-interest story there."

"Yes. You're not a writer?"

"I've been on a couple of newspapers, first reporting for a city one and lately doing editorial work on a country one."

"Really? I did features for a city paper all the time Rick was away. Which do you like better?"

"Well, put it this way — I learned a lot on both jobs, but I grew up in the country and I guess I'm a country boy at heart. How about you?"

"Oh, I grew up in a city but I'm certainly not a city girl at heart. All this is strange to me, but I love it. Rick grew up on the coast not far from here."

"His mother's people kept the Duck Point Light."

"Mrs. Morrison told you."

"That she did. What's become of Rick, by the way?"

"He took off on an errand. Said he'd be back soon."

"You really don't mind showing us through the house? We know it's an intrusion —"

"Of course not. We've had it all to ourselves for two weeks. Only I won't show you through. When you're ready, go right on in. Go where you like. Meantime, I'd fix you some lunch if you hadn't said you'd brought it with you."

"When we picked up the girls at Audrey's house this morning, they had it all packed. I had already stopped by for Dr. Gilbert at the Harbor Hotel, where he's staying. This is our second day of house-hunting with him. Yesterday we had trouble finding a place to eat —"

"*Dr.* Gilbert?"

"That's what Margaret calls him. It's an academic title. He's a retired professor."

"Of what?"

"Psychology."

"I wish I'd had a few like him."

"You wish that more the better you know him, I can tell you. I'd never met him until a couple of weeks ago, when he came to the Harbor. Margaret didn't meet him until maybe six months ago. But he was on the faculty of her father's college, and she heard him speak at some alumni meeting. Since then — well, we all think he's the greatest."

The others were coming out now. Andy went toward them.

"You must know that barn from stem to stern. Kim says we're welcome to go through the house, so let's go. It's now *twelve*-thirty, and you may not be able to bear it, Audrey, but I'm an hour hungrier than I was the last time I mentioned it."

"*I* think you're being very patient," Margaret said, smiling at him. "But that is the most beautiful barn! There's a looped rope from a high beam that we think must have been a swing. I've been trying to find the seat that went in it."

"Do you know what it would look like?" Kim asked.

"Dr. Gilbert said just a piece of board with crotched ends. Maybe not more than a foot long, but probably two feet or more; for two to sit on."

"I'll have a look for it. While you're looking at the house."

Anything for an excuse not to go in with them. Especially without Rick. Maybe before they finished, while she was still in the barn, she would hear Rick drive into the shed, where there was just space for his Volks beside what was left of the firewood Ellen had cut and split at the chopping block last fall.

The front door of the house opened into a small, square box of an entry, walled entirely in doors except for the jutting corner beams. Of the two narrow doors facing the wide front door, one was at the foot of a short, straight, steep flight of stairs; the other when opened revealed a sloping closet with side shelves and hooks for coats. The door on the right was open and Dr. Gilbert, the two girls, and Andy went through it into Ellen's kitchen. There were her floor of wide pine boards, uneven from wear and scrubbing, and her four walls of feather-edged boards nut-brown with age and raggedly spotted with what was left of a coat of blue paint like that on the haycart chained to the ridge-pole of the barn; her black cookstove with funnel reaching into the big central chimney through a sheet of zinc fitted precisely to the frame of a massive fireplace; her covered woodbox at the end of the stove and her braided rug before the oven door; her iron sink with bench for the water pail; her low couch and ticking clock . . .

The house faced south. Of four kitchen windows, two looked south and two east. The two doors on the kitchen's north side led to two bedrooms. The northeast corner room was very small; a three-quarter, low-posted bed left space only for a narrow passage beside it to the black chest of drawers under the single window; and Andy could not stand upright in it because the floor was raised by one high step from the level of the kitchen floor. To make more headroom in that part of the cellar, Andy said; a bedroom was not to stand in, but to lie down in. The middle room on the north side was no wider but much longer. It had admitted a three-quarter bed at each end, with two footed chests, painted green, under the two windows between the beds. The floor was even with the kitchen floor. There was a small open fireplace and on either side of it stood a Windsor chair, one a bowback and the other a rocker.

At the west end of the middle room a door opened into the northwest corner bedroom, identical to the northeast except that its floor was not raised. From this there was a door into the southwest room, which corresponded in size to the kitchen and which also had an open fireplace, smaller than that behind the zinc in the kitchen but larger than the one in the middle bedroom. All four rooms had been plastered above the pine wainscot on which the windowsills rested. None had been papered. The woodwork in the bedrooms had never been painted, but that in the southwest corner room had a thin coat of green stain to match the leafy pattern stenciled on the plaster there. The floors of all four rooms were covered with straw matting. The furnishings of the southwest room showed that it had been intended for use only on formal or special occasions — a bed folded into its walnut frame and standing like a great wardrobe

against one wall, a walnut commode with a flowered
bowl and pitcher on its marble top, a melodeon with
yellow keys, a family album and two books with faded
red bindings and gilt-edged leaves on a bamboo stand,
a late-Victorian sofa with matching armchair, platform rocker, and four straight chairs all upholstered
in green plush . . .

The steep staircase was lighted by a gable window
in the attic to which the stairs led. The bare bricks of
the chimney climbed on the right to emerge through
the ridgepole into the open air. Between stairs and
window on the left there were old trunks, wooden
boxes, chairs without backs or with broken legs, a
hooded cradle — all coated with dust — bulging
grain bags hanging from pegs in the roof, a few
warped baskets, the smell of mothballs. Beyond the
chimney there was a wall covered with faded, salmon-
pink building paper studded with big, scalloped brass
fastenings. Andy opened its pink-papered door into
a room with one gable window. Its floor and walls,
of which two sloped toward each other from the
floor to meet at the peak of the roof, covered with the
same thick pink paper. It had a spool bed with a corn-
husk mattress, patchwork quilts folded neatly on the
foot, two enormous goose-feather pillows, and an early-
pine blanket chest, a rabbit-ear chair with a split
plank seat, and a pine stand, with the drawer missing,
on which had been left a blue glass hand-lamp half
full of oil and a box of kitchen matches. In the pink
floor a circle had been cut through to the kitchen ceiling over the cookstove and a round lacy iron register

inserted. This was, of course, Ellen's bedroom, the room in which Ellen had died; but no one in the house now knew that . . .

This was all. Floor, walls, roof, and chimney; a door to go in and out by; two large square rooms, two very small square rooms, one long narrow room; a steep flight of ten stairs to an attic and a triangular room; twelve windows downstairs of six small panes in the upper sash and four in the lower, two windows upstairs with four panes above and four below. This was the house . . .

Kim had come up from the barn and taken a few stalks of golden glow from beside the door on her way in. They were now in an amber preserving jar in the middle of the kitchen table, which she had pulled away from the wall. She was setting out paper cups, spoons, plates, and napkins in packages when Andy came downstairs. She wondered what it meant that he was always the first to leave. She was glad it was he. She felt more at ease with him than with the others.

"You must be really hungry by now," she said. "Why don't you bring in your lunch and have it here at the table? I'm making sandwiches for Rick and me. He should be back any minute."

"Oh, we've spoiled enough of your day. We can strew our crumbs under a tree somewhere. Thanks just the same."

He wanted to get on now to where he could find out what Dr. Gilbert thought of the place. Margaret obviously loved it, but she had loved all the other places. If they were going to look at one or two more today, or go back to talk with the agent, they should be about it. The sun was already starting down the sky.

But Kim felt she must keep them, at least until Rick came; must get some idea of what they planned to do, must find out what, if anything, Rick had done.

She said, "I *wish* you'd stay. I *really* do. At least until Rick comes back. It's past time for him now."

"Well, let me find out what the others say."

He went quickly upstairs. She knew he wanted to get there before they started down, to speak to them where she could not hear what he said.

He found Margaret alone in the attic, moving, wonderfully young, clean, and absorbed, among the dusty trunks, boxes, broken furniture, and ragbags. As it was the first time they had been alone together that day, it was a minute or two before he said anything.

Then he whispered, "She — that Kim — wants us to bring in the lunch and eat with her. Seems rather intense about it. Rick hasn't come back yet. Maybe she's leery of being alone."

"Oh, I don't think it's that. Nobody who wasn't neurotic could be afraid here. She isn't the timid type. You know what I think?"

"What?"

"I think *they* want to buy it!"

"They're telling secrets out here, Audrey," said Dr. Gilbert in the door of Ellen's room. Then more loudly, "Excuse us, please! Coming through!"

"And we're right with you," Margaret sang out. "Kim's asked us to bring our lunch into the kitchen, and Andy's hopping right out to the car to get it. Imagine really sitting down to eat in that kitchen!"

A few minutes later Dr. Gilbert was seated at Ellen's table in Ellen's chair — a deep armchair with cushions covering the broken reeds in the seat and back — and Margaret and Audrey were filling his paper plate with sandwiches, olives, pickles, a stuffed egg, a whole tomato, while Andy dipped from the zinc pail water he had just pumped at the well. Kim was coming with her sandwiches in one hand and a big bowl of blackberries in the other.

"There's cream for these berries," she said, "but it's in the spring. I'll get it as soon as you're ready for it."

Dr. Gilbert drew a gusty sigh of pure pleasure and smiled on them all.

"I feel like a king," he said. He looked around the old room and sighed again. "King of the castle . . . Prithee, all be seated and partake of the feast."

A minute or two later, seeing that Kim had only broken off a corner of her sandwich and was sipping from her paper cup, he said, "Will you tell us what you know of the woman whose home this was for nearly a full century?"

She told them all she could remember of what her grandmother had told her of their schooldays and her visit to Ellen after they had been separated for many years, combining it with what the Morrisons had told her in the fortnight just past of Ellen's grandparents,

parents, husband, children, and her way of life after she was alone. Kim had only fragments of the whole Foye story, but even these took a long time to tell. Rick came in while she was talking, pulled up a chair close to hers, appropriated the sandwich she was neglecting, and listened as attentively as the rest. When she finished, he was ready for his share of blackberries, had noticed that the cream was missing, and left hurriedly to get it from the spring.

"It may sound tragic," Kim said. "So many deaths, and to be so long the only one here. But Gram, I thought, always almost — envied her, as if —"

"It's all the *living* one might well envy, isn't it? The eager wish and dogged determination to survive, without which, under the conditions, survival would have been impossible, and which could only have come from a way of life capable of producing and nourishing a spirit both blithe and tough, resourceful and purposeful."

Rick brought the cream in a dripping glass jar, unscrewing the cap as he came. They poured it over their saucers of glossy, ink-black berries as big as the ends of their thumbs. It was thick and yellow, from Ellen's Jersey cow. A dusting of sugar from Ellen's cracked bowl, brown from being set in the oven on winter days, and they had the flavor.

"Oh — luscious!" said Dr. Gilbert, and continued with the train of his thought. "Isn't that what has drawn us all to this place, whether we were conscious of it or not? Isn't that why the Tuckers have stayed two weeks, and why we are of no mind to hurry off to look at other country houses? Don't we all feel there is a vital secret here, if we can only find it? And elusive as it is, don't we all sense that if we stay a while we can find it, and build on it?"

"I do," said Margaret instantly.

"Come now," Andy said, resting his arm on the back of her chair. "Didn't you sense something like that in those places we saw yesterday?"

"Of course I did. Something like that *is* in every old country house. But nothing like so much as here. Here the vein Ellen Foye drew on for a hundred years is so rich that it is as if it had never been tapped. As if we were back at the beginning of the world, with everything clean and fresh and new, and could start all over again."

Dr. Gilbert smiled.

He said, "What was so remarkable about Ellen Foye, my dear, was that she never had anything new, never needed anything new. She took just what she had, and not only made it do, but demonstrated earth's potential for meeting every human need and aspiration, if wisely and capably used. Maybe what we see is the faint glow of a light she kindled. Have you ever read *Of Plymouth Plantation* by William Bradford, the colony's second governor? In it he said, 'the light here kindled hath shone unto many, yea in some sort to our whole nation . . .' "

"Look, I may be a bull in a china shop," said Rick. He sounded surly. "I guess I'm not a very imaginative guy. I agree Ellen Foye couldn't have survived here if she hadn't wanted to a lot, but it came to her to survive in and on, she was getting the knowhow from the time she was born, and all those last years she had nobody but herself to think of, no future generation to worry about. I can't see this place either as any new world or any part of the present one. What it is is an *escape* from the world, which I admit is something. It's what we've been using it for. It's what you would use it for if you owned it, isn't it?"

Dr. Gilbert turned a long, gently speculative look on Rick.

"Perhaps just at first . . . and in part . . . Perhaps later, at times . . . Which I believe is exactly what you and Kim have done and would do." He crushed his napkin, tucked it carefully into his cup, and then suddenly pushed back his chair, both hands grasping the edge of Ellen's table. "Let me tell you something, Rick. I've been looking for answers all my life. I'm an old man now, and I'm looking harder than ever. And you know where I look, and expect to find them, if I ever do? In people of your age. Not that I think any of you have them printed up on flyers ready to hand out to me. You're still looking for them, too. But the place to look is inside you, in your experiences and your reactions to those experiences, in what you have accepted and what you have rejected of what you've been taught, in what you have figured out and what you haven't figured out for yourselves, in your personal characters, in the minds and hearts and blood and bones of you. Because that is where the solutions are, and where the future of the human race is. In the last few weeks I learned a good deal from

Margaret and Audrey here, and Andy. But I don't know much yet about you and Kim, and you don't know much about us. Do you two have any special plans for the afternoon, or can we spend it getting acquainted?"

"Okay with me," Rick said, a bit sheepishly. "How do you propose to begin?"

"Oh, I know exactly how to begin," Dr. Gilbert told him. "I'm like a war-horse smelling smoke. The situation is readymade for me. I am in my element." He pulled a notebook from his pocket, slapped it down open on the table, and uncapped his pen. "We are all in this particular place at this particular moment to escape from something in the outside world which troubles us. Somebody tell the rest of us one thing out there which troubles him and which isn't here, or seems not to be. Say as much or as little about it as you like, and I'll try to get the gist of it into a word or a phrase or one sentence at most. Then we'll move on clockwise around the table. Margaret, you start . . ."

Fake "jewel" of progress; in staining, corrosive lead setting of apathy.

Smog of defeatism; pollution of pretense that man could make earth into heaven overnight, if he would, and may tomorrow.

Heavy pressures for conformity; and most of the rebellion against it peripheral, senseless, wild, self-destructive, horrifying — like fires set on the shores of an oil-slick lake.

Too many people lying to everybody, including

themselves; lying in what they do, as well as in what they say; lying about their motives, their ability, their purposes, what they want, what they feel; lying all the time and not even knowing it.

Organized confusion; unnamed streets crowded with strangers; elaborate mechanisms giving patently absurd signals; maps available are the maps of other cities, maybe, not this one; everybody pushing, breathing not only down your neck but into your face — and it's Bad Breath.

It had taken a long time in the telling, for Margaret had set the example of giving a brief rundown of her life, by way of introducing herself to the Tuckers and indicating what experiences had given her the feeling that so-called progress was creating far more important problems than it was solving and increasingly the challenge had become too great to face, for many, and so they refused to look, or learned to look without seeing. Then Andy and Audrey had followed in turn, Kim and finally Rick had done likewise. So that when he finished, they smiled around the table at one another with the sense of relief felt at any reunion where the reports of the separate pasts have been made and listened to with interest, as far as possible shared, and now all return together to the present.

Dr. Gilbert tore a single sheet from his notebook and passed it to Margaret, who read it at a glance and gave it to Andy with an appreciative nod at the author.

"Who but you," she said, "would sum it up that way?"

"I'm an old hand," he told her. "It's my trade. But you could do it, too, in your way. Next time we'll make you court stenographer."

No one else said anything until the slip had reached Rick and he had read it slowly, the last item twice. Then he grinned uncertainly at Dr. Gilbert.

"Is that what *I* said?"

"Isn't it?" asked the professor. "If I've misinterpreted you, I'll correct it."

Rick read it again, and his grin broadened.

"I guess that's it, but, man, how it improves in the translation!"

Then everyone laughed, except Dr. Gilbert. His eyebrows had shot up, his hand gone out to Rick's shoulder, his mouth opened to speak; and he waited with no change for the laughter to end.

Then he said, "And I thought I was fairly good at thinking up my own figures of speech, but you've given me the best one of the day! Once in a while something good does seem to 'improve in translation.' Nearly always we have to admit that it loses at least a little in translation, for those who can read the original. But in a poor translation it loses everything. And isn't that what is happening to the American dream — which has always been rooted in the human dream — that it is, at the hands of modern education, modern clergy, modern society, getting a new and very bad translation? If so, what is there to do but settle down to try to make a good one, enlisting the aid of every true scholar we can find? . . . Let's all give this some thought."

He pushed back his chair and stood up.

"I find that after a stretch of thinking I think better later if I stop thinking for a while. I don't know what system you young people may have for stopping thinking, but the only way I can do it is to go to sleep. Kim, you do have a lot of beds here. Is there one I could stretch out on for an hour or so?"

She said, "Please take your choice. The step-bedroom is probably the coolest now. It's been closed all day, and a woodbine grows over the window."

"The step-bedroom. Oh, I'd like that. Later, perhaps we can go at all this again."

When he had gone, Rick said, blinking, "What a guy! And at his age, too! Maybe you're all used to him by now, but I don't know as I ever would be. He's got me really churned up."

Andy nodded. "I know what you mean. Stimulating. He's what I expected to be surrounded by as soon as I got to college, and what I never saw a glimpse of when I went . . . If we're going to cut out for a while, how about a swim? Is there a rock where we can dive off into that pond we saw?"

"Sure is. I went yesterday."

"Rick and I are going swimming."

"Okay. May I have your car keys, Andy? At this rate, I don't know *when* Kim's going to be rid of us. Audrey and I'd better dash into town for some Italian sandwiches or something to bring back. You two'll be hungry again any minute now. Come with us, Kim?"

A few minutes later Vi Morrison rang up Dorrie.

"I thought you'd want to hear the next installment. After I told you about my whole forenoon being knocked into a cocked hat, what with a carful from across the state line pulling in here before I got my pies made and holding me up for most three-quarters of an hour and then just as we was going to set down to dinner that grandson of Suse Wentworth — or whatever he is — rushing in to ask a pile of questions about the Foye place that we didn't have any answer to — anybody'd think we had the selling of it! — and we told him he'd do better to go down and talk to Spike Bellamy unless he wanted to talk over the telephone and let everybody in town find out whatever he did. And he went. Well, he hadn't come back when I was talking to you, had he? No, I didn't think so. Well, he was gone a good hour, I'd say. Didn't stop in here on his way back, thank the Lord. I had a chance to stitch up the sides of that shift I cut out for you yesterday, and bind the neck and arms-eyes. I'll hem it tonight, if nothing more happens, but I don't know about that, a day like this has been. It's four o'clock, and that car the crowd come in this morning has just gone down the road, but there was only girls in it. They must have left the old man and the young one that come to the door over there, so they'll have to come back. If they stop here again, it'll like enough be just when your father's ready for his supper. Seems as if folks *know!* Well, I'd better go get it started, any-way . . ."

On the trip to town Margaret asked Kim if she and Rick had by any chance given any thought to buying the Foye place themselves, and Kim said they had, a little, for they loved it, but it was difficult to come to any decision as Rick was just out of the service and still had not made up his mind whether he wanted to try to go back to school or get a job; she couldn't see how he could do either and live here. Audrey said she could imagine that she and Walt would be in much the same situation when he came back and they were married, for Walt would have the same difficult decision facing him. Kim said it might not be quite the same situation right away, for she was almost certainly two months pregnant.

Margaret said, "Am I supposed to think that's tough? Here I am not even engaged!"

"It's heartbreaking about Margaret, you know," Audrey told Kim. "She could get engaged tomorrow and married next week, but she thinks she should teach another year and wants to open a school of her own, and seems to have some idea she might be a millstone around Andy's political neck."

"Must be she doesn't love him," said Kim. "I adore being a millstone."

"She will, too, once she gets used to it."

"Give me time," said Margaret. "Don't rush me. I have to find a way to do it *all*."

"Oh, if Andy can wait, I can. Personally, I'm in no hurry for you to move to Washington. Only some do say that's the best place to start saving the country."

"And I'm not so sure. Andy can start checking for us on that."

Rick and Andy, having dived into the pond and shaken the water out of their eyes, floated and talked. First of saltwater and fresh, coastal and inland boyhoods, islands and mountains; then of school, what you thought it would be like, and what it was; a little of war, a little of peace which was so often spoken of but they had never known; of loneliness, of which Andy had felt so much and Rick almost none until he had gone away from Kim but now was never free of except when he was with her and alone with her and they were not letting themselves think of what was beyond the small circle they had drawn.

"Until today," Rick said. "Until we got started with all that after lunch. I can't figure it out. I've never come across anybody like you folks. The things you think I seem to, you might say, recognize, only I know I never saw any of them before. It's like as if I knew they were there, but I couldn't get at them, and you and the professor took away a screen or something. Sometimes I feel as if it's a trick. I haven't trusted anybody but Kim much for quite a while. Then again I think it's because you've all been to college and learned how to say things I didn't know could be said, so I start thinking I'd better get to college as fast as I can, the way I planned to before I went in the service. Only whenever I've talked about that, since I got back, Kim just gets awfully quiet. That might be now because she thinks she's going to have a baby, but it was the same way before she was. She's suspicious of something, maybe a lot of things. And so am I, maybe everything and everybody but her — and I don't always understand her, which is a big part of what I want . . . This Dr. Gilbert — you've been to college, you say you're going back. Would you say he's a very brilliant guy?"

"Depends on what you mean by 'brilliant,' and what you mean by 'very.' I've studied under men who may have been more brilliant, but they never clarified my own thinking, just muddled me up. My idea of Dr. Gilbert is that he was a really great teacher, and still is, for two reasons. One, that he and Margaret are so much alike in their insatiable curiosity and determination to get at the truth, and the ability to fire up other people, and the delight they take in it all. And two, that they're so much alike in having strong convictions and respecting other people's convictions, whatever they are, and the capacity of every individual for having convictions. That's what makes a great teacher, and it does take brains, but not necessarily the brains of a genius."

"You and Margaret going to get married?"

"Sure. After I get around to ask her, which I'm not going to do until I think she's ready. And I don't think she'll be ready for a while. She's got unfinished business of her own."

"How long have you known her?"

"About six months now. Counting the two when we were writing to each other before we actually met. A — mutual friend introduced us by mail."

"Kim and I had never seen or heard of each other two months before we got married."

"Guess you didn't have anything holding you up."

"No. But we didn't have much to go on, either, as far as we knew or as far as we know yet. Only that we're a lot better off together than we were apart."

"Then you've sure made a good start."

"Yeah. And they're probably wondering by now if we hit bottom and never came up."

They dried themselves with their T-shirts and started back, bare from their belts up.

"You think Dr. Gilbert is going to want to buy this place?"

"I don't know, but I shouldn't wonder."

"What could he do with it, more than come here for a while in the summer?"

"Guess we'd only find that out from him."

"He got a family?"

"No. His wife died twenty years ago. She'd been an invalid for a long time. They never had any children. He says his students have always been his kids. He corresponds regularly with dozens of them all over the world. He does a lot of speaking at schools and colleges, churches, clubs — any group where one of his former students is a member and asks him."

"Can't imagine him alone here for a summer. Or a week even. Seems like a man with his pockets full of balls, used to tossing them out and having people around to hit them back."

"Must be plenty who'd jump at the chance to come with him if he asked them."

Andy's car was back in the dooryard. The girls had bought ice at a machine in town and were making lemonade in the kitchen. Across the entry the door was open into the southwest room, where there was the sound of music, faint and a little wheezy, but the notes and tempo varied. Rick and Andy went in far enough to see the professor seated at the melodeon in one of the green-plush-covered chairs. He nodded at them and played more softly but kept on playing.

"If I'd known anybody was coming who could play," Rick said, "I'd have taken those bellows apart. They waste too much air."

"I'm just trying to hold onto a mood, waiting for you boys to come back and the girls to finish making the drinks. You went swimming, they said. Good. I went to sleep, and had a dream. As far as I know, its the first one I've had in years. Must tell you about it as soon as we're all together . . ."

Because he kept on playing, the lemonade was brought into the southwest room, the china bowl and pitcher set in the corner and the marble-topped table rolled on its casters close to the sofa to hold the glasses and basin of potato chips. The girls appropriated the sofa and Rick and Andy pulled up two more green chairs. When Dr. Gilbert stopped playing they all applauded and when he turned his chair he was again at the head of a table.

"Oh, here we are then," he said. "Since we were together, I've slept and had a dream. Shall I tell it to you?"

"The professor has had a dream," said Andy. "Give him a glass of lemonade all frosty, with clinking ice, and he will tell it to us."

"A glass for each, and toast the dreamer," said Margaret. "Hear! Hear!"

"What was your dream, sir?" asked Rick.

"Well, now, you may not believe it really was a dream, or that I slept, and I shall not try to convince you, for at my age, as in early childhood, there is such a delicate line between thinking and nightdreaming, tangible reality and daydreaming, what is past and what is present, what is present and what is future, that often one cannot see it, much less point it out to another. Yet in this mysterious borderland one may encounter something ordinarily highly elusive and which is none the less real for being intangible. Let us say that I had a most interesting experience while lying down in the step-bedroom, and that *dream* is the most acceptable name I can think of to give to it. I had lain down with the intention of going to sleep, I had been sleepy, I had felt myself drifting off . . . and then I heard a girl's voice asking me a question. I seemed to know she was asking it of me, even before I was awake enough to hear the words she used, though I am sure she did not call me by name.

"She was saying quietly, 'Will you come outside, please?' After a minute, when I did not answer, she repeated, 'Will you come outside?' I asked stupidly, 'Where are you?' adding, 'I cannot see you.' And she answered sensibly, 'I am outside. I am at the window which is overgrown with woodbine. Come out and you will find me sitting on the doorstep.'

"Then I rose, straightened my tie, put on my seersucker jacket which I had hung on the bedpost when I lay down, ran a comb through my hair without benefit of looking glass as I could find none, and went to the door. She was there, as she had said she would be, sitting on the step with her hands folded in her lap. Her back was to me. From the door I could tell only that she had broad shoulders and a long, very thick braid of dark hair, and that her hands, though handsome, were as large as some men's hands, and folded rather awkwardly as if unaccustomed to the position. When I had gone down the steps and turned to face her she looked up at me with an oddly quizzical expression and I saw that she was perhaps fifteen years old, and hauntingly beautiful. I can describe her only as a young Mona Lisa, and she was wearing a brown calico dress which came to the tops of her heavy boots."

Kim started, and both hands flew to her mouth.

Dr. Gilbert nodded at her.

"You were right, my dear. Exactly as you thought . . . While I was trying to think how to address her, she said, 'I came to ask you what you want with this house.' She had the voice of a girl but the tone of adult authority. I was never thereafter aware of any age difference between us.

"I sat down beside her, saying, 'It is your house, isn't it?'

"She said, 'It was built by a Foye and has always been owned and lived in by Foyes. What do you want with it?'

"I said I was eager to learn from it, to read what Foyes had written here, to cultivate all that was here which they had planted, to see and hear and feel as much as I could of what they had seen and heard and felt, and to make and keep it available to others to learn from, to cultivate, to gain strength and courage and hope and love of life from.

"She interrupted me with a one-word question. She asked 'Who?'

"I said that if possible I would begin with her old school friend's granddaughter and her husband, who had come here to call on her and found her away. That if I could buy her place, I should ask them to live in it for a while, for as long as they liked, to keep it warm and the chimney clean and the road open, providing only that they would set aside a room in it where I could sleep from time to time and would let me join them for meals when I was here. I said that by and by there might be children.

"She said, thoughtfully, 'It has been a long time since there were children.' We both thought about that, and then she said, 'There have been more than two here with you today.'

"I said yes, we had had three visitors, a girl who was a teacher, a girl who was preparing to be a teacher, and a young man who would soon go to the nation's capital to help with the American government.

"She said, 'Foyes have never had much to do with the government. It is very far away.'

"I said, 'Now it comes closer to us every day, and we must have to do with it, or it will cease to be the government we, the people, need and want.'

"She seemed not to hear me, or not to comprehend. She said, 'When there were children, the teacher used to come to supper. Sometimes the teacher boarded round. That is, she stayed a week, or two, or three, depending on how many families had children in school, at each house where one of her pupils lived. Every house had a map of the United States, and a wide board painted black, and after supper when the teacher was here we played geography and arithmetic games and had spelldowns and made cornballs and molasses candy.'

"I told her that is the way to learn, mixing work and play and generations. I said one of my young friends had set her heart on having such a school, and another of them would like to teach in it, that I should like to teach in it, too.

"She asked me another one-word question. 'Where?'

"I said I believed she had not yet decided where or when. But that it had occurred to me today as I stood on the rim of the hill and looked down through the trees to the lake that if I had this place, she might begin by having a summer camp-school here. Children could live in tents, climb in the trees, swim in the lake, swing in the barn, eat in the kitchen, study and talk in the parlor evenings and on rainy days.

"She said, 'When there are children, they always do these things.' Her smile reached her eyes as she thought about this. Then she asked, 'Would there be changes made?'

"I said yes, some changes would have to be made. That if we had this place, I would hope someone would always be in it, that it would never be closed and alone, but there would be much more coming and going than there had ever been, so a good road must be built to it. More kinds of work going on would mean that housekeeping must take less time, and we should need the conveniences of electric power, central heating, plumbing.

"Again she was not listening, or not comprehending. She asked, 'Would you keep stock?'

"I said I hoped Rick would, that I should like to buy back her Jersey cows and maybe two more Jersey cows, and some chickens from Paul Hurd.

"She asked, 'He a farmer?'

"I said, 'Rick? No. He's a lobsterman and his folks kept the Duck Point Light. But if he doesn't know how to milk a cow and wants to, its one of the things I can teach him while he is making up his mind whether or where he wants to go to college. I grew up on a farm something like this. I can milk the Jersey cows. And if by and by he and Kim have to be away, maybe Audrey and Walt will take a turn at being my caretakers and students. When boys come home from war, they need a little time, a little peace . . .'

"She said, with no sadness, 'Your boys came back from the war.'

"I said, 'Not all of them. But Rick did. And Walt will.'

"It was very quiet there on the step. Then I heard what I thought might be a motor, still far away, perhaps on the main road. I don't think she heard it. But that was when she spoke again. She said, 'I'm glad there will be cows. And children.'

"I said, 'We are all children, in a sense. We have many problems which we can never stop working at, as long as we live, unless we solve them. That is what brought us together — the feeling of kinship which comes of seeing the same problems and sharing a determination to work at them. We must work at them, often, where they are. But, to have any hope of success, we must also study them apart, where they are not. And that is here.'

" 'What we must do,' I told her, 'is to find out at least an infinitesimal part of what I am sure you now know.'

"She was looking off across the field and woods. She had never moved, you understand, from the position in which I had found her. Not so much as a finger. I was sure I could hear a motor now. It was quite close.

"She asked suddenly, still looking off, 'Have you tried out the melodeon?'

"I said no, that I was no musician, played only in private, to please myself.

"She said, 'Nobody has touched it since there were children. See if you can pick out the Doxology.'

"I came in, and, after a few false starts, managed to combine the footwork and the chords for 'Praise God from Whom all blessings flow, praise Him all creatures here below, praise Him above, ye heavenly host —' and about then I heard you girls in the kitchen . . . But there was no one on the step when you drove up, was there? So mustn't it have been a dream? Only one strange thing is that I have no recollection of waking and thinking that I would come in here and try the melodeon, since I was alone. None whatever . . ."

The lemonade had not been touched after he began. In the late-afternoon heat six small pools of water had gathered around the glasses on the marble slab.

Rick heard himself burst out with, "I don't know whether I'm supposed to or not, but blessed if I don't believe you."

"*Blessed* either way," said Audrey softly. "Would you really — give Walt a steer when he comes home?"

"You *know* he would," Margaret said. "Dream or more or less conscious planning, Dr. Gilbert, you've managed to pick up and put together, I'd say, everything that's been floating around in all our heads ever since we got here. You could have done it without Ellen, but if you say she came and helped you, as far as I'm concerned she did."

Kim jumped up and ran out into the kitchen. Rick followed and found her in tears.

"What's the matter, honey? Does the idea scare you? Or don't you like what he's planning? Or what?"

"Oh, Rick! *Scare* me! *Like* it! The whole thing is just so fabulous. We don't have to leave, and we can save our money, and you can begin studying with somebody who *is* somebody, and Margaret may start a kind of school right here, and I never felt so *with* so many people in my life. Did you? Rick, you *didn't* go to see the real estate man, did you?"

"Sure, but what's the harm? I took an option on the place, got a first refusal. I'll just transfer it to him."

"But what will he think? It seems so awful now. We were trying to get ahead of him, right when he was trying to figure out something for us!"

"Kim, I'll explain it to him. He'll understand. That's one of the greatest things about him. You can tell him *anything*, as long as it's true, or anyway, you think it's true. And as far as I can see, that goes for the rest of them, too. They just want to be themselves and want us to be ourselves. That's why you feel *with* them. It's the only way you can be *with* anybody."

Now the others came hesitantly to the door.

"Is she all right?" Audrey asked Rick.

Kim pulled Rick's handkerchief out of his hip pocket, scrubbed her eyes, blew her nose, and laughed.

"Of course I'm all right," she said. "I'm just silly. I'm just pregnant. Like Ellen said, there are going to be children. Look, gang, could you stay overnight? Would you have to telephone somebody, if you did? There are plenty of beds, and we have so much to talk over."

Margaret looked at Audrey.

Audrey said, "I'd want to call home. They'd worry."

"You can call from Morrisons'."

"Okay, Audrey. We'll take you down. You'll have to come, Andy. Your cousin married Paul Hurd."

"Hurry up. Rick's happy, so he must be hungry. We'll have supper on when you get back."

"I don't have to call up anybody," said Dr. Gilbert. "I'm going out and sit on the step and savor belonging to a gang."

A few minutes later Vi Morrison said to Chet, "I knew it! Here they come again!"

She snatched up a deep dish of beef stew, hurried with it into the shed-room, turned it into a kettle on the back of the stove, and went to the screen door.

"Hi," said Andy. "Sorry to bother you again. This

is Audrey Mason. Could she use your telephone? We're going to be your new neighbors, but we won't keep on being a nuisance, honest. We'll get a telephone over there, first thing we do."

"You going to buy the place? I kind of thought the Tuckers might."

"Oh, they're going to be your new neighbors, too. The whole kit and caboodle of us."

"Well, I declare!"

She showed Audrey into the sitting room where the telephone was. Andy had gone back to the car and Margaret.

Vi said low to Chet, "Did you hear what he said?" Chet nodded.

"Said they're *all* going to buy it. And this morning they'd never heard of the Tuckers, nor the Tuckers of them. Did you ever hear tell of anything so crazy in your life?"

Chet shook his head.

Vi tucked the cloth closer around the pan of hot johnny cake on the table.

"We'll eat just as soon as she's gone," she promised. "Then I'll have to call up Dorrie. Wonder what she'll have to say to *this!*"